Praise for Robert Thorogood

I love Robert Thorogood's writing.
Peter James

'This second *Death In Paradise* novel is a gem.'
Daily Express

'Deftly entertaining … satisfyingly pushes all
the requisite Agatha Christie-style buttons.'
Barry Forshaw, *The Independent*

'For fans of Agatha Christie.'
Mail on Sunday

'A treat.'
Radio Times

'This brilliantly crafted, hugely enjoyable
and suitably goosebump-inducing novel is
an utter delight from start to finish.'
Heat

'A brilliant whodunit.'

Robert Thorogood is the creator of the hit BBC 1 TV series *Death in Paradise*.

He was born in Colchester, Essex, in 1972. When he was 10 years old, he read his first proper novel – Agatha Christie's *Peril at End House* – and he's been in love with the genre ever since.

He now lives in Marlow in Buckinghamshire with his wife and children.

Also by Robert Thorogood

A Meditation on Murder
The Killing of Polly Carter
Death Knocks Twice

Murder in the Caribbean

Robert Thorogood

ONE PLACE. MANY STORIES

HQ
An imprint of HarperCollins*Publishers* Ltd
1 London Bridge Street
London SE1 9GF

This paperback edition 2018

1

First published in Great Britain by
HQ, an imprint of HarperCollins*Publishers* Ltd 2018

 RED PLANET PICTURES

Robert Thorogood asserts the moral right to be identified as the author of this work.
A catalogue record for this book is available from the British Library.

ISBN: 978-0-00-823819-3

MIX
Paper from
responsible sources
FSC
www.fsc.org
FSC™ C007454

This book is produced from independently certified FSC™ paper to ensure responsible forest management.

For more information visit: www.harpercollins.co.uk/green

Printed and bound in Great Britain by
CPI Group (UK) Ltd, Croydon, CR0 4YY

For Rosie Evans

Where do you want me to start? At the beginning? Okay. Then you have to go back twenty years. That's when it all began. With a single gunshot. Nothing before then matters. I was born, I lived my life, but it was in that moment that everything changed. Everything. You can't even begin to imagine what that's like. You think you can, but you can't. I used to think the feelings inside me would go away. Somehow. That it wasn't possible to feel like this forever. But guess what? It is. Not that I let on. I got good at hiding it. It used to surprise me, how everyone would look at me and think I was normal. They didn't know about the furnace I had churning inside me. It became like a game. I'd see how normal I could be. No-one ever knew the truth. And over the years, the decades, that fire inside me changed. It got tighter and denser. And then one day, I realised it wasn't a fire at all. It had become like a diamond. A diamond of pure hate. It made me laugh to feel that power inside me. Knowing that it was what was keeping me sane. And then, finally, the twenty years were up, and I knew I was ready. It was time. Time for revenge.

CHAPTER ONE

Ordinary Police Officer Dwayne Myers had lived in the same house his whole adult life. It was a concrete-poured bungalow that was set in lush jungle that rose behind and above the sleepy town of Honoré on the western coast of the Caribbean island of Saint-Marie.

Where the money had come from to buy such a desirable plot of land was, fortunately for Dwayne, never quite established by the Saint-Marie Tax Office. He was also lucky that he'd not had a visit from the island's Planning Officer since then because, while he'd started building a two-storey house, his money had run out half way through. This meant that when he took occupancy of his new home, his builders had only completed the ground floor, although they'd left the necessary steel rods poking up out of the 'roof' should Dwayne ever wish to finish building the floor above.

He never had.

In fact, as the years passed, Dwayne had come to like the way the steel rods jutted out of his bungalow. You always knew which house was his, he'd say proudly to anyone who asked.

But then, the unfinished house was entirely in keeping with the decades-long decline that had gripped Dwayne's front yard. Where there wasn't dirt, there were rusting motorbike parts, and where there was neither, there were weeds, some of which had grown into fully fledged bushes. And littered around as though dropped by an absent-minded giant was the front end of an old taxi, a trailer on tyres that had lost their rubber years ago, and a wooden speedboat that was rotting into the ground where it lay.

However, on this particular morning, perhaps the most surprising feature of Dwayne's garden was the Englishman in a suit who was holding a pair of binoculars to his eyes while hiding in a bougainvillea bush by the front gate.

The man was Detective Inspector Richard Poole.

He'd been staking out Dwayne's house for the last hour, and he was deeply unhappy. Not that that was much of a change for Richard. He'd been born unhappy.

As for why he was hiding in a bush, that could easily be explained by the fact that, three weeks before, Dwayne had announced that he wanted to study for his sergeant's exam. Richard had been suspicious from the start, if only because Dwayne had never before tried to advance his career in any way. Frankly, it was sometimes a struggle to get him to attend his annual appraisal.

Something was up. Richard was sure of it. And when he learned that Saint-Marie Police regulations allowed officers studying for exams to spend a morning a week at home for 'personal study', he realised what it was. Dwayne had embarked on the whole endeavour as an elaborate ruse to bunk off work one morning a week, hadn't he?

That's why Richard had spent the last hour hiding inside a bush, a pair of binoculars clamped to his eyes while trying to ignore the spiders and other stinging insects that could at any moment be crawling into his shirt collar. Or up his trouser leg. And he was very definitely ignoring the rivers of sweat that were running down his back, and the feeling of itching and prickly heat as it built up on his skin where it was touching his thick woollen suit. But he wasn't leaving his bougainvillea bush. Not until he'd proven that Dwayne was skiving.

Richard saw movement and swivelled his binoculars just in time to see Dwayne throw back the curtains of his bedroom window and yawn. Luckily for Richard, the windowsill and brickwork saved him from finding out if the bottom half of Dwayne was as similarly naked as the top half, but this was the confirmation Richard had been looking for. He checked the time on his wristwatch. It was nearly 11am.

'Got you,' Richard muttered to himself.

Richard smashed out of the bush, opened the crumbling picket gate that led onto Dwayne's property – and then, when he found that the picket gate had come off in his hands, he put the whole thing to one side so he could stride unencumbered up to Dwayne's front door.

With a sharp rat-a-tat of his knuckles against the door, Richard announced his presence.

There was no answer, but Richard wasn't in a rush. He waited a little while longer and then he knocked on the door again. But much louder this time. After a few more seconds, Richard was gratified to hear the slap of feet as Dwayne approached. The security chain rattled as it was unhooked, and the door finally opened.

'And what time do you call this?' Richard said, pointing to his wristwatch, before realising that the door hadn't been opened by Dwayne.

In fact, it had been opened by a woman with mussed-up blonde hair. And she was barefoot, Richard noticed, just before he realised that this was because she wasn't wearing any trousers for that matter. As for the rest of her clothes, it very much seemed to Richard as though the woman was holding a bath towel loosely across her front, and was possibly otherwise completely naked.

Oh heavens, Richard realised in a panic, the woman had answered the door wearing next to no clothes! He immediately fixed his eyes on an area of space directly above the woman's left shoulder, causing the woman to laugh easily as she turned her head to call back into the room.

'Dwayne, it's your boss,' she said with what Richard recognised as an Edinburgh accent.

Before Richard could ask how this woman could possibly know who he was, she turned and padded off into the recesses of the house, Richard making sure to keep his eyeline fixed firmly mid-air.

'What are you doing here, Chief?' Dwayne said as he

came to the door. Richard finally lowered his eyes and was relieved to see that Dwayne had thrown on a bright blue silk dressing gown that depicted Chinese fighting dragons, even if it only just reached down to the top of his thighs.

'What am *I* doing here?'

'Sure. You're supposed to be at work.'

Richard was rendered almost speechless. Almost.

'You answer the door and have the gall to say that it's me who should be at work?'

'Oh I see, something's up at the station, and you've come to pull me from my books.'

'Your books?'

'Sure. You know what it's like. Thursday is for home study.' As Dwayne said this, he winked slowly for his boss's benefit.

'Why did you just wink at me?'

'Because, Chief, Thursday is for "home study",' Dwayne said with another slow wink.

'But that's clearly not what's going on here. Especially as I just saw you open the curtains to your bedroom wearing next to nothing. Not to mention your friend I just met, whoever she is.'

'That's Amy,' Dwayne said with a delighted smile. 'She's something, isn't she?'

'I'm sure we can all agree she's something, but she shouldn't be walking around in a towel on Police time.'

'But she's not on Police time. She's on holiday.'

'I don't care what she's doing on the island,' Richard

interrupted, 'it's what you're doing on the island that bothers me. Because you're supposed to be using Thursday mornings for personal study time.'

'Why do you keep saying that?'

'Because it's supposed to be what you're doing!'

This statement seemed to take Dwayne by surprise.

'But you never really meant that, did you?'

'Of course I meant it!'

Richard took a deep breath to steady his rising blood pressure. Dwayne was a good copper in many respects, but it was safe to say that his and Richard's approach to work weren't entirely universe-adjacent.

'Oh right,' Dwayne said, understanding finally coming to him. 'You actually want me to be doing personal study on my mornings off.'

'They're not mornings off, they're study periods!'

'Okay okay,' Dwayne said, holding up his hands, 'you've made your point. I'll make sure I work every Thursday from now. But don't worry, no harm done. I mean, it's not like there's much going on on the island at the moment.'

Before Richard could reply that it really wasn't for Dwayne to decide what was or wasn't 'going on' on the island, they both saw a flash of light from the direction of Honoré harbour that was followed a few seconds later by the crack and boom of a massive explosion.

'What the hell was that?' Richard said as a thick cloud of black smoke started to blossom from about half a kilometre out to sea.

'I don't know about you, Chief, but that looked to me like an explosion.'

Richard turned back to his subordinate and dead-eyed him.

'Dwayne. Get dressed. Personal study's over.'

By the time Richard and Dwayne arrived at the harbour, the smoke from the explosion had long since cleared, and they found Detective Sergeant Camille Bordey and Police Officer Fidel Best securing the Police launch, which was really no more than an old wooden skiff that had a pair of massive engines strapped onto the back and the words 'Saint-Marie Police' written in white down the side.

'Did you see that, sir?' Fidel asked, as he pulled the old tarpaulin off the steering position.

'Of course I did, or what do you think I'm doing here?'

'Anyone know what it was?' Dwayne asked.

'I was on the veranda of the station when it happened,' Camille said, 'and I saw a ball of fire out in the harbour. I think a boat went up.'

'Then we need to get out there,' Richard said as he boarded the boat and sat down on the bench that ran down one of the sides.

'Yes, sir,' Camille said, joining him as Dwayne cast off. Camille started the twin engines, Dwayne stepped onto the boat and it started to move off.

'Not too fast!' Richard yelped as Camille opened the throttle and the boat started to surge through the water.

'What's that, sir?' Camille asked over the roar of the engines.

'Not too fast!'

'Can't hear you, sir,' Camille shouted as Richard's old school tie freed itself from his suit jacket and started flapping wildly behind him. It was perhaps a sign of how seriously Richard was holding on for dear life that he didn't make any attempts to grab it and force it back down the front of his suit jacket so that sartorial decorum could be restored.

As Camille drove the boat in a wide arc around the clutch of yachts that were at anchor, she, Dwayne and Fidel shared grins, knowing how much their boss hated any kind of physical danger, real or imagined.

They came across their first piece of debris from the explosion less than a minute later and Camille cut the engines, the launch slowing to a slooshy stop almost immediately.

Looking about themselves, the Police could see that it was one of those days in the tropics of almost perfect stillness. There wasn't a cloud in the sky, the sea seemed to be breathing as it gently rose and fell, and there were sparkling diamonds of reflected light all around them on the water. But there were also what looked like thousands of different-sized pieces of ripped-up wood floating on the surface of the water.

'Look, over there!' Fidel said, and they all saw that there was something much larger floating in the water just off their port bow.

With a quick squirt of power, Camille steered the launch towards the object, and it revealed itself to be the back end of an old boat. The prow should have been pointing vertically downwards towards the sea bed, but Richard could see that the front half of the boat was missing from where the explosion had split it in two.

The section of the stern that was still just above the water line had the boat's name written in white letters. It was called *Soundman*.

'Anyone know who owns the boat?' Richard asked, before he realised that his team was looking at an area of the hull just above the painted name. As Richard looked for himself, he could see why. There was a bright smear of what looked like blood. In fact, the way the smear ran down the wood, it was easy to imagine that someone who was heavily bleeding had briefly clung to the side of the boat before subsiding and slipping into the sea. There even appeared to be a rather macabre handprint in blood just to the side of the smear.

'I'll call the coastguard,' Dwayne said, pulling out his phone. 'They can maybe winch the boat out of the water and help us get it back to shore. And in answer to your question, Chief, *Soundman* belongs to a guy called Conrad Gardiner. He lives in a house on the beach to the side of the harbour.'

'And what do you think happened here?'

Richard's subordinates looked at each other, nonplussed.

'It exploded,' Fidel eventually said.

'I can see it exploded,' Richard said in exasperation. 'But how did it explode? Do boats normally explode?'

This time it was Dwayne's turn to answer.

'No, Chief.'

Richard pulled a hankie from his jacket pocket and wiped the sweat from his brow, his face, and then the back and front of his neck.

'Very well,' he said, 'we need to keep this bit of boat above water. And we also need to keep our eyes peeled for any survivors.'

Even as Richard said this, he could see that there was no-one in the water near the debris, either alive or dead.

Within half an hour, the coastguard's bright yellow rescue boat had arrived and was starting to winch the rear end of the boat onto its deck. This allowed Richard to order Fidel and Dwayne to stay with the coastguard and coordinate the safe return of the boat while he and Camille drove the Police launch in wide circles through the expanding spread of floating debris. All they found were various pieces of detritus – from plastic jerry cans to kitchen implements and even an old white plastic chair – but they couldn't find anything that seemed to shed any light on exactly what had happened.

Once it became apparent that there was nothing left to find on the surface of the water, Richard ordered Camille to drive them back to harbour. When they arrived, Richard saw a small crowd of locals gathered on the quayside. Richard couldn't imagine why. After all, the explosion had happened hundreds of metres away, there was nothing much for the crowd to see, but then he noticed that everyone seemed to be clustered around one woman in particular.

While Camille tied the boat up, Richard saw the crowd

jostle the middle-aged woman forward, and he went to find out what was happening.

'I'm afraid I'll have to ask you all to move on,' he announced as he came within earshot. 'There's nothing to see here.'

'But is it true?' the woman at the front asked.

'Is what true?'

'That it was Conrad's boat?'

'It's still early in the investigation.'

'But was it Conrad's boat?' she said again, almost begging.

Before Richard could reply that he couldn't possibly comment, Camille pushed past him and took the woman's hands in hers.

'Natasha,' she said, 'I'm so sorry. It was Conrad's boat.'

'Detective Sergeant?' Richard said, irked that Camille had so effortlessly taken control of the situation.

'Yes, sir?' Camille replied.

'You know each other?'

Richard indicated the woman. He could see that she was perhaps in her late forties, and was dressed somewhat dowdily, with a simple skirt, blouse and cardigan.

'This is Natasha Gardiner,' Camille said. 'Conrad Gardiner's wife.'

'Oh,' Richard said. 'I see.'

'But it was definitely his boat . . .?' Natasha asked, her eyes desperate with worry.

'I'm sorry,' Camille said. 'It was.'

'Then where is he?'

'We don't know. But we didn't see him in the water, so maybe he got away before it happened.'

Richard decided that enough was enough. If it was unprofessional that they should be talking about the incident before they'd even finished their first survey of the scene, it was doubly bad that they'd be doing so in front of a crowd.

'Perhaps we could have this conversation somewhere a little more private?' he asked Camille.

'Good idea,' Camille agreed. 'Natasha and Conrad live only a couple of houses away, we can talk there.'

Natasha's house was precisely the last place on earth Richard wanted to visit, but he couldn't see a diplomatic way of explaining this to his partner, so he just harrumphed by way of an answer.

'Good!' Camille said, and then started to lead Natasha off, telling her how she shouldn't prejudge the situation, there were a million things that may have happened, and maybe they'd find a very damp and embarrassed Conrad already waiting for them back at her house. This seemed to settle Natasha a little, but it did nothing to improve Richard's mood as he followed behind.

Natasha's house was a one-storey bungalow that led directly onto the little beach of Honoré. It had a green and white striped awning out front, and a couple of hanging baskets of flame-red flowers either side of the front door. The inside of the house was just as quaint, with simple furniture, and sea shells arranged on shelves.

'Now, why don't I get us all a glass of water,' Camille said, heading to the sink. 'And maybe you could tell us a bit about where Conrad was going this morning.'

'Well, I don't know. Not exactly. Only that Conrad always goes out fishing every morning.'

'He's a fisherman?' Richard asked.

'Oh no, he's a music producer. Or he was for a time.'

'So what does he do now?'

'Well . . . you know. This and that. I mean, we don't need so much money to get by, now we're older.'

'But he goes fishing every morning?'

'Not every morning. Sometimes he doesn't get up in time. But most days.'

'And do you ever go out with him?'

'Me? Oh no, I'm not welcome. You see, Conrad never catches anything much. For him, it's more about getting away, I think. You know what men are like.'

Natasha addressed this last comment to Camille as she came over with two glasses of water.

'Here you go,' Camille said.

'Thank you,' Natasha said gratefully as she took her glass. 'And you think he maybe wasn't on the boat when it went up like that?'

'It's a possibility,' Camille said.

'But we can't really talk about specifics this early in the investigation,' Richard said. 'Although you should perhaps know that we found a smear of blood on the one remaining part of the hull we could find.'

'Oh,' Natasha said as this information sank in.

'It may not be blood,' Camille said with a warning glance at her boss to soften his approach. 'And even if it is, it's possible it belongs to someone other than your husband, of course.'

'But he always goes out on his own. No-one else would have been with him. If you found blood . . .?'

Richard could see tears forming in Natasha's eyes.

'Can I ask,' he said, 'was your husband's boat safe?'

'How do you mean?'

'Well, are you surprised he had this accident?'

And with that, the tears came.

Richard looked at Camille, partly in helplessness, and partly in irritation. As far as he was concerned, it was entirely his partner's fault that they now found themselves in this situation. This was far too soon to be talking to a key witness.

For her part, Camille ignored her boss's disapproval and went and knelt by Natasha.

'You mustn't worry. We still don't know what happened.'

'But where is he?'

'We'll find him. If he's out there, we'll find him.'

As Camille continued to console Natasha, Richard realised that he was now something of a spare part to the whole conversation. So he wafted his arms a bit. He didn't quite know why, but as he did so, he had the flash of a memory of being at college parties where, no matter what room he went into, no-one seemed to want to talk to him. In fact, Richard remembered how college parties had been a type of living hell. They were full of all of the beautiful and confident people, and he'd drift from room to room being roundly ignored. Before his memories spiked too painfully, Richard decided to keep himself busy by poking around.

On a nearby shelf, he found a collection of photos that charted the growth of a young woman from a baby up to the day she graduated from college, a mortar board on her head and a scroll in her hand. This was no doubt Natasha's daughter. But Richard could also see photos of Natasha and a man he presumed must be Conrad, her husband. The photos were taken at parties, and Natasha and Conrad were laughing or dancing together in all of them. They looked a handsome couple, Richard thought to himself, and he realised he had trouble matching the vivacious young woman in the photos with the older woman he'd just met. But then, he had to remind himself, Natasha had just discovered her husband had possibly recently died.

As for the photos of Conrad, he looked as though he was always having a good time. He was laughing in every photo, or smoking a cigar, or raising a toast with his bottle of beer.

Seeing that Natasha was still crying, Richard slipped into a little corridor that led from the main room. He saw an open door. Telling himself that seeing as Natasha had invited him into her house he didn't need a warrant, he pushed the door open a bit further, and what he saw inside shocked him.

The room had been trashed, with all its contents tipped over or dashed to the floor. What's more, Richard could see that the room's one window had been smashed, and there was a fist-sized chunk of concrete lying in the middle of the glass-strewn rug.

Clearly, someone had thrown the chunk of concrete in through the window, but what had happened next? Had this person then climbed in afterwards looking for something? Or had the room been smashed up just for the hell of it?

Richard was about to return to Natasha to find out what she knew about the break-in, when his eye caught something red and shiny sitting in the centre of a small writing desk to the side of the room. Unlike the rest of the furniture, this one table had been left standing. But what was on it?

Richard picked his way across the room until he could see the object more clearly..

It was a ruby.

A big, fat red ruby that was significantly larger than any jewel Richard had ever seen before. In fact, it was so large, Richard knew it couldn't be real. It must have come from some kind of theatrical costumier's or joke shop.

But what on earth was a ruby doing in the middle of the desk?

CHAPTER TWO

Richard returned to the main room of the house and explained what he'd just seen.

'I don't understand,' Natasha said. 'There's been a break-in?'

'It's how it looks,' Richard said, and then he asked Natasha what the room was usually used for.

'It's Conrad's. His den. It's where he likes to go. You know, when he wants some peace and quiet.'

'Then can I ask, have you been in his room today?'

'No. Conrad doesn't like me going in there.'

'Do you recall hearing the sound of glass smashing at all today?'

Natasha rose from her chair.

'What's happened?' she asked.

'If you could just answer the question.'

Natasha looked to Camille for support, and she nodded kindly, which seemed to give her strength.

'Okay. Well, no, I didn't hear any glass smashing today.'

'Thank you. And have you been in the house all day?'

'I've been cross-stitching a kneeler for the church.' As Natasha said this, she indicated some brightly coloured threads that were piled on an occasional table nearby.

'I see. You're involved in the local church?'

'Of course. Aren't you?'

Richard didn't quite know how to reply, if only because he always felt a touch bashful that religion had never quite 'taken' for him. As he tried to think of a suitable reply, Camille stepped in.

'And what church do you belong to?'

'Father Luc Durant's. He's such an impressive priest. Don't you think?'

Richard had no idea who Father Luc was, but he recognised that he was in danger of losing control of the interview entirely.

'Then can I ask,' he said, 'if you didn't hear any glass smashing, and you were here all morning, what time did you leave?'

'How do you mean?' Natasha asked.

'Well, we first met you at the harbour. So when did you leave your house for the harbour?'

Natasha frowned as she considered her answer.

'That's easy enough to explain. I left when . . . you know, I heard the . . . the boat . . .'

'You heard the explosion?'

'Not that I knew what it was. It was just this terrible noise.'

'What time was this?'

'It was just after eleven, I think. I was listening to the news on the radio.'

'And then what did you do?' he asked.

'Well, I got on with cross-stitching. I didn't think it had anything to do with me. But about five minutes later, Morgane Pichou came and knocked on my door. You know Morgane? She runs the tourist centre in Honoré. Anyway, she said she'd been down at the harbour when the explosion happened, and she'd heard that it was Conrad's boat that had just . . . well, that it had just happened to. I didn't know what to think. And then my phone rang. It was the harbour master, Philippe. He said I should come down to the harbour at once. There'd been an accident. I still didn't believe it could be true – I still don't believe it . . .'

'So what time did you get down to the harbour?' Richard asked, aware that Natasha was about to start crying again.

'I don't know. Twenty past. Something like that.'

'And just to be clear, you were definitely in the house the whole morning before the explosion?'

'Yes.'

Richard paused to collect his thoughts, because this meant that if Natasha could be believed, the break-in must have happened *after* she'd left her house following the explosion. After all, if it had happened at any time before, she'd surely have heard the glass smashing. But what sort of person would break in to Conrad's house after his boat had just exploded? Were the two facts connected, or was it just a coincidence?

'Mrs Gardiner, could you follow me?' Richard asked,

before leading Natasha and Camille into the corridor where Conrad's room was. As he pushed the door open, Natasha gave a little gasp and her hand shot to her mouth.

'Is this a surprise to you?'

'Of course,' Natasha said, deeply shocked. 'I mean, Conrad's not the tidiest person, but he's not this bad. Everything's been thrown onto the floor. Hasn't it? And the window's been smashed.'

'I think it was smashed with that piece of concrete there,' Richard said, indicating the chunk in the middle of the room. 'Which is why I was asking if you'd heard the sound of any glass smashing today. I think it would have made a considerable noise when that rock came in through the window.'

'Of course. I didn't hear any smashing this morning.'

'Can you see if anything's been stolen?'

Natasha scanned the room from the doorway.

'I don't know. I don't think so. I wouldn't say Conrad had anything worth stealing.'

'Then can you tell me if this belongs to him?' Richard said, entering the room and going over to the table where the bright red ruby was sitting.

'What is it?'

'It looks like a ruby.'

Natasha's expression of concern briefly froze, and Camille and Richard exchanged a glance – both knowing that the ruby had just registered with her.

'A what?' Natasha asked.

'A ruby,' he replied.

Natasha didn't speak for a few moments.

'Does it mean anything to you?' Camille asked as kindly as she could.

Natasha seemed to come to a decision.

'No,' she said firmly. 'But you're saying it's a real ruby?'

'I don't know,' Richard said. 'I doubt it. It would be worth millions.'

'Then I've no idea how that got there,' Natasha said with finality.

'Do you think it belongs to your husband?' Camille asked.

'Oh no. Where would he get something like that from?'

Richard bent down to give the jewel a good inspection. It lay on its side and was cut so that it was fat at one end but sharpened to a point at the other. Richard could see tiny air bubbles trapped inside, making it clear that it really was just a trinket made of plastic.

'So you're saying this jewel doesn't belong to your husband, and doesn't belong to you, either?'

'That's it exactly,' Natasha said, happy with Richard's assessment. 'I've never seen it before in my life.'

'Then I wonder who put it there?'

'I've no idea.'

'Don't you? Only you seemed to recognise it.'

'I didn't,' Natasha said, and Richard could see how sincere she was. 'I was just surprised. I couldn't work out what it was doing there.'

'Which is very much the question, isn't it? Can you imagine

why anyone might have wanted to smash that window there, break in to your house, and then place a paste red ruby on this desk here?'

'No.'

'Are you sure about that?'

'Oh yes. I've no idea what it can possibly mean.'

Natasha seemed to have got control of whatever doubts she'd previously had, and Richard could see that he wouldn't be getting any more from her for the moment.

'Okay, we'll have to treat this room as a secondary crime scene, so we'll need to have our officers process it. And we'll need to take your fingerprints as well, Mrs Gardiner. Just so we can exclude them from whatever we find in this room, of course. And can I ask where we might be able to find sample fingerprints from your husband?'

Natasha looked into the room and indicated a spilled bottle of rum on the floor that was lying next to an old metal tumbler. 'That's Conrad's bottle. And his glass. His fingerprints should be on both of them.'

Richard thanked Natasha for her time and told her they'd update her with news of her husband the moment they had any. In the meantime, she was to wait until one of his officers returned to take her fingerprints and start processing the room.

'So what do you think of Mrs Gardiner?' Camille asked as they walked the short distance back to the Police station.

'I think she's in shock.'

'But the ruby didn't surprise her entirely, did it?'

'I'd agree with you there, Camille.'

'So why did she deny all knowledge of it?'

'Indeed,' Richard said as he stopped at the bottom of the slope that led up to the Police station. As he did so, he saw two people emerge from the station.

'Oh no, no, no, no, no, no,' Richard said, and started racing up the steps two at a time.

Camille had no idea what Richard was doing, but, looking up, she saw that Dwayne was standing on the veranda and was chatting easily to a very attractive blonde woman. Camille smiled to herself. So that's what had upset her boss.

As for Richard, he was a man on a mission as he strode onto the veranda of the Police station and found Dwayne talking to Amy, the woman who had answered the door that morning wearing only a towel.

'Officer Myers, what the hell is going on?'

'Chief?' Dwayne said, startled by his boss's sudden arrival.

'What are you doing here?'

'How do you mean, "here"? I work here.'

'But I left you strict instructions to get the remains of the boat to shore. So how come you've been inside the station with a civilian?'

'Whoa,' Dwayne said, holding up his hands. 'Back up there a moment. Fidel and me have got the boat to shore. But we need to process the blood we found on it. And lift whatever prints we can find. So I came back to the station to pick up the Crime Scene Kit. And when I got here – only minutes ago, I can tell you – I found Amy waiting for me.'

'You came back to get the Crime Scene Kit?'

'I said.'

'So why haven't you got it in your hands right now?'

Dwayne was puzzled that his boss was so interested.

'I was thirsty after all that hard work in the sun. So I got a drink of water with Amy here, and now — what you're interrupting — is me telling her I'm busy on a case and we'll have to meet up later on.'

Richard didn't believe a word Dwayne was saying. He'd been sloping off work and hanging out with his new girlfriend again, Richard was sure of it.

'I'm sorry if I've caused a problem,' Amy said in her lilting Edinburgh accent.

'It's not you who's caused a problem,' Richard said, stiffly.

'And anyway, it wasn't Dwayne I came down here to see,' she continued, and then she gave Dwayne a playful punch on the arm. Dwayne winced in melodramatic pretence that the punch had caused him mortal pain. Amy pulled a shocked face, and Richard sighed internally at the whole teenage horseplay of it all. As far as he could tell, Amy was in her early forties, and she and Dwayne were surely old enough to have got beyond what his mother called the 'giggling and pinching' stage of courtship.

It was only once he'd finished his thought process that Richard realised that he'd not quite registered what Amy had said.

'How do you mean, you didn't come to see Dwayne?' he asked, as Camille joined them on the veranda.

'Well, isn't it obvious?' Amy said. 'I came to apologise to you.'

'Apologise?'

'Of course. For answering the door to you wearing only a towel this morning.'

Richard's face flushed, and Amy smiled with an understanding of his embarrassment that just made his cheeks burn an even deeper shade of red.

'Yes, well,' he blustered. 'It wasn't quite what I expected, but don't worry, I've seen worse. I mean, better. Or not better – that's not right. I just mean, I've seen . . . if I'm honest,' Richard said in quiet despair, 'I don't quite know what I mean.'

'You just mean,' Amy said, smoothing over Richard's awkwardness, 'you're used to seeing semi-naked women.'

'Well, normally only on the mortician's slab, if I'm honest,' Richard said by way of keeping things light, but it was only as he looked at Camille and Dwayne's horrified faces that he realised how creepy he must have sounded.

'Anyway,' Amy said awkwardly, 'no harm done. I just wanted to apologise. And introduce myself properly to you. I'm Amy McDiarmid.'

Amy held out her hand, and Richard was relieved finally that normality had resumed.

'Richard Poole,' he said. 'How do you do.'

'Very well, thank you,' Amy said, as amused as Richard's team was at his formality. 'Although, I wanted to ask. Did you manage to see any birds this morning?'

'How do you mean, did I see any birds?'

'Well, it's just, I couldn't help noticing. When you came to the door, you had a pair of binoculars around your neck.'

'You did?' Dwayne said. 'I didn't notice.'

'That's right,' Amy said. 'A nice pair of binoculars.'

'But you're not into birdwatching, Chief,' Dwayne said.

'I don't think he was birdwatching,' Camille said as she realised what the binoculars meant. 'You were spying on Dwayne, weren't you?'

'It's not how it looks,' Richard said weakly.

'You were *spying* on me?' Dwayne said, amazed.

'But Thursday mornings are for revising for your sergeant's exam. And I've never seen you with any of the revision materials in the office. Or talking about how hard the work is. In fact, I've seen no evidence you've even started work on your exams. So I just wanted to check up on you. You know, that you were actually studying.'

Dwayne stared long and hard at his boss.

'You know,' he said, 'if you'd been using your binoculars to get a glimpse of a beautiful naked woman, I reckon I could understand where you were coming from. But snooping on colleagues to check they're looking at a load of old books . . .?'

Richard didn't quite know what to say. Dwayne was making it sound like he was in the wrong and not Dwayne.

'Now, I've got a Crime Scene Kit to get,' Dwayne continued primly. 'Amy, I'll see you later.'

Dwayne gave Amy a quick kiss on the cheek, and then he turned and entered the Police station.

'Don't worry,' Amy said kindly, touching Richard's besuited elbow. 'You know what Dwayne's like. He'll forget about all this in no time at all. He doesn't bear grudges.'

Richard's mobile phone rang in his jacket pocket.

'If you'll excuse me, we're in the middle of an active case, I'll need to answer my phone, it could be important.'

Richard stepped to one side, which gave Amy a moment alone with Camille.

'You really answered the door to him wearing only a towel?' Camille asked.

'I'm afraid I did.'

'I'd have paid anything to see his face.'

'He went bright red.'

'I bet he did.'

'You know what? Your boss is just like Dwayne said he'd be. But even more so.'

Camille smiled. She'd spent a long time with Richard, and she'd long ago realised that most of his sudden squalls of anger and stick-in-the-mud curmudgeonliness came from an upbringing that had straitjacketed him from the moment he put on his first suit, shirt and tie aged four. Camille believed that inside her boss, just as surely was the case with every human, there was a free spirit bursting to get out. In the meantime, she found herself a wry spectator to his wrecking-ball social interactions. And the fact that Richard was utterly dedicated to solving crimes went a long way in her mind to making up for all his other inadequacies. Mind you, she thought to herself, he'd crossed a line when he'd started spying on Dwayne with a pair of binoculars. She knew she'd have to speak to him about that later on.

Richard returned from his phonecall, energised.

'Okay, that was Fidel, Camille. He says he's found something on the boat we need to see. At once. Amy, you'll have to excuse us.'

'Of course,' Amy said, and called out, 'Send my love to Dwayne,' as she started clipping down the stairs to leave the Police station.

'I'd rather not,' Richard replied before turning back to Camille. 'Right then, seeing as we've now got two scenes to work, I suggest we split up. You take the Crime Scene Kit back to Natasha and Conrad's house. Dust the window frame and windowsill for fingerprints. Also, someone should see if there are any prints on that chunk of concrete that was used to smash the glass. And while you're about it, check for footprints in the soil outside the window, and do a quick door-to-door. Did any of the neighbours see or hear anything suspicious like breaking glass before or after the explosion this morning? And above all else, make sure you bag the paste ruby. It was left on the desk for a reason, and I suggest we find out what it was.'

'Yes, sir.'

Dwayne came out of the station holding the large metal flight case that was the station's Crime Scene Kit.

'Dwayne,' Richard said, 'Camille will need the kit for herself, she's working a secondary crime scene. So I want you down at the harbour running a door-to-door. And also go yacht to yacht for that matter. Did anyone see Mr Gardiner go out on his boat this morning? And was anyone with him, or was he on his own? We still don't know who was on his boat when it exploded.'

'Were you really spying on me?'

'We don't have time for this now, Dwayne. I also need you to get onto the Saint-Marie dive school. I want them in their scuba kit and scouring the sea bed where the boat went down. I want a list of everything that sank from Conrad's boat.'

'Don't worry,' Camille said to Dwayne. 'I'll talk to him about snooping on you.'

'Not now you won't,' Richard said, heading down the stairs. 'I need to see Fidel, and you both need to get on with your jobs.'

A few minutes later, Richard was striding along the concrete quay towards where he saw the back half of Conrad's boat resting on its side. Fidel was erecting 'Police – Do Not Cross' tape around it, and to the side of the quay, the Saint-Marie Coastguard were making good the winch on their boat.

'Okay, Fidel, what have you got for me?' Richard called out as he approached.

'Well, sir, the explosion wasn't an accident.'

'You know that?'

'I do, sir.'

'How can you be so sure?'

'Let me show you.'

Fidel led Richard around the structure, and Richard could

see that the wooden sides of the hull were jagged and torn in a way that looked as though a leviathan had risen from the deep, snapped the boat in two with its jaws – and this was the bit of the boat it had then tossed aside.

Passing the sharp edges of the hull, Richard saw that the interior of the boat had been mostly ripped out by the explosion, although there were still plenty of old pipes and rusting metal fixings sticking out at crazy angles. Mercifully, there were no smears of blood here, but Richard watched as Fidel stepped up to a dirty grey tube that ran along the inside of the boat and which was fixed with red cable ties.

'Okay, sir,' Fidel said, 'I think that this section of the boat was once the engine compartment. And this tube here was the fuel inlet to the engine.'

'So where's the engine?'

'I imagine it got blown from its housing and sank with everything else. But the thing is, on boats like this, the engines tend to be at the rear. In a tight and enclosed space directly under the driving position.'

'Okay,' Richard said, wondering where Fidel was going with this.

'It can make them seriously dangerous if there's any kind of cut or tear in the fuel inlet. Like we've got here.'

Fidel indicated a point on the pipe with his forefinger, and Richard could see that there was a deep cut that ran along it for about three inches.

'How did that get there?'

'I've looked at it, and it's pretty neat. I think someone slit it open using a sharp knife.'

'But why would they want to do that?'

'Well, a tear in the fuel line like this isn't enough to let much petrol leak, but it's enough to let fumes from the petrol get out.'

'Oh,' Richard said, understanding finally coming to him. 'Petrol fumes that then build up inside the enclosed space.'

'Exactly, sir. And then, the tiniest spark and the whole thing goes up.'

'But how did you find that rip?' Richard asked, looking at all the dozens of feet of pipes that ran around the inside of the boat's hull.

'Well, sir, I was carrying out a visual inspection of the wreck when I found this.'

Fidel walked around the inside of the boat and pulled down a mess of what looked like electric cables that were tied together with parcel tape. But as Richard looked more closely, he saw that there was something else that the parcel tape was holding in place.

It was a mobile phone.

What was a mobile phone doing taped to the inside of an engine compartment?

As Richard looked again, he could see that it was one of the old-fashioned plastic phones that had no touchscreen, it just had buttons and the smallest of screens for the minimum of text.

But there were also two thin electric cables emerging from

the housing of the phone – and the plastic at the end of each cable was stripped back to reveal copper wires. Richard took a step back, the sheer enormity of what Fidel had uncovered hitting him.

'Good grief,' he said.

Someone had sliced into the fuel pipes of the boat so that the enclosed engine compartment would fill with petrol fumes. But this person had also taped a doctored phone inside the same engine compartment. When the boat was heading out to sea, the compartment filled with petrol vapour, and this person had then rung the number of the mobile phone. The incoming call had turned on the circuit that was supposed to drive the motor that made the phone vibrate, but it had been re-routed to a couple of cables that led outside the casing. And once the current was flowing in these two little cables, the electricity had arced and caused the tiniest of sparks.

The spark had caused the petrol to explode, and the boat had blown apart.

Despite the heat, a shiver ran down Richard's spine.

Fidel was right. Conrad hadn't died in some tragic accident at sea.

He'd been murdered in cold blood.

CHAPTER THREE

Of the many things that irritated Richard about the tropical island of Saint-Marie, perhaps the one that infuriated him the most was just how small it was. It's not that he had an objection to its size *per se*. After all, as he often had occasion to tell his team, he'd holidayed many times on the Isle of Wight as a child, so he knew something about island living. But it was one thing to take a vacation on an island, and quite another to run a Police investigation on one.

For starters there were no forensic or pathology labs on Saint-Marie, so whenever Richard needed to process any kind of physical evidence, it had to be sent 'off island' to Guadeloupe. But the island's size also meant he only had access to two Police vehicles. One of these was a battered old Mark II Land Rover that was painted mustard yellow and had the crest of the Saint-Marie Police Force on the bonnet and sides. For all Richard publicly grumbled about the vehicle, he couldn't help but feel a grudging affinity with it. Like him it was British, hadn't even been remotely designed for tropical climes, and yet here it was, chugging along and doing the best it could in very testing circumstances.

But if Richard tolerated the Police Land Rover, the same couldn't be said for the other Police vehicle, a sputtering Harley Davidson motorbike that had an attached, almost-certainly illegal sidecar. Only Dwayne was qualified to drive the infernal machine, and Richard only travelled in it under sufferance. After all, as he'd tell anyone who asked, if the answer is ever 'get on a motorbike driven by Dwayne', you've very definitely been asking the wrong question.

However, the most irksome aspect of island living, as far as Richard was concerned, was that the distances were often so small that the quickest way to get somewhere was to walk. And while Richard loved the idea of walking in theory – particularly on a crisp winter's day, the grass stiff on the ground with frost – it was quite a different matter yomping through the blistering heat of the tropics wearing a thick woollen suit.

Sweating heavily, Richard arrived at Mrs Gardiner's house, and found Camille inspecting the earth beneath the smashed window. Having updated her that he and Fidel now believed Conrad had been murdered, Richard asked what Camille had so far been able to find.

'Not much of anything, sir,' she said. 'There are no foot-prints out here. And no cigarette butts or anything else that suggests anyone was here. And the window's not overlooked by any of the neighbours, so they didn't see anything, either.'

'Did they hear the moment the window was smashed?'

'I've asked whoever I can find who was nearby at the time, and no-one saw or heard anything suspicious.'

'I see,' Richard said, disappointed. 'Then what about the window frame?'

Camille explained that she'd just finished inspecting the outside frame, and it was so rough and weather-beaten it wasn't possible to lift any fingerprints from it.

'Then what about the break-in? Has Mrs Gardiner got any theories?'

'None. Although I asked her to have a proper look at everything that was thrown on the floor, and she said she's not sure, but she thinks nothing's been stolen.'

'In which case, the break-in was all about leaving the ruby.'

'Which is kind of crazy, sir.'

'I'd agree with you there. Because, why bother?'

'It's a message, isn't it?'

'That's what I'm thinking. It's got no intrinsic value, so it must be symbolic somehow. Or a warning of some kind.'

'To Natasha?'

'It's a possibility. Because it wasn't a message for Conrad, was it? I mean, with him dead, he's not going to receive it, is he? Look, let's talk to Natasha again. We need to tell her the explosion wasn't an accident, and I want to press her a bit more about this ruby.'

Richard and Camille went into the house, but Natasha was nowhere to be found. However, the French windows were open, and they could see that she was standing on the beach down by the sea.

'Oh, bloody hell,' Richard said to himself as he stepped out of the house and onto the bright white sand. He hated walking on beaches in his brogues, and he still couldn't quite believe that it was an occupational hazard he had to endure on an almost daily basis.

'Mrs Gardiner?' Camille asked as they approached, but Natasha didn't turn round. She just kept staring out at the distant horizon.

Richard cleared his throat to get the woman's attention.

'If he's in the water, he'll come in here, won't he?' Natasha said, almost to herself. 'I mean, this is the nearest beach.'

'It is,' Camille said, kindly. 'But there have been developments. It looks like maybe your husband's boat didn't explode by accident.'

Natasha's brow furrowed, but she didn't say anything.

'It looks like it was set off by an IED,' Richard said. 'An improvised explosive device.'

This finally registered with her.

'I'm, sorry . . .?'

'Now, I understand this is a terrible shock,' Camille said before her boss could be any more insensitive, 'but if someone was behind this terrible event, then every passing hour will make it harder for us to catch them.'

'You're saying it *wasn't* an accident?'

'I'm sorry.'

'But why would anyone want to do that to Conrad?'

'That's what we'd like to know.'

Natasha took a moment to compose herself, and then she said, 'No, it's not possible. It's monstrous.'

She then headed back to her house. After a quick glance of surprise at each other, Richard and Camille followed her across the sand.

'You don't think anyone could have wanted to harm your husband?' Camille asked.

'No way.'

'Even though it looks as though someone did?'

'But who'd want to harm him?' Natasha said, turning and looking at the Police officers with what Richard realised was a fair amount of desperation. 'Everyone likes Conrad, that's the whole point of him. He's popular.'

'Do you mind me asking, what exactly does he do?'

'Well, it's like I told you before. He does this and that.'

'But what sort of "this and that"?'

'He used to be a record producer. With his own recording studio and everything. He's always been a champion of island music.'

'He *used* to be a record producer?' Richard asked

'For many years. But you can't keep making hit records. Your luck eventually runs out, and that's how it went with Conrad. He hit a bad patch, and when the money ran out he had to let his studio go.'

'That must have been hard,' Camille offered.

'Not to Conrad. Nothing is ever a problem to him. If we're rich, and we've had plenty of money in the past, he's happy. If we're poor, he's also happy. He's just happy with everything and everyone.' This comment really seemed to resonate with Natasha. 'So it's just impossible that anyone would do this to him. You must have made a mistake.'

'You think so?'

'I know so.'

'Then perhaps you could explain why a ruby was left on a table in your husband's study?'

There was a flash of surprise in Natasha's eyes that Richard could see her quell just as soon as it appeared.

'I don't understand.'

'Because I think you know what it means.'

'I don't.'

'It's better if you tell us what you know now,' Camille said, playing the role of the 'Good Cop'.

'But I don't know anything about why that ruby was put there. Nothing at all. I promise you.'

Natasha said this statement with such finality that Richard was left in no doubt that she meant it. The only problem was, both Richard and Camille knew she was lying. But why would she lie about why a ruby was left in her house?

Just before it was time to finish for the day, Richard gathered his team at the whiteboard in the Police station.

'Okay, so what have we got so far?' he asked, popping the lid on a fresh board marker.

'Well, sir,' Fidel said, 'I've lifted the prints from the bottle of rum you got from Natasha's house. And assuming those prints belong to Conrad, I can say that they match the fingerprints we've been able to lift from the blood we found on Conrad's boat.'

'It was his handprint in the blood?'

'I've got definite matches for his first, second and third fingers on his right hand, and matches for his left thumb and first finger.'

'So it really was Conrad who was injured in the explosion.'

'And who then slipped down the side of his boat into the water,' Dwayne added. 'Which means he went into the water bleeding.'

Richard shuddered. They all knew how slim the chances were of a heavily bleeding man lasting long before attracting the attention of a nearby shark.

'And it was a big explosion,' Dwayne said. 'Anything that could do that to a boat could do a lot worse to flesh and bone.'

'Poor man,' Camille said.

'Although,' Richard asked, 'are we *sure* he didn't survive?'

'I don't see how he could have done,' Fidel said. 'I reckon we were at the scene within twenty minutes. So if he was alive – either on his boat or in the water – we'd have seen him.'

'Then could he have swum ashore before we got there?'

'No way. The nearest land was Honoré beach, and that's where we came from. If he was in any condition to swim to safety, we'd have passed him on our way out. And I was checking the water the whole time, sir. I didn't see anyone swimming anywhere.'

'Very well. We'll need to tell Mrs Gardiner that her husband is missing presumed dead. Camille?'

Camille sighed, but knew it made sense that the task fall

to her. After all, she was the only detective at the station who wasn't Richard Poole, and that was reason enough for her to handle all of the conversations that required any kind of sympathy.

'Okay,' she said, and went to her desk to get ready to leave.

'Then, Dwayne,' Richard said, 'what did you get from going door-to-door at the harbour?'

'Well, Chief, I spoke to whoever I could find, and three witnesses all said that they saw Conrad get onto his boat on his own this morning.'

'No-one else was with him?'

'That's what they're saying. And the harbour master, Philippe, said he talked to Conrad this morning and was sure he was on his own. In fact, Conrad asked Philippe to help load his scuba kit onto the boat because there was no-one else around to help.'

'He took scuba diving kit out with him?' Richard asked.

'That's what Philippe said. But the important thing is, Philippe's ninety-nine per cent sure that no-one else was on the boat with Conrad. Unless they were hiding in the cabin.'

'I see,' Richard said, already feeling frustrated that the explosion had ruined their primary crime scene. How could they run forensics or test any of their theories when half the boat had sunk to the bottom of the sea?

'Then did you speak to the Saint-Marie Dive School?'

'I did. And tomorrow they're putting together a team to scour the seabed under where the boat went down.'

'Oh, Camille,' Richard said to his partner as she headed

for the door, 'were there any fingerprints on the ruby that was left at the scene?'

'No, sir. There wasn't a single fingerprint on it.'

'Now, that is interesting, isn't it?'

'You're right, sir. Whoever put it there made sure there was no way of tracing it back to them,' Camille said, and then she headed off.

'And yet, it must have been bought from somewhere on the island. Dwayne, can you ring all the shops where you think it would be possible to buy a fake ruby. I want to know where it came from.'

'Okay.'

'Which brings me to you, Fidel. What have you been able to glean from the mobile phone detonator you recovered from the boat?'

'Well, sir,' Fidel said, leading them over to his desk where he'd separated the mobile phone from the wires, and had also removed its back cover and battery. 'I dusted the tape and outer casing for fingerprints. There aren't any.'

'Like the ruby,' Richard said. 'Which, again, makes sense. Our killer's got to be careful.'

'But I also removed the battery and casing and dusted them all over as well. You know, just on the off chance I could find a fingerprint or trapped hair or something.'

'Of course. But nothing?'

'Got it in one, sir. Nothing. Or so I thought. Because I then decided to dust the SIM card before I tried to work out what the number was and where it had been bought from.'

Richard was impressed.

'You dusted the SIM card for prints?'

'You've got to be thorough, sir,' Fidel said, believing that Richard was chastising him. 'And I found a partial fingerprint on the contact side of the SIM card.'

'You did?'

'Better than that, I was able to lift it. And the thing is, it doesn't match any of the exclusion prints we took for Conrad Gardiner. Or his wife, for that matter.'

'The print from the SIM card belongs to some unknown third party?'

'I believe so.'

'Have you uploaded the print to the CPCN?' Richard asked eagerly.

The Caribbean Police Computer Network was one of the few saving graces of working on Saint-Marie as far as Richard was concerned. It was a database of information that unified all of the Police forces in the Caribbean, and also linked to data held by the FBI and Europol.

'I uploaded it as soon as I could,' Fidel said, 'and I've set it looking for a match.'

'Very good work. Very good work indeed. Although, did you by any chance learn anything from the information on the SIM card?'

'Nothing that I think will help us. Because it's got its IME number, so I ran it through the computer. It's a Saint-Marie number, but it's a prepaid phone that was sold just over a year ago.'

'Has the shop that sold it kept any details?'

'They haven't. In fact, it's that dodgy phone shop down by the harbour. Just by the booth where you buy tickets for the glass-bottomed boat.'

'And they won't tell us who they sold it to?'

'No way.'

'Can't we get a warrant and force them?'

'When I spoke to them, they said they've lost their records. And anyway, the phone was sold for cash, there'd be no way of tracing who they sold it to.'

'So the phone is a dead end?'

'Not necessarily, sir. Seeing as it was used to set off the bomb, it must have received a phonecall at 10am this morning. I've put in a request with the phone company. They're going to let me know what calls were made to or from that SIM card as soon as they can.'

'Good stuff, Fidel,' Richard said. 'Then what do we know about Conrad Gardiner? His wife Natasha said he was a record producer or something back in the day.'

Dwayne laughed.

'"Or something" more like, Chief.'

'How do you mean?'

'I mean, he played at being a hotshot record producer, but he had no taste. So he'd scout whatever talent he could find. You know, a young band, or a guy who did his own thing and reckoned he needed a great producer to take him to the next level. Anyway, Conrad would convince these people to sign to his label. He'd then cut a record in a studio he had built, and then he'd announce the band by throwing a party. And they were great parties, I can tell you. But the bands were always the worst, and the records never sold.'

'Then what made him go into producing?'

'No idea.'

'And how did he carry on if he was so unsuccessful?'

'You mean, building a studio, and then launching band after band and never making any money?'

'It doesn't seem like a very sustainable business model.'

'It wasn't. But then, the rumour was he used mob money to set up his studio.'

'He had links to gangsters?'

'That's what people used to say. That the money he had wasn't clean. And I can tell you, Conrad used to hang out with some pretty shady people back in the day.'

'He was a gangster himself?'

'I don't know I'd go that far. But his friends were. No doubt about it. He was the sort of guy who, when he builds a studio, you don't ask where he got the money from.'

'So what's he been doing since he gave up record producing?'

'He's like a lot of men on the island. He does what he can to get by. You know, seasonal work when the tourists are around, and who knows what the rest of the time.'

'But he's dodgy?'

'He *was* dodgy. I don't know about recently. I've not heard anything.'

'But if he's got that sort of background, it could explain why someone wanted him dead.'

'It could, although he was never a big fish. So whatever he's been up to, it's been pretty low grade stuff for a number of years.'

'Did you know him?'

'Sure. Enough to say hello to, anyway. I liked him.'

Richard was slightly wrongfooted.

'Despite him being a criminal, Dwayne?'

'Of course,' Dwayne said easily. 'But there are worse crimes than being a criminal.'

At this pronouncement, Richard threw his hands up in the air and returned to inspect the information on the whiteboard.

'Then what of the wife, Natasha?' he called back to the room. 'Anyone have anything on her?'

'Not me,' Dwayne said.

'She said she went to church, didn't she? Fidel, do you know Natasha Gardiner?'

Fidel, as a good family man, attended Sunday services at Honoré church every week.

'I don't think so, sir,' Fidel said. 'If she goes to church, it's not the church here in Honoré.'

'That's interesting. She goes to church, but not to her local church.'

Richard went to his desk to check his notes. He found what he was looking for almost at once.

'Here it is,' he said. 'She told us she goes to Father Luc Durant's church. Anyone know where that is?'

Richard's team didn't, so Richard decided to do some

digging for himself. It didn't take him long to discover that Father Luc was a Catholic priest who ran a church on the south side of the island, but there didn't seem to be anything else of note about him or Natasha's role in his church. So Richard tried to see what he could dig up on Natasha on the Police Computer Network, but didn't get anywhere. She had no presence as far as he could tell, and he couldn't find any specific references to her on any of the government databases or on the local newspaper website, either.

She seemed to be entirely without interest.

And yet, Richard knew that she hadn't told them the whole truth about the ruby.

In lieu of having any character references for Natasha, Richard decided to ring her church and spoke to a woman who explained that she was Father Luc's secretary. When pressed, she was able to reveal that Natasha came to church every week, she was heavily involved in all of their charity endeavours, and there was no way at all that she would participate in anything 'dodgy'. She was an upstanding member of the community.

This wasn't exactly what Richard wanted to hear, so next he got the number for Morgane Pichou at the tourist office, seeing as she'd been the person to tell Natasha that there'd been an explosion in the harbour. Unfortunately for Richard, when he spoke to Morgane, she made it clear that there was no way Natasha could ever have been mixed up in her husband's disappearance. According to Morgane, although Conrad was a bit of a layabout, Natasha loved him deeply and had done so ever since they'd met decades before.

It was all hugely frustrating for Richard, and his mood didn't improve when Camille returned.

'Sir,' she said as she sat down at her desk, 'I'm convinced there's something Mrs Gardiner's not telling us.'

'Go on,' Richard said.

'I mean, she was hit hard when I told her that we now think her husband was missing presumed dead. She was distraught. And I believed her. But I got the feeling that she was also guilty somehow. Or maybe that's too strong. But something was gnawing at her.'

'You think she could be involved in his death?'

'I don't know.'

'Because the two people I've spoken to say she couldn't have been. So why's she acting so strange?'

'I don't know, sir.'

Fidel called over from his desk.

'Oh okay, sir, I think you need to see this. The computer's got a match for the fingerprint I lifted from the SIM card.'

'It has?' Richard said as he headed over to Fidel's desk.

'It sure has. The fingerprint belongs to a man called Pierre Charpentier.'

'And who's he when he's at home?'

'Well, this is where it gets interesting. His prints are on the system because, twenty years ago, he committed murder during a robbery in London. So he's been serving a life sentence. First in Holloway prison in London. And then, five years ago, he was transferred to the Central Prison on Saint-Marie.'

'Hang on,' Richard said, trying to process what Fidel had just said. 'You're saying that the print on the SIM card you found on Conrad's boat belongs to a man who's in prison for murder?'

'What's more, he committed his murder all those years ago while he and his gang were robbing a jewellery store in London.'

This got the team's attention, and now it was Camille and Dwayne's turn to head over to Fidel's desk.

'He knocked off a jewellery store?' Dwayne asked.

'He sure did. And now we find his fingerprint on the detonator of a bomb, and a big fat fake jewel left at the victim's house. It's all connected, isn't it?'

'But hold on,' Richard said. 'How could Pierre whoever-he-is have killed Conrad at all, seeing as he's currently in prison?'

'That's the thing, sir. He isn't in prison.'

'But you just said he was.'

'That's the whole point. He's been in prison for the last twenty years. But he was released three days ago.'

The team looked at each other, absolutely stunned.

Richard was the first to recover.

'Then I suggest we find this Pierre Charpentier as a matter of some urgency,' he said. 'Don't you?'

It's amazing what you learn in prison. Who knew you could make an improvised bomb out of an old phone and a few wires? And it was so easy to set up. Conrad had no security on his boat. The hatch to his engine compartment wasn't even locked. It was simple. Under cover of night, I taped the phone inside, and then it was just a case of working out which tube was the fuel line that led from the petrol tanks. A quick slice with a knife, and the job was done. It was amazing. The rush I felt knowing I now had his life in my hands. After two decades of waiting. One call, that's all it would take. And that's all it took. I dialled the number when his boat was out in the harbour where everyone could see it. I then waited a few seconds for the call to connect, and then the boat went up. Just like that. Boom. Then, when everyone rushed to the bay, I went to his house and smashed in the back window. Wrecking his study wasn't part of the plan, but I couldn't help myself. I felt alive. Finally alive. And then I left the ruby. That had always been the plan. To leave the ruby. Because it wasn't enough to kill Conrad. I wanted to make a statement. To let the whole world know. I was back.

CHAPTER FOUR

It took a quick phonecall to the administration department of the Central Prison to find out that Pierre Charpentier had indeed left prison three days before, and his registered address was a halfway house a few miles away.

When Richard told his team Pierre's address, Dwayne offered to come along.

'Why?' Richard asked.

'Let me put it this way,' Dwayne said. 'It's not the sort of place someone like you wants to get lost in.'

As the Police jeep arrived, Richard found himself agreeing with Dwayne's analysis. For the last few minutes they'd travelled down a narrow dirt road that cut through a field of sugar cane, the thick stalks pressing in on either side. Then, once the field ended, the track opened up into a dirt clearing that contained half a dozen clapboard houses that were nestling in scrubland right next to the sea.

Camille parked the Police jeep by some overflowing bins. There was no-one around. Just some laundry drying on a line and a scrawny dog sleeping in the shade of an old pick-up.

It felt like something out of the Wild West, Richard thought to himself.

'Come on, let's get this over with,' he said, heading to the crumbling building that was listed as Pierre's halfway house.

Stepping up onto the porch, Richard knocked loudly on the wooden door. There was no answer from inside, although Richard saw a net curtain twitch in a house nearby. Interesting, he thought to himself. The enclave wasn't as deserted as he'd first thought.

Richard took a few steps back and looked at the upstairs windows of the old building. They had yellowed copies of the Saint-Marie *Times* taped to the inside, and there was a bush of some sort growing out of the gutter above.

'Let me see what I can do,' Dwayne said, heading around the side of the house.

'Dwayne!' Richard called out after him. 'We don't have a warrant.'

'I know that, Chief,' Dwayne replied, before disappearing.

Richard knocked on the door again, but there was still no answer.

'Mr Charpentier!' he called out. 'Saint-Marie Police. Are you there?'

Richard noticed the net curtain at the nearby house twitch again. Whoever was inside was very interested to see what was going on.

After knocking on the door for a third time, Richard was

gratified to hear the sound of footsteps approaching from inside. He took a step back to make sure he wasn't within striking distance of Pierre when he opened the door and pulled his warrant card, ready to show it.

There was the sound of various chains being lifted, bolts being slid back, and then the door opened inwards.

'Detective Inspector Richard Poole of the Saint-Marie Police Force,' Richard said.

'I know who you are,' Dwayne said as he finished opening the door.

'How did you get in there?' Richard asked, quietly furious.

'Well, that's the funny thing, Chief. The back door was open, so I just walked in.'

'The back door was open, was it?' Richard asked, sceptically.

'I mean, it took a bit of effort, but it was definitely open. Eventually.'

After a moment's indecision, Richard pushed past Dwayne into the house, his interest in Pierre's whereabouts drawing him in. After all, if the back door really were open, they could claim that they were investigating the security of the house as a matter of community policing. If Dwayne had broken in, then that was something he'd have to explain to a tribunal if it ever came to that.

As Richard looked about himself, he saw that the house was shabby, and was only furnished with the bare minimum. He saw a little sidetable with an ashtray and packet of cigarettes and matches next to it. There was also a bottle of beer that Richard saw was half full.

Pulling on a pair of crime scene gloves, Richard went into the kitchen at the back of the house and saw a brown paper bag on the worktop. Inside there were a few basic groceries, none of them unpacked. And from the smell coming from the bag, Richard guessed that it had been sitting out in the heat.

There was also a see-through folder to the side of the groceries that contained all the literature from the prison explaining the ups and downs following a spell inside. Richard also found an open brown envelope, and he used his pencil to raise the flap so he could see its contents. It was full of what looked to be about a hundred dollars in low denomination notes.

'He left in a hurry, didn't he?' Camille said from the doorway. 'He's not even finished his beer.'

'That's what it looks like to me,' Richard agreed. 'And, from the state of his food here, I don't think he was here for very long.'

'So what happened?' Dwayne asked.

Richard looked about himself. There were no signs of a struggle. In fact, it looked as though Pierre had only just popped out for a few minutes. As Richard went back into the front room, he half expected to find a cigarette still smouldering in the ashtray.

'Dwayne,' he said, 'I want you to bag the physical evidence.'

'Yes, sir.'

'As for you and me, Camille, I think we've got a lead to follow up.'

'We have, sir?'

A few moments later, Richard and Camille had gone to the house next door where Richard had seen the curtain twitching. Having knocked loudly on the door, they soon heard a shuffling of feet from inside the house.

'Hold on, hold on,' a voice called out.

The door opened to reveal an ancient woman who was almost entirely bent over, and seemed only to be kept upright by a claw-footed hospital walking stick that she was gripping firmly in her right hand.

She lifted up her head, and Richard could see that her eyes were cloudy.

'Are you the Police?' the woman asked.

'We are,' Camille said. 'We just wanted to ask you a few questions about your neighbour.'

'What neighbour?'

'The man who moved into the house next door three days ago,' Richard said. 'I'm sure you saw him.'

'I didn't,' the woman said before retreating from the door and trying to shut it. 'I can't help you.'

Richard put his hand out to stop the door from closing.

'But you see everything around here, don't you? I saw you checking us over when we arrived.'

'And there's been quite a serious crime committed,' Camille said, far more kindly. 'If you could give us any help, we'd be so very grateful.'

The old woman considered her answer for a moment, and then she sighed.

'Alright. What do you want to know?'

'Did you see the man who moved into the house three days ago?'

The woman laughed with a wet cackle.

'I don't see anything. Can't you tell?'

The woman made an extra effort to lift her head, and indicated her cloudy eyes.

'Is it your cataracts?' Camille asked.

'Everything's a blur to me now.'

'But you were spying on us,' Richard said, unable to keep the note of disapproval from his voice.

'I was robbed last year. I have to be careful.'

'So you can see some things.'

'I can't see much, but I know where you are.'

'Then did you see someone move in three days ago?'

'I did. A taxi arrived in the morning. I could tell it was a taxi from the colour. It was deep red. And a man got out. I heard him thank the taxi driver. It was a man's voice.'

'And he went into the house next door?'

'You know, the prison use it for people who are just released from jail?'

'They do?' Camille asked innocently.

'So you get all kinds of goings on. I don't like it. But I'm old, no-one cares what I think.'

'Do you remember what time this was?' Richard asked.

'I don't know. It was in the morning. Maybe after eleven? It was before I'd had lunch, and I always have lunch at midday.'

'And what did this man do once he'd arrived?'

'Well, nothing that I know of.'

'Nothing?'

'He went into his house, and I didn't think about him again until that afternoon.'

'Well, that's very helpful, thank you,' Camille said. 'Although, why did you think about him that afternoon?'

'Because of the men who came to see him.'

'What's that?' Richard asked.

'Well, I was sitting on the porch in the afternoon when I saw a car arrive. I don't know what sort it was, before you ask, it parked too far away. It was just a blur. But I saw three men come from it and then go into the house next door.'

'And you're sure there were three of them?'

'Oh yes. I could see the shapes of three people.'

'And they were all men?'

'I heard three voices. They were all male. In fact, they were arguing as they approached.'

'Do you know what they were arguing about?'

'I'm sorry. I wasn't listening too closely.'

'Then do you perhaps remember anything they said? Any phrase, or even just a single word?'

'I'm sorry, all I can tell you is they were three men, and they were arguing about something. Mind you, that was nothing compared to what happened next.'

Richard was about to ask the old woman to explain, but Camille put her hand on his elbow, indicating that he should keep quiet. She'd recognised that their witness had finally warmed up and was enjoying the sound of her own voice.

'The man who'd arrived first – he was wearing a blue

jacket – was happy to see them to start off with because he greeted the three men like old friends. But after a few minutes I heard the man in the blue jacket start to get angry.'

'Did you hear what was said?'

The woman thought hard.

'It was something about him wanting his share, I think. That's right, he kept saying "where's my share?" over and over. And then the three men who'd arrived together started arguing among themselves as well. It got quite heated, and it ended with the man in the blue jacket telling them he wanted them all to leave. And a few minutes later, that's what they did. But I got the feeling the three men left with their tails between their legs. They weren't so chatty on the way out as they'd been on the way in.'

'And it was the same three men who left as who'd arrived?'

'I think so. The man in the blue jacket was still in his doorway after the others had left.'

'I appreciate you don't see too well,' Camille said, 'but can you describe any of these men at all to us?'

'I'm sorry. I think one of them had a red top. Like a T-shirt. But I couldn't tell you anything else.'

'Did you maybe see what colour their skin was?'

'They were dark-skinned.'

'And did they speak with local accents?'

'Oh yes, very definitely. They were all from Saint-Marie. Or from an island nearby.'

'So they were three dark-skinned men who you think were from the island?'

'That's right,' the old woman said with another chuckle. 'Which isn't bad for someone who can't see, is it?'

'It sure isn't,' Camille agreed.

'Then what happened?' Richard asked.

'How do you mean?'

'Well, we've just looked around your neighbour's house, and it looks like he left somewhat suddenly at some point.'

'Oh, that was later that day.'

'It was?'

'I was in my kitchen when I heard a car pull up outside. I didn't think much of it, and I didn't even see which of the men had come back, but I saw the first man who'd arrived that day – the man in the blue jacket – step out of his house. I could see that from my window. He said something and then I saw him leave. A few seconds later, I heard a car start up and drive off.'

'Did you hear what he said?'

'I think he said something like, "I thought I'd never see you again."'

'"I thought I'd never see you again"?'

'And I'm sure he said something else, but I didn't catch it. But he then walked from the house, and you know what? Now you mention it, I've not seen him since. Or any of the other three men, either, for that matter. Not that I'd recognise them, of course.'

'Have there been any other visitors since then?'

'No. No-one.'

Richard looked back over the notes he'd taken, trying to

make sense of what he'd just learned. Who were the three men who'd visited Pierre on the day he left prison? Where had Pierre then gone off to when one of them returned later on? And, seeing as Pierre very obviously hadn't been back to his halfway house since then, where was he now?

As for the identity of the three men who'd visited that day, Richard had a theory he wanted to test, especially considering how Pierre had apparently been overheard demanding to know where 'his share' was.

Richard asked Camille to take the old woman's formal statement, and while she was doing that, he drove back to the Police station.

As he entered the main office, Fidel stood up excitedly.

'Sir, I've got something.'

'You have?' Richard said.

'I sure have, because I've been processing the evidence Camille bagged from Conrad's office. And you know that chunk of concrete that was used to smash in the window? I've been checking it for fingerprints, and guess what? It's borderline admissible, but I was able to lift half a thumbprint from a pebble that was buried in its side.'

As he spoke, Fidel led Richard over to his desk and showed him the chunk of concrete. Bending down to inspect it more closely, Richard could see that it was rough – there'd be no way to lift any kind of usable fingerprints from it – but Richard could also see that a few smooth pebbles were embedded in the block, and Fidel had dusted each of them with graphite powder.

'And?' Richard asked.

'The fingerprint also belongs to Pierre Charpentier, sir.'

'It was Pierre who threw the rock through the window?'

'It was.'

'Then that's *exactly* what I wanted to hear.'

'It is?' Fidel asked, surprised.

'Oh yes, because I think Pierre killed Conrad for a very specific reason and then left that fake ruby behind for the exact same reason.'

As Richard went and sat down at his desk, he told Fidel that a taxi had taken Pierre to his halfway house on the morning he was released from prison.

'So contact the prison, would you? Find out what taxi firm picks up prisoners, and see if you can talk to the driver who drove Pierre that day. In particular, I want to know what sort of mood Pierre was in on the journey.'

'Yes, sir.'

As Fidel started making calls, Richard logged on to the Saint-Marie Police Computer Network and called up the case file for Pierre Charpentier's original crime. And what Richard read held him spellbound. Because, as he'd already guessed, Pierre hadn't robbed the jewellery shop in London twenty years before alone. He'd been part of a gang of four. The men had driven up to the store on motorbikes just as a consignment of jewellery was being delivered. They'd then smashed up the shop with baseball bats until the manager handed over the delivery. Then, as they were leaving, one of the men pulled a handgun and shot a member of staff dead.

Richard read that the man who was killed that day was called André Morgan. He'd only been with the shop for three months, but what Richard noticed at once was that André was originally from Saint-Marie.

That would have to be followed up.

As for the men in the gang, they'd fled on their motorbikes just before the Police arrived at the scene.

However, the robber who'd fired the gun made one mistake. As he jumped onto the back of his partner's bike to make his escape, his gun fell from his grasp and he wasn't able to pick it up before the bike had driven off. This meant that although the bank robbers got away with their loot, the murder weapon was left behind at the scene, and was later retrieved by the Metropolitan Police. They were then able to lift a couple of fingerprints from the barrel of the gun. But the fingerprints didn't match anyone on the UK Police database. Nor did they match anyone on Interpol's database. In fact, the Police weren't able to match the fingerprints with anyone. Even worse, although the motorbikes were later found dumped in a back street, the men had vanished into thin air. And the bikes had been stolen from Brick Lane the night before, so that was a dead end as well.

All told, over two million pounds' worth of jewels had been stolen that day, and the Police didn't have a single credible lead.

Then, a week after the jewellery heist, the Police received an anonymous phonecall. The message was left by a woman who, according to the notes Richard was reading, 'had a thick

Caribbean accent'. She told the Duty Officer that the jewel heist had been carried out by men from Saint-Marie. The woman hung up before she could be quizzed any further. The anonymous phonecall was later traced to a phone booth near Willesden Green Tube station, but the Police were never able to identify who the caller had been.

However, the tip-off meant that the Police in London sent copies of the fingerprints they'd retrieved from the murder weapon to the Police in Saint-Marie. It took quite a few days for the answer to come back to London, but it was worth the wait.

The Saint-Marie Police had a match for the fingerprints. They belonged to a well-known local hoodlum called Pierre Charpentier. And, even better than that, their records showed that Pierre had left Saint-Marie three weeks before the jewel heist, and had returned to Saint-Marie two days after it had been carried out.

The Saint-Marie Police swooped on Pierre and charged him with theft and murder. He was then extradited to the UK where he stood trial at the Old Bailey. When he was cross-examined, Pierre claimed that he'd had nothing to do with the jewel heist, and he was being set up for the murder as well. His defence was that he may have been in the UK, but he was nowhere near Bond Street at the time. As for the fingerprints that were found on the murder weapon, Pierre just kept saying that he was being set up.

The jury didn't believe him, and Pierre was convicted of murder and robbery, and was sent down for twenty-five years.

For the first fifteen years, he was incarcerated in Holloway prison, but, as was usual for foreign offenders, he was repatriated to a Saint-Marie prison for the last few years of his sentence. The fact that he'd finally left prison after serving only twenty years suggested that he'd also been given time off for good behaviour.

Richard leant back in his chair to try to process everything he'd learned, but he was interrupted by the arrival of Camille and Dwayne. Dwayne was holding a cardboard box of possessions.

'What did you get from the halfway house?' Richard asked.

'Nothing we hadn't already seen, Chief,' Dwayne said. 'But I've got the bottle of beer and glass Pierre was drinking from, so we can check them for fingerprints.'

'As for me, sir,' Camille said, plonking herself down onto the chair behind her desk, 'once she got going, Pierre's next-door neighbour never stopped talking, but I think I got everything.'

'Did she give you anything new in her statement?'

'Not really. It's the same as she told us. Pierre turned up three days ago. Three men arrived soon after, argued with him, and left. And then, later that afternoon, one of the men returned, and Pierre left with him in his car.'

'And he's been in hiding ever since,' Richard said, finishing Camille's story.

'Got it in one.'

'But who were the men who met him?' Fidel asked. 'And which of them was the one who came back?'

'Well, Fidel,' Richard said, 'I think that's a very good question indeed.'

Richard explained how he'd just read Pierre Charpentier's original case file, and how Pierre had been part of a four-man gang who'd robbed a Bond Street shop of over two million pounds' worth of jewels. And how Pierre had shot a member of staff dead before he made his escape.

'Then how did they catch him?' Fidel asked.

'Pierre left his fingerprints on the gun he used.'

'He did?' Dwayne asked, surprised. 'That's not too clever.'

'Maybe he wasn't too clever.'

'Did they positively identify him in any other way?' Camille asked.

'I don't believe so.'

'There wasn't any CCTV inside the store?'

'The case notes don't mention anything about CCTV.'

'And he never took off his motorbike clothes, gloves or helmet at any time during the robbery?'

'That's right.'

'So no-one was able to place him visually at the scene?'

'This, I believe was very much the point Pierre's defence brief tried to make.'

'So the only thing that actually links Pierre to the murder is a weapon that had his fingerprints on?'

'Not quite the only thing,' Richard said. 'He was from Saint-Marie, and he was in London at the time. Oh, and the man he shot dead was also from Saint-Marie. We'll have to look into him. His name was André Morgan. But you're right, Camille. If it was indeed Pierre Charpentier who committed murder that day, he was very foolish leaving his own gun behind at the scene. But that's not what interests me. What interests me is, where did Conrad get his money from?'

This statement took everyone by surprise.

'What?' Dwayne asked.

'Well, it was you, Dwayne, who said that despite having no real talent, Conrad "came into money" about twenty years ago. And you also said it could have been mob money that funded him. So what I'm wondering is, what if it wasn't mob money?'

'Do you think he was maybe one of the robbers?' Fidel asked, his eyes widening.

'Well, let's look at what we know. Pierre was jailed twenty years ago. Not just for murder, but also because of his part in a four-man heist of a jewellery store in London. Even though he always denied he was involved in any way. But then, according to our witness next door to Pierre's safe house, on the very day he got out of prison he was met by three men.'

'Oh I see!' Fidel said. 'They were the other three members of the gang.'

'That's what I'm thinking,' Richard said. 'And although our witness's sight isn't what it might once have been, her hearing's good enough, and she said very specifically that these three men were already arguing before they arrived, and then Pierre joined in the argument soon after. And the nub of the matter was the fact that he was demanding they hand over "his share". In fact, he kept asking, "where is my share?". Now, what do you think that could refer to?'

'His share of the jewels!' Fidel said.

'Exactly. Despite his protestations of innocence, Pierre was one of the robbers that day. And I think that for the last twenty years, as he rotted in a high security prison, there was only one thing sustaining him. And that was the knowledge that all he had to do was keep quiet and the moment he left prison, he'd finally get his share of money from the heist.'

'You really think he kept quiet all that time?' Dwayne asked sceptically.

'I think anyone with the right incentive would keep schtum. And two million pounds' worth of jewels is quite the incentive. I imagine that once the rest of the gang had paid their fence and any other intermediaries to re-cut the stones, they'd maybe have cleared as much as a million pounds by the end. So, divided by four people, that's a quarter of a million pounds each. And in Saint-Marie dollars that's maybe as much as three to four hundred thousand dollars per gang member.'

'Yup,' Dwayne said, now in accord. 'I'd keep quiet for a lot less. Especially if I was already in jail for murder.'

'So what are we saying?' Camille asked. 'Was the day Pierre got out of prison the day he also found out he wasn't going to get any of his money?'

'That's exactly what I think happened,' Richard agreed. 'His share of the cash had been spent. Or mismanaged. We don't know. But we do know how angry Pierre was to find out that his share was missing. And this was after he'd spent twenty years believing he'd be rich when he left prison. Just imagine what it must have been like if he really did find out his share of the loot no longer existed. It would push anyone over the edge.'

'So that's why he killed Conrad,' Camille said. 'And why he then broke into Conrad's house immediately afterwards and left that fake ruby. It *was* a message. Just like you said.'

'But who was the message for?' Dwayne asked.

'I don't know,' Richard said darkly. 'And that's what's worrying me.'

CHAPTER FIVE

'Okay,' Richard said to his team, 'imagine you're Pierre Charpentier. If you wanted somewhere secret to hide on the island, where would you go?'

Fidel, Camille and Dwayne were full of ideas. It was possible Pierre was hiding in a nearby boarding house or hotel, or was staying in the local homeless shelter, or maybe just living rough in the jungle. Really, he could be anywhere. And as the suggestions arrived thick and fast, Richard made a list of them on the whiteboard. Having done so, he then divided the list up among himself and his team. But first, Fidel was to go to the Prison and speak to the guards and whoever else he could find to discover who Pierre was friends with, Camille was to try to discover what kind of digital footprint Pierre was leaving now that he was out of prison, and Dwayne was to go and tap up whatever contacts or informants he could find, to see if Pierre's return to civilian life had caused any ripples on the island.

As Dwayne put his Police cap on and left, Richard ghosted out after him and stopped him on the veranda.

'And Dwayne?' he said. 'About the whole spying thing . . .'

Dwayne smiled easily.

'You want to apologise?'

'Apologise?' Richard said, confused. 'No, I just wanted to say that I may not be able to keep tabs on you while you're visiting every dodgy bar on the island, but if I find out you've actually sloped off and hooked up with Amy McDiarmid again, there'll be trouble, I can tell you.'

'Hang on. You're *not* apologising to me?'

'What is there to apologise for?'

'You ran an observation on my house.'

'You make it sound like a bad thing.'

'It was.'

'Anyway, it wasn't anything so formal as an observation. I just hid in a bush.'

'You hid in a *bush*?'

'But you were with your girlfriend when you should have been working on your sergeant's exam.'

'So?'

'*So?*'

'I can revise any time, Chief. But I only met Amy a few weeks ago. What we've got's really special. And you know, we're still at that stage of our relationship.'

'And what stage would that be?'

Dwayne looked at his boss, trying to work out if he was pulling his leg. '"What stage"?'

'That's right. I said, "what stage"?'

'You honestly don't know what I'm talking about?'

'All I know is, you were with your girlfriend when you should have been revising. And you even let her visit you at the Police station.'

'But she only came here to see you.'

'I don't want to meet your girlfriends, Dwayne. I'm trying to solve a murder case. And so are you, I'd like to add.'

Dwayne cocked his head to one side as he considered his boss. He knew that Richard was English, and uptight and repressed, but was he really *this* English, uptight and repressed?

'Good,' Richard said, misreading Dwayne's silence as agreement. 'I'm glad we've finally sorted that out.'

And with that, Richard tried to return to the main office, but he found that Camille was standing in the doorway holding a printout, and, seeing the look of disapproval on her face, he realised she'd been standing there for some time.

'What?' he asked defensively.

'Oh, nothing, sir,' Camille said, 'I just wanted to let you know what I'd got on Pierre so far.'

Richard grabbed the piece of paper from Camille's hand and headed back into the office. After a sympathetic glance at Dwayne, Camille followed.

Richard read the printout as he sat down behind his desk.

'So, Pierre Charpentier is fifty-four years old. He's got no siblings. No wife. No children. And his parents died when he was fifteen. So that pretty much rules out his family as the people who could be providing a refuge for him. And as for his record, I see that before he committed murder, we'd had him in for questioning on seventeen separate occasions. For acting as a fence, aggravated assault, burglary – this is quite the rap sheet, Camille.'

Richard didn't look up from the printout, because he could sense that Camille was standing in front of his desk, a hand on her hip and an eyebrow raised. And once again Richard was getting the distinct impression that he was 'in the wrong', but he refused to give in to it.

'Yes, quite the rap sheet,' Richard repeated, in the hope that Camille would perhaps get bored and wander off.

She didn't, so Richard eventually lifted his eyes from the paper.

'What was that?' Camille asked.

'What was what?'

'You have to apologise to him.'

'To whom?'

'You know who. Dwayne.'

'Now, don't you start,' Richard said.

'But he's in love!'

'In love,' Richard snorted. 'For this week perhaps. But that man has more girlfriends than I've got . . .' Richard couldn't quite find the right word to end his sentence. 'Socks,' he eventually said.

'Socks?'

'Yes. Socks. Anyway, you know what I mean,' Richard said, getting up and heading in a huff to inspect the whiteboard.

'But I think this time it's different. She seems really into him. And I know he really likes her.'

'Look, Camille, no-one is more thrilled than me that Dwayne is "loved up", but that's no excuse for slacking off.'

'But what if you found love, sir?'

As Camille said this, Richard was popping the lid on his favourite black board marker, and it pinged into the air and dropped to the floor.

'Now look what you've made me do,' he said irritably as he bent down to pick up the lid.

'Because if you found love,' Camille continued, 'I know we'd all be pleased for you. And if you then spent a bit too much time with that person, I know we'd all understand. No, better than that. We'd be happy for you. And we wouldn't interfere.'

'I haven't been interfering.'

'You went and spied on him.'

'That wasn't interfering. That was being a responsible line manager. Now, if you don't mind, we've got a killer to catch. And seeing as your background check suggests that Pierre Charpentier doesn't have a ready network of family to rely on, the question of where he's hiding becomes even more acute.'

'You're right there, sir,' Fidel said, relieved that the conversation had moved on from his boss's love life. 'And I'm still not making much progress on that front. Although I've spoken to the taxi driver who drove Pierre to his halfway house that morning. He said Pierre seemed really pumped to be out of prison. He noticed because he's had the prison contract for years, and most people are a bit lost when they first come out. Or are emotional. But he said Pierre wasn't like that at all.'

'He was "pumped"?'

'It was like he had a sense of purpose. That's how the taxi driver put it to me.'

'I see,' Richard said as he went back to study the white-board where the names Conrad Gardiner, Natasha Gardiner and Pierre Charpentier were written up in big bold letters.

'You know what?' Richard said after a few moments. 'If Conrad's dead and Pierre's in hiding, that doesn't mean we're without leads.'

Richard pointed at Natasha's name on the board.

'Because we now know the ruby was left behind because of the burglary twenty years ago. And Natasha Gardiner was married to Conrad twenty years ago. I think it's time she told us the truth.'

Leaving Fidel in the station, Richard and Camille returned to Natasha's house. They found her sitting in the front room.

'Mrs Gardiner?' Camille asked as she and Richard entered the room.

'Have you any news?' Natasha asked.

'I'm sorry, we haven't.'

'He can't be dead. I just don't believe it.'

'We'll let you know the moment we have anything defi-nite. But in the meantime, there has been a development elsewhere in the case. We'd like to see if you recognise this man.'

Camille handed over a copy of Pierre's mugshot and, as Natasha looked at it, she seemed to crumple.

'Oh god,' she said, her hand going to her mouth.

'You recognise him?' Camille asked.

'It's that Pierre man, isn't it?'

'You know him?'

Natasha nodded.

'And he's the reason why a ruby was left behind in your house, isn't he?'

Richard could see that Natasha had no ready reply.

'Mrs Gardiner?' he asked sternly, but Natasha only had eyes for Camille.

'You go through life,' she said, 'and you just hope the past won't catch up with you. But that's not how life works, is it?'

'The ruby is connected to your past?' Camille asked.

'Not mine,' Natasha said. 'And I wasn't sure when I saw that ruby. I mean, I had an idea. I worried, but I didn't know for sure. That's why I didn't say anything. But if that man Pierre is behind all this, then I know exactly why he's done what he's done.'

As Natasha said this, she burst into tears.

Richard rolled his eyes to himself. Bloody hell, why was it always so hard getting witnesses to talk without them turning on the water works?

Natasha pulled a hankie from the sleeve of her cardigan and tried to wipe the tears from her face.

'My husband was a good person,' she said in between her sniffs. 'You have to believe me. He was kind to me, and a loving father to our daughter. He meant well in so many ways. But he was also weak. In the past more than now, but what he did caused a stain it's not possible to wipe away. And it was all because of him,' Natasha said, indicating the photo of Pierre. 'Because if Conrad was a good man under it all, Pierre was the worst. I knew he was trouble from the start.'

'You knew Pierre from before he went to prison?' Richard asked.

'I married Conrad twenty-five years ago. I was flattered by his attention, and I just ignored my parents who said Conrad wasn't any good. I was full of myself. Feeling all grown up at nineteen years old. Having a boyfriend with a motorbike. If I could reach back in time, I'd slap myself in the face and tell me to walk away.'

'You now feel your parents were right?'

'They were right. But they were also wrong. Conrad *was* a good man. Like I said. It's just he loved money. And music. He loved the whole music scene. I always encouraged him to become a roadie or sound technician, but it required too much work. He just talked about this amazing career in music he was going to have, but he never did anything about it.

'Then, a few years into our marriage, he started hanging out with Pierre. That was the worst time, because I could see how dangerous he was. He had these dead eyes, you know? And you could tell, when he was looking at you, he was just trying to work out how much use you were to him. Conrad and I argued a lot about him. And my husband became secretive. I knew he was seeing a lot of Pierre, but what could I do? Our daughter Jessica was two years old and quite a handful. And then one day, Conrad said he was going away for a few weeks, and the next time he saw me, we'd be rich. I knew that this was somehow connected with Pierre, and I begged him not to go, but Conrad wouldn't listen. He said my responsibility was to Jessica, and his responsibility was to provide for us. That's what he was doing. And then, one day, Conrad was gone. He didn't leave any details of where he was. He just vanished into thin air.

'I was so worried. And alone with Jessica. I didn't know what to do. After a few days, I even went to the bars where I knew Pierre drank, and I started asking around. All I learned was, Pierre had vanished as well. Just as I suspected. Whatever Conrad was doing, he was doing it with Pierre. And the days turned into weeks, and I was falling apart. I heard no word from Conrad in all that time.

'Then, three weeks after he'd gone, Conrad walked back in through that door.' Natasha pointed at the door behind Camille and Richard. 'And he was so full of himself, he said he'd struck gold. We were rich. But he wouldn't tell me what he'd done to get the money. And even so, he said it would take a while to get his full share. I didn't know what to think. I mean, Conrad had just vanished, and now he'd returned saying he was rich? There was no way what he had done was legal, and this is my shame. Although I tried to say I wouldn't touch any of his money unless he told me how he'd come by it, my resistance wore down. If I'm honest, I was just so pleased to have him home. And so was Jessica. And the thing is, Conrad really was rich. Within a few weeks, he had all of this money. And it seemed to keep coming. He was throwing parties, wanting everyone to have a good time. It was so exciting, and I turned a blind eye to it all.

'And a few months later, he bought that old recording studio up behind the old Priest's house. It didn't cost him much. You see, it was in a terrible state. But then he spent a lot of money on getting the best equipment shipped in. And signing young talent, as he called it. So he could promote these bands, and also record their music. He was so sure of himself. He was finally going to be a success. But there was still something not right about it all, I could tell. And I knew there was *definitely* something not right when I asked him if he was still seeing Pierre. You see, since he'd come back with all this money, he'd not mentioned Pierre once. Or gone drinking with him. But when I asked, Conrad just shut down and said he had nothing to do with Pierre any more. But I could see that Conrad was worried about it.

'Anyway, I tried to stop worrying about what had happened to Pierre and just get on with my life. And there was so much that was good during that time. Jessica was just beautiful, Conrad had his music career going, and I should have been happy. But I kept worrying about Pierre. Where had he got to? What had gone wrong between him and Conrad? So, one day, I got up my courage and went back to one of the beachside bars. It was just a shack, really. When I asked the barman where Pierre was, he told me that he was in a prison in the UK for murder. I was shocked. And I went straight to the library where I did some research on the internet, and that's when I found out the truth. Pierre had robbed a jewellery shop in London with three other men. He'd then murdered one of the employees in the shop and left his gun behind. And I could see the dates of the robbery matched the time that Conrad had been out of the country.

'I confronted Conrad that night, and that was the only time he physically hurt me. He grabbed me so tight I had bruises on my arms for days. It was like he was trying to crush me, but Conrad said, if I wanted to live, I had to never mention Pierre's name again. I didn't know what to think. What had Conrad done? Or rather, I now suspected what Conrad had done. He'd been one of the other men, hadn't he? That's where our money had come from. It had been stolen, and a man had died. Our money was blood money.

'But what was I supposed to do? Shop my own husband to the Police? And I read all the reports I could on the robbery and the trial, and I could see that the only person who'd used any violence was Pierre. In the end, I decided that the fact that Conrad had been so angry when I'd mentioned Pierre's name was enough for me. It told me he'd not wanted what had happened to that poor man to happen. And then, I saw that the jewellery shop they'd robbed was part of a chain that had branches all over the world, and they'd even been insured. They'd not lost any money because of the robbery. So that's what I kept telling myself. What had happened was in the past, and I couldn't change that. And you know, the years passed, and we had other problems to deal with.'

'Like what?' Camille asked.

'Well, it turned out Conrad wasn't a very good music

producer after all. I mean, he wanted to be. He worked hard. Up to a point. But he slowly slipped into his old ways. Hanging out with the wrong sort of people. And somehow, he seemed broken. By the time he'd spent whatever money he had, he'd lost all his confidence. His swagger. And he was distant from us.'

'Including your daughter?' Camille said, indicating the old photos on the mantelpiece.

Natasha looked at the photos, and a deep sadness overcame her.

'As she got older, Jessica couldn't understand why her dad didn't want to spend any time with her. But I think it was shame that kept him out drinking in the bars or on his boat. That he'd not made anything of his life. You know, Jessica went to university on St Lucia, and Conrad didn't visit her even once. I went when I could. It's a good few hours on the boat to St Lucia, but I'd try and see her once a term. When she graduated, she stayed on St Lucia, and we don't have the sort of money to keep going there, so we don't see so much of her any more. And she's not even coming back now. Even with her father . . . dead.'

'You think he must be dead?' Richard asked, picking up on the certainty in Natasha's voice.

'I do. For the last few months, Conrad had been getting quieter and quieter. Even more withdrawn. And then, a couple of weeks ago, he just told me everything. How my suspicions all those years ago were correct. He'd been in Pierre's gang and had carried out the robbery. I had no idea why he was finally telling me, but I had the good sense to stay quiet, so he'd continue talking. And tell me he did.'

'Did he say who the other members of the gang were?' Richard asked.

'He just said it had been him, Pierre and two other men from the island.'

'All of the men were from Saint-Marie?'

'Yes. But he never knew Pierre was carrying a gun that day. That's what he wanted me to know. You see, Conrad had been one of the two men who were waiting on bikes outside the jewellery store while the robbery happened inside. He didn't even see the moment Pierre shot that poor man dead. It all happened inside the store. And he didn't see a gun in Pierre's hand when he came out and got onto his bike afterwards, he wanted me to know that as well. The way Conrad told it, he didn't even know that anyone had fired a gun – or been killed – until much later. But then, he said, he was so terrified as he sat waiting outside on his bike, it was a miracle he didn't have a heart attack there and then.'

'Did he really not say who the other two members of the gang were?'

'I'm sorry. He didn't. And I didn't ask. I was too busy trying to work out why Conrad was suddenly telling me all this. But then he explained that Pierre had been moved back to a Saint-Marie prison a few years before. And it was when he told me this that he started crying. I had no idea why, but whatever was causing him so much pain, was hitting him real hard. I just held him, and he cried and cried.

Eventually, he calmed down enough to say, "and I've got to tell him it's gone."

'I didn't know what he meant, but he told me in bits. I think Conrad was in charge of Pierre's share of the money. Or he said he'd look after it. But what I eventually realised was, Conrad had spent it.'

Richard caught Camille's eye.

'How had he spent it?' Camille asked.

'He'd not meant to, that's what he kept saying. But when his music business was going under, he was convinced it was a temporary setback, so he borrowed some money from Pierre's share. That's how he put it. It was just a short-term loan to tide him over. As cashflow. He was convinced the music business would finally start making money, and he'd be able to return the cash he'd taken. But he lost that money as well, so he took even more. And when he lost that as well, he said he had to take the rest of Pierre's money. He had no choice. It was the only way of keeping the business alive, and the business was the only way he'd ever be able to repay Pierre. But he lost it. He lost it all.'

'When was this?'

'He said this all happened something like ten years ago. And I began to realise why Conrad had become increasingly withdrawn since then. He was terrified. All that time. Because he knew Pierre had already killed once. And one day he'd leave prison, and he'd want his share of the money.'

'So did he tell you why he was suddenly confessing all this?'

CHAPTER SIX

Back in the Police station, Richard called his team together.

'Okay, I think it's fair to say we've got a ticking clock here. Who's got anywhere with working out where Pierre's hiding?'

'Well, Chief,' Dwayne said. 'I've put the word out on the street that we're looking for him, but I can tell you, the people I've spoken to haven't heard anything. In fact, I struggled to find anyone who even remembers Pierre Charpentier. As far as I can tell, he's not been in touch with anyone on the island for the last twenty years.'

'That fits with what I learned,' Fidel said, going to his desk and picking up an old buff folder. 'I spoke to the guards at the Prison, and they all said Pierre was something of a loner. He didn't mix with people. I'm sorry to say I didn't get much of anything, but I was able to get his personal file.'

Fidel handed the file over to Richard, and, as he started flicking through it, he could see that it contained Pierre's record of behaviour, annual reviews, a log of visitors, and so on. He'd need to read it later on.

'Good work, Fidel. But you got no hint of where Pierre might have gone to next?'

'Nothing at all,' Fidel said.

Richard updated Fidel and Dwayne with what he and Camille had just learned from Natasha, in particular, the fact that Conrad had been one of the original members of Pierre's gang, and that Pierre had apparently threatened to kill them all one by one.

'If we could work out who the gang were . . .?' Fidel said.

'We'd be able to warn them their lives are in danger. But how to identify them after all this time?'

'What about the original case notes from the murder?' Camille asked.

'There's nothing in there that suggests who the other two people could be. In fact, about the only lead I could find that even remotely suggests a link to Saint-Marie – other than Pierre – is the anonymous tip-off the Met got to check Saint-Marie criminals for the killer.'

'What's that?' Camille asked.

Richard explained how a woman with a thick Caribbean accent had rung the Met Police from a telephone number in Willesden Green tipping them off that they should look for the robbers on Saint-Marie.

'A woman?' Dwayne asked. 'Who could she be?'

'No idea,' Richard said, 'and I don't know how we're going to find out two decades later. But we need to keep our eyes peeled for a woman who could turn out to be our mystery informant.'

As Richard said this, he wrote 'Anonymous Tip-Off Woman???' on the whiteboard.

'But we need to focus on what we do know, and that's basically that Pierre went to his halfway house that morning. He had a sense of purpose according to his taxi driver. But then he threatened the other gang members with murder, according to Natasha. And then, according to his half-blind neighbour, one of the gang members came back later on, Pierre got in his car, and that's when the trail goes cold. So I suggest the four of us return to the halfway house. There's got to have been other people around that day who maybe saw something.'

Fidel made photocopies of Pierre's mugshot from prison – and also copies of a recent photo of Conrad – and they all returned to the halfway house to make enquiries door-to-door. It was sweltering work in the afternoon sunshine, and the task wasn't made easier for Richard when a chicken bonded with him and decided to follow him wherever he went.

The team – plus their new chicken recruit – met up an hour later under the shade of a massive banyan tree.

'Okay, what have you got?' Richard asked, using his hankie to wipe the sweat from his brow, face and neck.

'I didn't get much, sir,' Fidel said, 'but a direct neighbour to the halfway house said he recognised Pierre's face when I showed him a photo. He said he saw him arrive in a maroon taxi that morning. He didn't know the time, but he said it could have been 11am.'

'Which would fit with what we'd already learned. Just ignore the chicken,' Richard added as the chicken started pecking at his left shoe. 'What else have we got?'

'Well, sir, I've maybe got something,' Camille said. 'But don't get your hopes up too much. There's a guy in that house over there.' As Camille said this, she pointed at a lean-to on the furthest edge of the clearing.

'I'd call that more of a dwelling than a house,' Richard corrected.

'And you've not even met the man who lives in there. He was pretty wild-looking. And had a white beard and crazy hair. You know the sort.'

As Fidel and Dwayne smiled, Richard realised that he didn't know the sort at all, thank heavens.

'But I bet you charmed him,' Dwayne said with a grin.

'It's funny you should say that, Dwayne. Before too long, he told me he recognised Pierre's photograph, and he also remembered Pierre arriving in a taxi that Monday morning.'

'Okay,' Richard said. 'So that's three neighbours who all place Pierre arriving here on Monday morning.'

'And he also remembers seeing an old black car arriving soon after, and three men getting out.'

'Did he identify Conrad being one of those men?'

'When I showed the photo of Conrad to him, he said he wasn't sure. He might have been one of the men, but he said he was out on his stoop gutting some fish he'd caught for his lunch. He wasn't paying much attention. He said he only noticed the three guys at all because they started arguing.

When that happened, he didn't stay around to find out what it was about. He said the less you know around here the better. So he took his fish inside and thought no more of it. And then, about an hour later, he came out again to feed his dog, and he saw that the black car was gone, and the men with it. But there was now a grey car parked outside the halfway house.'

'A *grey* car?' Richard asked. 'Not a black one?'

'That's what he said. It was a grey Citroën.'

'He could tell that?'

'He said, in a former life, he'd been a mechanic. He recognised the model, it was a Citroën CX. A real beauty of a car, he said, but it's an old model, and this one wasn't in good shape.'

'Okay,' Richard said, pulling out his notebook and making a note. 'So who was driving it?'

'He didn't see.'

'He didn't?'

'He said he wasn't paying attention, it was only the car he really noticed – because it was such a classic. He didn't see who was driving.'

'Then how do we know which gang member it was?'

'Well, there we have a bit more luck. He said he started to walk to the car to give it a quick once over when he saw a man in a blue jacket leave the halfway house and get into the car.'

'And that was definitely Pierre?'

'I showed him Pierre's mugshot, and he positively identified him. It was Pierre who was wearing the blue jacket, and who got in the grey Citroën.'

'Did he see who was driving as he got closer?'

'That's the thing. He said that as soon as Pierre got in the passenger side, the car did a three-point turn and drove out of here. He never saw who was driving.'

'Look,' Richard said, suddenly angry. 'Would someone *please* get rid of this bloody chicken?'

'You just had to ask,' Dwayne said, reaching down to pick up the offending creature. He then took hold of the bird's head and gently tucked it under its wing.

'Don't worry, Chief,' Dwayne said. 'Chickens are so stupid, if it's too dark for them to see, they go to sleep.'

And with that, Dwayne put the chicken back on the floor, its head still tucked neatly under its wing.

The chicken didn't move. It just stood there stock still.

'Dwayne,' Richard said. 'I take back everything I've ever said about you. Thank you.'

Despite his words, Richard was a touch unnerved that there was what appeared to be a headless chicken standing on the ground in front of him – it felt too much like a metaphor for how he was leading the case – so he decided they should all return to the Police station.

Over the next few days, Richard set his team the task of discovering how many Citroën CX owners there were on the island. Fidel rang round the list of names he was able to pull from Government House while Camille rang Natasha Gardiner. Did her husband by any chance own a grey Citroën? She replied that the only car she and Conrad owned was a black Toyota. This was welcome information in that it fitted with the witness who'd said that three men had arrived after Pierre in an old black car. But it was less welcome information in that it also implied that it *hadn't* been Conrad who'd later returned. So who had it been?

Richard also wanted to know how Dwayne was getting on with identifying the shop where Pierre had bought the red ruby. Unfortunately, Dwayne said that he'd rung every jewellery and tourist knick-knack shop he could think of, but he'd drawn a complete blank. No-one he spoke to sold anything like fake red rubies, and nor did they know where you'd go on the island to buy them.

Fidel also didn't get good news from the phone company about the SIM card from the phone that had been used to set off the bomb.

'Sir,' he'd said to Richard. 'The SIM card did indeed receive a call on the morning the boat exploded. And the call came in at the right time. But the number that dialled in to the phone came from another pre-paid mobile phone that was bought on Saint-Marie over a year ago. Just like the phone on the boat. Which suggests to me the killer maybe bought the two phones as a pair. With cash. So they'd be totally untraceable.'

It was another dead end.

As for the Saint-Marie Dive School, their search of the sea bed under the area of the explosion proved just as fruitless.

The remaining bulk of the boat had split into three different sections as it sank to the bottom of the sea, and they'd found a considerable spread of debris lying in the sand all around. Remembering how the harbour master had said that he'd seen Conrad load some scuba tanks onto his boat on the morning that he was killed, Richard asked if any diving tanks had been found on the sea bed. This was his way of working out how diligent the divers had been, and how reliable their testimony was. Unfortunately for Richard, he was told that no such equipment had been found. It was possible they were still trapped inside one of the sections of boat, of course, but this was the last thing Richard wanted to hear. After all, if the scuba tanks were there but the Saint-Marie Dive School hadn't found them, then that begged the question, what else were they failing to find?

And throughout all this, Richard kept working on trying to identify where Pierre was now hiding. But there was no evidence of Pierre staying in any of the local hotels, hostels or B&Bs. So where was he? And there was another aspect of Pierre's vanishing act that increasingly irked Richard. Pierre had left prison with only one hundred dollars to his name, and he'd left the cash behind when he'd driven off in the grey Citroën later that afternoon. So, wherever he was hiding, Richard was increasingly of the opinion that someone must be helping him. Either financially, or by offering him a safe place to hide. But who was it? If Dwayne was right, the various hoodlums and ne'er-do-wells on the island had all forgotten about Pierre years ago – decades ago, even – so who could be offering him sanctuary?

Richard tried to glean what he could from the prison record Fidel had brought back, but it didn't offer much by way of new information. Pierre kept himself to himself, he didn't belong to any of the gangs, and he didn't take or deal drugs. As far as Richard could tell, he'd been something of a model prisoner. Even his personal statement for the Parole Board was down-the-line 'correct'. In it, Pierre had said how he acknowledged what he'd done, he'd regretted it ever since, and now he felt he'd paid his debt to society.

As for visitors, the only person from outside the prison who'd had any contact with Pierre while he was inside was the prison's official prison visitor, Father Luc Durant. When Richard read the name Luc Durant, he remembered that Natasha Gardiner had said that she went to Father Luc Durant's church. This gave Richard pause. Although it wasn't unheard of on a small island like Saint-Marie that the name of a person tangential to the case should crop up more than once, Richard didn't like the coincidence.

He decided he'd call the Governor of the Saint-Marie Prison, ostensibly to garner whatever background information he could on Pierre, but also because he wanted to ask about Father Luc Durant.

'Sure, I know Pierre,' the Governor said in a weary voice as the call was put through to him. 'But I don't know him, if you know what I mean.'

'Not really,' Richard said. 'Could you explain?'

'Well, I was on the review board when he came up for parole, so I met him then. And I've been through his prison record. But before that I wouldn't have been able to pick him out from a crowd. Sorry.'

'And how did he seem when he came up for parole?'

There was a dry laugh from the end of the phone.

'That's the one time in a prisoner's sentence you know you're not seeing the real man. It's understandable. It's a job interview, isn't it? For the job of being allowed to operate in freedom outside the prison again.'

'But you've seen a lot of prisoners, what did you pick up from him?'

'That he was bone tired. That he was sick of the prison. Sick of us.'

'Did he seem dangerous?'

'Obviously not,' the Governor said with an edge to his voice. 'Or we'd not have let him out early.'

'Then can you tell me something about Father Luc Durant?'

'What do you want to know about him?'

'He's the only person I can find who ever visited Pierre.'

'That's hardly surprising. Father Luc Durant visits all our prisoners. But you're right, if you want to know what Pierre was really like, talk to Father Luc. He'll be able to tell you a bit more about him.'

'And is Father Luc entirely trustworthy?'

'Of course. He's one of the most trustworthy men I know. He's always here for prisoners, and there's precious few people I can say that about, I can tell you.'

Thanking the Governor for his time, Richard ended the call and then phoned Father Luc's church. The call was answered by a man who high-handedly informed Richard that Father Luc was leading a funeral and couldn't possibly come to the phone. However, he'd pass on the policeman's message just as soon as he returned.

Richard hung up the call with a growing sense of frustration. It was all very well trying to find out what Pierre was like, but that didn't answer the question, where was he now? They had no real leads, and every day that passed brought them one day closer to the next murder, he was sure of it.

Richard decided to go back to the original case notes on Pierre's robbery. As he did so, Richard remembered that the man who'd been murdered – André Morgan – had come from Saint-Marie.

Richard clicked forwards in the digital archive on his screen until he was looking at what the Met Police had on André Morgan. He could see the contact details of his parents, both of whom lived in Honoré. He also saw that André had left school at eighteen, and had become an assistant in a jewellery shop in Honoré three years later. The manager of the Honoré branch had been interviewed by the Police after the murder and had said that André was hardworking, and superbly attentive to his customers. A year after starting as a trainee, he was promoted to a full-time job, and within another year he'd been made senior salesman for the shop. Then, two years later, André decided he wanted to travel, applied for a salesman's post at the flagship store in Bond Street in London, and got the job.

Richard carried on reading the manager's statement, and

was intrigued to see how he'd said he'd not been entirely sorry to see André leave. Because, although he'd had so much potential when he'd started out, he felt that André had perhaps 'taken his foot off the pedal' recently. The manager went on to say that he'd turned up late for work a couple of times, and he'd even given the impression on other occasions that he was suffering from a hangover. It wasn't appropriate behaviour for a member of staff in a shop that had such an exclusive clientele.

Wondering what had prompted this possible change in André, Richard scrolled on through the notes the Metropolitan Police had taken after talking to André's boss in the London store, and here Richard could see that things seemed to have returned to normal for André. According to his London manager's statement, André worked hard, was punctual, and was an exemplary member of the team. He'd been working at the store for nearly three months without blemish when he was murdered.

In fact, Richard saw from the statement that the manager of the London store had been present when the robbery had taken place, and he said André didn't interact with the robbers at all. He thought the robbers' focus was entirely on the security man and the manager himself, and making sure they got hold of the briefcase of jewels. It was only as the robbers were leaving that one of them pulled a gun, turned to André and shot him dead in cold blood.

It was as Richard read this fact for the umpteenth time that he realised something.

Why hadn't Pierre shot the manager? Or the security guard? Seeing as he was prepared to commit murder, surely they were far more likely to be able to testify against him later on? So why, considering the fact that André hadn't interacted with the robbers at all, had Pierre shot him dead?

What if it was because he *was* connected to the robbers somehow?

And in a world where he was running out of lines of enquiry, Richard decided that he should pursue the André Morgan angle. But how could he even begin to do that seeing as the young man had been dead for the last twenty years?

Richard looked back in the file to the contact details of André's parents. That was as good a place to start as any. He picked up his phone and dialled the number that was listed. The phone was answered on the second ring.

'Honoré Bakery,' a male voice said.

'Is that Mr Morgan?' Richard asked.

'It is.'

'This is Detective Inspector Richard Poole. Can I ask, are you the father of André Morgan?'

There was a silence from the other end of the phone. Richard listened carefully and began to worry that the man had hung up.

'Why are you asking?' the man eventually said.

'Can I first just check? You're the father of André Morgan, who died in a jewellery robbery just over twenty years ago?'

This time the silence on the other end of the call was filled with breathing that Richard could hear had suddenly got heavy.

'Why are you ringing?'

'Are you André Morgan's father?'

'Yes, but why are you ringing? Is this to do with Pierre Charpentier?'

Now it was Richard's turn to be surprised.

'You know about him?'

'Of course. I was there the day he left prison.'

'You were?'

'The man who killed my son? Yes. I was there. Look, I can't talk to you over the phone. Come to the bakery. I'll tell you what happened when he got out of prison if you come to my office.'

Richard said he'd be along in a few minutes, and hung up. He then called across the room.

'Camille, I think we've just got ourselves a lead.'

CHAPTER SEVEN

As it happened, Richard knew Mr Morgan's bakery well, as he had a secret weakness he didn't like to admit to his team. He adored French pastry. Every buttery crumb of it. In particular he loved glossy *éclairs* full of whipped Chantilly cream. But he also loved delicately layered *mille feuille*, sugar-glazed *babs au rhum*, and pretty much anything that contained chocolate. So, if Richard ever had a taxing day at work – and, if he were honest, these seemed to happen more often than not – he'd pick up a delicate pastry on the way home. At first, Richard had worried that his ardour for this most fancy of French cooking would result in him piling on the pounds, but he soon realised that the sweltering heat of his walk home was negating the calories the pastry would otherwise have been putting on. In fact, Richard increasingly believed that a quick macaroon – which, after all, was mostly coconutty air surrounded by an almond case of brittle wonder – was the necessary fuel he needed to get home.

Not that he did it every day, of course. Or had become obsessed in any way.

The young man behind the counter looked up as Richard and Camille entered the shop.

'Your usual?' he asked, and Richard blushed bright red. This was exactly the start to the conversation he'd been hoping to avoid.

'Your *usual*?' Camille asked, deeply amused.

'Oh yes,' the assistant said. 'The Detective Inspector is a most valued customer. But tell me, did you bring that spoon back?'

Much too late, Richard realised that he did indeed have a used and washed-up spoon in his inside pocket. He'd borrowed it the day before, when he'd said he'd like to be able to eat his *crème au caramel* on the way home.

Somewhat shamefacedly, Richard reached into his jacket pocket and pulled out the little spoon.

'Thank you,' he said.

'No worries. Now, how can I help you?'

Richard realised he didn't quite have the energy to continue his end of the conversation, so Camille stepped into the breach.

'We're here to talk to your boss, Stefan Morgan.'

'Of course. He's in his office at the back. Come on through.'

The assistant indicated a little door to the side of the counter, and Richard and Camille went through, finding themselves in a gloomy corridor that was full of tall metal stands that smelled of sugar and flour.

'Come here often, do you, sir?' Camille asked, unable to let her boss's recent encounter pass without comment.

'Hardly.'

'But I thought you were one of their most valued customers?'

'He exaggerated.'

'Even though you've always told me, the problem with France is that it's full of French food.'

'I never said that.'

'You're always saying that! How you can't get a decent meal in a French restaurant.'

'Well, you can't. Unless you want to eat pigs' trotters or snails.'

'Or frogs' legs, I know,' Camille said, completing Richard's sentence for him. 'In fact, as you keep telling us, the French are terrible chefs. And now I realise why you've been so rude about us all of this time. You're repressed.'

'I beg your pardon?'

'You love the French really, but you're in denial.'

'I don't, and I'm not.'

'But you love our pastries, don't you?'

'Okay, I admit I quite like the pastries from your country, but they're not that special, you know. The British have pastries, too.'

'Oh they do, do they?' Camille said, putting her hand on her hip.

'You'd better believe it. I mean, we've got . . .' Richard said, wracking his brain to think of a single British pastry. 'Sausage rolls,' he eventually said. 'They're pretty special. And your humble pork pie's a pastry, too. Don't forget that.'

'Pork pie? What's that?'

'Well, it's bits of pork moulded into a cylinder that's then sealed in meat jelly. And it's surrounded by the most delicious pastry, cut through with lard, which is of course the secret.'

'Lard?'

'That's right. Lard.'

'What's lard?'

'Well, if you're going to put it like that, it's pig fat.'

Richard's words hung in the frangipane-scented air.

'I don't think I've quite done it justice,' he added.

'No, it sounds lovely. Pig meat in pig jelly surrounded by pig fat.'

'You've got to taste one.'

'No,' Camille said, going in for the kill. 'I want you to admit it right now. French pastry is superior to British.'

'Different, I'll grant you. Not superior.'

'But you love it, don't you? Which is why you come in here every day, and the assistant greeted you by asking, "your usual"?'

Richard couldn't quite see a way of denying what was so obviously a self-evident truth, so he decided to do what any true-born Englishman does when confronted with an embarrassing fact: he'd just pretend the conversation wasn't happening.

'We can't stand here all day gassing,' he said, walking away. 'We need to interview Mr Morgan.'

Before Camille could reply, Richard opened the door at the end of the corridor, and walked in on a very plump man who was sitting behind an enormous desk. He had a wooden box open in front of him, and he was looking at old newspaper cuttings and photos.

'Mr Morgan?' Richard asked.

The man looked up, as though he was surprised to see the Police.

'That's right. I'm Stefan Morgan. You'd better sit down,' he said in a wheezy voice, indicating a couple of plastic bucket chairs nearby.

As Richard pulled out his hankie and dusted the thin sheen of flour from his chair seat, he saw that Stefan was probably in his sixties, and he was one of those men who was so plump that his breathing, even in repose, required a degree of effort. But it was more than that, Richard thought to himself as he folded his handkerchief and slipped it back into his jacket pocket. The man looked defeated.

'He was such a good boy,' Stefan offered to no-one in particular as he went back to looking at the old documents in the box.

'Do you have a photo of him?' Camille asked.

Stefan handed over a photo of a young, smiling man standing behind a jewellery counter. His skin seemed to glow with good health, and there was a sparkling intelligence in his eyes. Richard could see why he'd been a shop assistant. He looked keen and ready to serve.

'That was taken in Honoré,' Stefan said. 'Just after André started at the jewellery shop.'

'He looks like a lovely boy,' Camille said.

'He was,' Stefan said in a whisper. 'And his life was taken from him.'

'By Pierre Charpentier,' Richard added, wanting to get Stefan to focus on the issue at hand.

'By Pierre Charpentier,' Stefan agreed, and Richard could see a stiffness come into Stefan's demeanour.

'Who you saw when he left prison.'

'Oh yes.'

'Why?'

Stefan turned to look at Richard, puzzled.

'Do you have kids?'

'No.'

'Then you have no idea. No idea what it's like to hold that new life in your hands. And that feeling of love – the unconditional love you feel for that life. How desperately you realise you'd do anything for them. Lie, steal, cheat and kill if necessary. And that's the very first moment you meet them. You just know you've got to protect this young baby. It's overwhelming. And then when someone takes that child's life from you? There are no words to describe what that's like. The horror.'

Stefan stopped speaking so he could re-catch his breath.

'It killed my wife,' he said.

'It did?' Camille said.

'She couldn't handle the grief. She got so weak that first year after André's death, she got a virus. We never knew what it was. But she didn't fight it, and then she got pneumonia. And when she went to hospital, it was like she gave up. She was dead two weeks later. From a broken heart. And it was that man's fault. That man who killed my son. He has the blood of two people on his hands. My son. My wife. The only two people I've ever cared about.'

'I'm so sorry,' Camille said.

'And as you can see, I now hide in the back office.'

Stefan reached for an opened can of Coke on his desk and took a large slug from it.

'Can you tell us the last time you saw Pierre Charpentier?' Richard asked.

Stefan paused briefly, mid-gulp, and then he put the can back down on his desk.

'You want to know about the day he got out of prison?'

Stefan plucked a tissue from a box and daintily wiped his lips, although Richard got the impression that he was trying to buy himself a few moments to ready his story.

'It was simple. I just needed to see him. That man. And I needed him to see me. He had to know I was still out here.'

'So you waited for him before he left prison?'

'I knew he'd be released just after 10am. That's when all prisoners are released. So I drove up to the prison and made sure I was waiting there from nine.'

'What car do you drive?' Richard asked.

Stefan was surprised by the question.

'An old Nissan.'

'What colour is it?'

'White.'

'You drive a white Nissan car?'

'That's right.'

'And do you own any other cars?'

'No.'

'So you drove up to the prison in your white Nissan, and were waiting outside. Do carry on.'

'That's right. And I knew he was coming because a taxi pulled up outside the main gate just before ten. This was it. The moment I'd waited for for twenty years. And then the doors to the prison opened and there he was.'

As Stefan said this, both Richard and Camille could see that he was reliving every moment.

'The man who'd murdered my son. He also saw me.'

'He did?'

'He put his hand up to his head to block the sun. So he could see me.'

'What did you do?'

'I took a step forward so I was standing in the road, and I just looked at him. I wanted him unsettled.'

'Was he?'

'He took a few steps towards me, and then he stopped. I think he recognised me. I mean, it had been twenty years since he'd seen me. My wife and I had attended every day of his trial, and I've changed a lot since then . . . but I think he worked it out. He took a step back, it was like he stumbled. And I started walking towards him, I couldn't help myself. I mean, he looked pretty lean and fit, like he had when he went into prison. And I'm just this fat old man who eats too many pastries, but I couldn't help myself. As for what I was going to do when I reached him, I had no idea. But I wanted to see him up close. And as I crossed the road, he turned and got in the taxi, and it drove off. I think I scared him.'

Stefan paused to collect his breath, and Richard could see a sense of pride burning in the old man's eyes.

'So that's all I know about Pierre. But what I want to know is, why are you so interested in him?'

'Well,' Richard said, not wishing to reveal his hand entirely, 'since he left prison, his name has come up in conjunction with another investigation. Since which time he seems to have done a runner.'

'He's committed another crime?' Stefan asked. 'I don't believe it. He only got out of prison last week.'

'At this stage, all I can say is that we just need to ask him a few questions. So, do you know where he is?'

'No. I've no idea.'

'Or have you had any contact with him?'

'No. I didn't even have contact with him when he got out. I just walked towards him, he got in his car, and that was that. The last time I saw him.'

'Okay. Then do you mind me asking, what do you know about the explosion that happened in the harbour last Thursday?'

'You mean, Conrad's boat?'

'Oh, you know him?'

'Of course. It's a terrible thing that's happened.'

'I'd agree with you there. Can you tell us a bit about your relationship with Conrad?'

'Well, I've known him for years. As a person you could talk to in a bar. Or go to if you needed someone to do the odd job for you. You know, he built the store room round the back of the building.'

'Did you know him when he was a record producer?'

For the first time, a laugh bubbled up in Stefan's throat.

'Record producer? I don't know what you think he was, but he was no record producer.'

'But he made records,' Richard said, puzzled.

'He threw parties, that's what he did. Don't get me wrong, they were good parties, but they were terrible records. That man had more money than sense. No-one was surprised when his business collapsed. I think he'd just used the whole thing to hang out with young people. And girls in particular.'

'He liked hanging out with young girls?' Camille asked.

'He'd always have a string of hopefuls on his arm.'

'Even though he was married?'

'But he's married to Natasha, isn't he? I don't know if you've met her, but she's a weak woman. She could never control her man. So Conrad just slept with who he wanted. Or he did back in the day.'

'Have you seen him at all in the last few weeks?'

'No. Can't say I have. But are you saying Pierre Charpentier is somehow connected to his boat exploding?'

Richard ignored the question.

'Can you tell us where you were last Thursday at about 10am?'

'I'm sorry?' Stefan was thrown by the question.

'Just so we can rule you out of our enquiries.'

Stefan didn't know what to say, but he reached for a little diary on the desk in front of him.

'Okay,' he said, turning back the pages with his chubby fingers. 'So, if you're asking where I was when Conrad's boat exploded, I can tell you I was on Guadeloupe, at the General hospital. If you must know.'

'Why?'

'I was . . .' Stefan said, not entirely comfortable with the direction the conversation had taken. 'Do you really need to know?'

'It would be a great help,' Camille said.

'Okay . . . so I was having an MRI scan.'

'You were?'

'I recently had a fall, and when I went to the local hospital, they found a shadow on my X-ray. In my liver. They were worried it was cancer, and the blood tests weren't good. So yes, last Thursday I had to go to Guadeloupe and have a full body MRI scan.'

'Have you had the results?' Camille asked.

Stefan noticed the empty Coke can on his desk, picked it up, crushed it in his hand, and dropped it in the empty waste paper basket under his desk.

'They need to run more tests before they can be sure. But at this stage, it's a question of what stage cancer I've got, and where it's spread, not whether I've got it.'

'I'm so sorry,' Camille said.

'Can I pick you up on something you said?' Richard

asked, unaware of how crassly he was shattering the mood in the room.

Stefan shrugged.

'Whatever you like.'

'It's just, you said you and your wife both attended Pierre's original trial in London.'

'That's right. We attended every single day. And stood and cheered at the end when he was convicted. Cheered and cheered.'

'And you also said your son was a good boy. And I'm sure he was. In fact, I've read the case notes, and his manager at his store in Honoré was very positive about him.'

'He was always a hard worker.'

'At first,' Richard added. 'Because the manager also said André had perhaps taken his foot off the pedal in the time just before he left for London.'

'That was that woman,' Stefan said dismissively.

'And what woman would that be?'

'A few months before he left the island, Stefan started staying out late. I wasn't joking when I said he was a good boy. It wasn't like him at all. He was a good Christian boy before then. But he started going to bars and drinking too much. And we could smell cigarette smoke on his clothes. And found ganja in his room. We were horrified. This wasn't our son. And it wasn't. He'd started dating this girl, and she was corrupting him.'

'What was her name?'

'That was the thing, we never met her. She refused to

come to the house when we were here, and Stefan wouldn't tell us her name. He said that if we knew who she was, we'd try and split them up. And he was right, because it was his manner changing that hurt us the most. He became insolent. Like he didn't care.'

'Hang on,' Richard said, trying to make sense of what he was being told. 'You never knew her name?'

'He wouldn't tell us. It was his secret, he said. But then, after a few months of this, the manager of the jewellery store rang us and said he wasn't happy with André's work. So we banned him from seeing her again. We were the enemy to him by this stage. But he wasn't earning enough money to move out and get his own place, so we knew he'd have to do as he was told. And my wife started spending much more time at home. To make sure André and his girlfriend stopped using our house for their . . . encounters. You see, we always got the impression that this girlfriend of his didn't have a place of her own, so we hoped this would stop them meeting up. And it seemed to work. André was still just as sullen, but he seemed to have stopped seeing the girl. And then I got a phonecall from our local priest. He said he'd seen André and a young woman going into the family crypt in the cemetery just outside Honoré.'

'You have a family crypt?'

Richard had always found it odd that on Saint-Marie families didn't bury their dead in military rows with headstones all neatly aligned. Instead, each family would often have a crypt in which they buried their whole family. And, as humans would be humans, some of these would be bigger and more ornate than others, so the graveyards of Saint-Marie were full of structures that often had stairs that led to floors and even verandas above the crypt so that candlelit celebrations could be held on feast days like the Day of the Dead. And, although Richard knew there was no health or safety or planning permission attached to these haphazard structures, they all conformed in the sense that every inch of every structure was always covered in alternating black and white square tiles, as though the buildings were made from massive chess boards. When visiting a graveyard in Saint-Marie, it was like being trapped in an *Alice in Wonderland* maze of crazy and improbable two-tone buildings.

'Our family have had a crypt at the Honoré cemetery for nearly one hundred and fifty years,' Stefan said proudly. 'It's on the main avenue. Right at the top of the hill. And there's still space inside for another hundred years.'

Richard didn't quite know what the correct response to this sort of crypt-based bragging was, so he just said, 'Well done. But, before André left for the UK, are you saying that your son was visiting the family crypt with his girlfriend?'

'That's what the priest said. It didn't seem possible. Not when I had the only key. But I decided to go and check. There's a locked metal grille that stops people going down the steps to where the bodies are kept. And I could see that no-one had tried to force it. I was surprised. How could André have been going into the crypt if he hadn't broken in? Anyway, I used my key to open the gate and went down into the chamber. It's not that big. There's a wall of metal drawers where the coffins go. And some stone sarcophaguses that used to be used for the laying in of bodies, but we haven't done that for decades. Anyway, once I was in there, I also found a pile of clothes on the tiles in the corner. And there was an old turned-over hubcap from a car that was full of cigarette butts and crushed roaches from spliffs. And empty bottles of rum. My perfect son. My kind, sweet son. I couldn't believe it. We'd banned him from meeting this woman, so he'd started going to the family crypt with her. It was disgusting.'

'So what did you do next?' Camille asked.

'I confronted him about the crypt, and he just admitted it. Like it wasn't a problem. He said we couldn't control his life. He was an adult. So he'd got my key to the family crypt copied, and that's where he'd been taking his girlfriend. Well, I don't need to tell you, this caused the greatest of all possible rifts, because André was desecrating our family ancestors' resting place, but he just didn't care. Not that it was his fault, I had to keep telling myself. It was this woman he was with who'd led him astray. Who'd bewitched him. That's how André's mother and I looked at it. He'd been bewitched. Then, a few days later, André announced he'd applied for a job at the head office in London, and he was going to move there. Just to get away from us.

'And then, just like that, he was gone. And he didn't ring. Didn't write. Didn't text. We didn't know what to do. He was our only son, and he'd just gone away. And we told ourselves this was a natural part of growing up. That we had to let him go so he could come back. And then, about three months later, we got a knock on the door from the Chief of Police in Honoré. He said he'd just got off the phone with the Metropolitan Police in London, and he had some very bad news.'

Stefan couldn't continue as he remembered the day he was told that his son had been murdered. Camille reached over, squeezed the old man's hand, and he looked at her with tears in his eyes.

Richard wasn't quite ready to let Stefan off the hook just yet.

'What happened to the girlfriend?' he asked.

'I'm sorry?'

'The woman who you think bewitched your son?'

'I've no idea. I suppose she's still on the island somewhere.'

As Stefan said this, Camille's phone started to ring. She made her excuses and left the room to take the call.

'Can I ask one last question?' Richard asked.

'Shoot,' Stefan said.

'After you saw Pierre on the day he was released, what did you do?'

The question surprised Stefan.

'I'm sorry?'

'Did you follow Pierre when he got into his taxi?'

Stefan looked deeply uncomfortable.

'No.'

'So what did you do?'

'Do I have to answer this?'

'Eventually,' Richard said, his voice hardening. 'Either here now or back at the Police station later on.'

'Alright. I suppose it doesn't matter. After I'd seen Pierre, and he'd gone off in the taxi, I got back into my car and drove to Honoré cemetery. It's where André's buried. I didn't go into the crypt, but I just stood outside. I told my son I'd confronted his killer and he'd run away, his tail between his legs. I hoped it would make me feel better, but it didn't, because all I kept thinking was, that evil man was now free, and my beautiful son was still dead, and had been for the last twenty years.'

Richard could see the pain in Stefan's eyes, but there was also an anger there, too. Understandably, Richard thought to himself.

'Sir, that was Fidel,' Camille said, returning to the room. 'He's just taken a phonecall from a member of the public. A grey Citroën car has been found abandoned in the jungle.'

'A grey Citroën car?'

'And not just any kind, sir. It's a Citroën CX.'

Richard understood the importance of the point Camille was making. Pierre had been picked up from his halfway house by one of the gang members driving a grey Citroën CX.

'And you should know, sir,' Camille continued, 'whoever left it in the middle of nowhere, they also set fire to it. The car's been completely burnt out.'

CHAPTER EIGHT

Richard never understood why people would come from all around the world to holiday in the Caribbean. The place was too hot and too humid. And if the heat wasn't enough to put you off, there were creatures on land, sea and in the air that could hospitalise or outright kill you. As for the beaches, they were covered in a fine sand that, frankly, got *everywhere*. And, as he'd tell anyone who cared to listen, the sea was the wrong temperature. After all, when you're boiling hot, the last thing any sane person would want to do is get into a sea that was as warm as a bath, especially considering that this particular bath contained killer sharks.

However, if he couldn't understand why anyone would want to book a beach holiday to Saint-Marie, Richard really didn't understand why anyone would then travel to the interior of the island. This was only partly because the centre of Saint-Marie was dominated by a dormant-but-nonetheless-not-yet-provably-dead volcano. It was also because every inch of the island that wasn't coastline was basically jungle.

Sometimes the jungle was only scrubby, or had been cut back to make space for goats or gardens, but as you travelled further inland, the tropical rainforest got thicker, the creepers that hung from the trees all the more creepy, and the sense that there was danger lurking behind every trunk became all the more justified.

It was fair to say that Richard didn't like travelling around Saint-Marie. And yet, here he was, deep in the jungle, looking over the edge of a hairpin bend, where a burnt-out Citroën had come to rest at the base of a tree quite a few feet down the slope that led away from the road.

The car was almost completely blackened.

'I'm not going down there,' Richard said to Camille.

'What are you talking about? It's not steep. Look at Dwayne and Fidel working the scene.'

Richard looked over, and Dwayne and Fidel were indeed moving around the car without any noticeable side effects.

'But what if there was a sudden mud slide, or earthquake?' Richard said, looking about himself as though he was expecting the ground to open up and swallow him whole.

'Okay, sir, you stay here. You can always read my report,' Camille said, and headed down to the car, knowing full well her boss was too much of a control freak to leave her in charge of anything.

Richard frowned to himself. He knew exactly what his Detective Sergeant was up to, but what could he do? He couldn't possibly stand on the road watching his team work such an important crime scene without him. There was nothing for it. He'd have to go down and join them.

Gritting his teeth, Richard took a first step onto the slope. His foot seemed to hold. That was good.

He placed his other foot onto the dirt, but made sure that his body was turned so he was facing to the side of the slope.

'You want any water?' Dwayne said as he passed Richard on his way back to the Police bike on the road.

Richard realised that maybe the slope wasn't as vertiginous as he'd first thought. He took a couple of steps further downwards and put his hands out to break his fall if he toppled over. He checked his footing again. It seemed secure enough.

Dwayne passed him again, glugging on a bottle of water.

'You sure you don't want any of this?' he said, pausing long enough to offer his bottle to his boss.

Richard realised that maybe the slope really was a lot more safe than it had at first looked.

'Thank you, Dwayne,' he said as he took Dwayne's proffered bottle.

Richard took a long, deep drink. There. That was better. He handed the bottle back.

'You can just walk up and down, Chief,' Dwayne said.

'Yes. I see that maybe I can.'

'Come on, let me show you what we've got so far,' Dwayne said and headed over to the car.

Richard followed Dwayne and tried to avoid Camille's eye as he increasingly realised how very firm the ground was.

'So there was a guy up here on his motorbike,' Dwayne

said. 'He stopped just up on the road back there, and that's when he saw the burnt-out car down here.'

'Do we know the witness?'

'He's an American tourist from Miami. And he didn't come down here to check. He just called the car in and then went on his way.'

'I see.'

Now that Richard was closer, he could see that the car had come to rest on the slope somewhat askew, and it was the 'uphill' section of the car that had burnt through most thoroughly. There was an area to the front left of the car that was the furthest down the slope which hadn't burnt at all.

The paint on this undamaged section of the car was grey.

'And it's a Citroën CX?' Richard asked, going to look at the paintwork.

'Sure is, Chief. Just like the CX that apparently picked up Pierre from his house.'

Richard looked high above the car, and saw sunbeams slicing through the canopy of trees. He could well imagine someone driving or pushing the car off the road, and then setting fire to it. The dense foliage above would help diffuse the smoke, and he knew that the road was rarely used. If you wanted somewhere to set fire to a car, it was almost ideal.

'What about the car's owner?' he asked.

'Whatever documents were inside were burnt when the car went up,' Fidel said. 'But we've got the number plate. We'll run it through the computer back at the station.'

'What else did you find?' Camille asked.

'Nothing much,' Fidel said. 'Although Dwayne thinks the car was maybe stolen.'

'You do?' Camille said as she went around to the driver's side where Dwayne was indicating, and he showed her a flatheaded screwdriver that was jammed into the melted steering wheel column.

'Someone used a screwdriver to hotwire the car?' Camille said, surprised. 'I didn't think that worked any more.'

Like any good copper, Camille knew that before electronic keys became common, criminals could hotwire some models of car by hammering a large screwdriver into the ignition slot. It destroyed the lock, but it was then possible to twist the screwdriver handle as though it were a key and start the engine that way.

'It worked up until about the early nineties,' Dwayne said, and then he realised that he'd perhaps revealed a bit too much about his past. 'Not that I've used the technique myself, you understand. I've just got friends who have. But this is a seriously old car. Easily from before 1990, so the screwdriver in the ignition must have worked.'

'Which suggests the car was stolen.'

'I reckon so. And I bet it was chosen *because* the old trick of the screwdriver would work.'

'And then our car thief drove the car to pick Pierre Charpentier up from his halfway house. And then what?'

'No idea, but the car ended up here, didn't it? We know that much.'

'But why?' Fidel asked.

'Good question,' Camille said. 'If this is the car that was used to pick Pierre up, what's it doing all the way up here? What do you think, sir?' Camille asked, looking over at her boss, but Richard had vanished.

'Sir?' she asked again.

There was still no sign of Richard.

Camille went down the slope and skirted around the bonnet of the car until she found Richard on his haunches examining the front left wheel of the vehicle with a magnifying glass. It was the only wheel on the whole vehicle that hadn't caught fire.

'Sir,' Camille said. 'Dwayne thinks the car was stolen.'

'Quiet, Camille. I'm concentrating.'

Richard fished out his pearl-handled pocket knife and oh-so-carefully inserted it into the tread of the tyre. Camille got down to look at what her boss was doing and saw that there was a tiny but bright-white piece of gravel stuck in the rubber of the tread.

'What is it?'

'Gravel.'

'Gravel?'

'Yes, Camille,' Richard said testily. 'Gravel.'

Taking out a little see-through evidence bag, Richard used his knife to prise the tiny bit of gravel out of the wheel and into the bag.

'But not just any gravel,' Richard said, prising out another piece that was jammed into the tread and placing it into the bag to join the first sample. 'This is white gravel. And you'll notice that there's no white gravel on the ground here in the jungle. And none on the road back up there. And you'll also recall I'm sure how the area around the halfway house where Pierre was staying was just dirt as well. So where did this white gravel come from?'

'Well, anywhere on the island, sir.'

'Oh no, I don't think so. But I'll know it for sure when I compare these samples against my soil collection.'

'Oh okay, you've got to stop right there, sir. You have a *soil* collection?'

'Of course,' Richard said. 'I put it together when I first arrived on the island. I went to all the beaches, dirt roads, tracks and so on I could find and took samples of the soil, sand and gravel. I then labelled and categorised them for just this situation.'

Camille stifled a laugh.

'What?' Richard said.

'Oh nothing, sir. That's all normal.'

'What is?'

'Collecting samples from every dirt track and beach on the island.'

'It's normal for a Police officer who wants to solve crimes,' Richard said, straightening to his full height, although he was still downhill from Camille, so his eyeline was below his subordinate's. 'Now, I suggest we go post-haste to my shack and see if we can find a match for these bits of gravel. Then maybe we'll find out where this car was before it came here.'

Leaving Dwayne and Fidel to finish processing the scene,

Richard got Camille to drive him to his home on the beach. There was still a part of her that thought her boss was joking, but she realised how serious he was when he pulled out a cardboard box from under his bed and opened the lid to reveal hundreds of test tubes of different soil, sand and gravel samples, all of them labelled and dated.

'Wow,' Camille said.

'Wow indeed,' Richard said, misunderstanding entirely the angle at which his partner was entering the conversation.

Camille made her excuses and left, but Richard hardly noticed. He was already beginning to work through his library of soil samples.

A few hours later, Richard strode back into the Police station and announced, 'Well, that was *very* interesting.'

He was gratified to see that Dwayne and Fidel had returned from processing the burnt-out car. This meant they could share in his discovery, too.

Camille looked up from her desk and decided that she was happy to play along for once.

'Okay, sir. What did you find in your collection?'

'It's what I *didn't* find, that's what's so interesting,' Richard said.

Camille reminded herself that she should never 'play along' with her boss's games.

'Okay. Then what didn't you find, sir?'

'A match, that's what I didn't find. I went through my entire library of gravel samples, and couldn't find a single sample that in any way matched the white gravel I got from the tyre treads of the Citroën.'

Camille didn't immediately reply.

And nor did Fidel or Dwayne.

'Because that means,' Richard said, ploughing on regardless, 'that the gravel I found in the Citroën's tyre is almost certainly not from any naturally occurring source nearby.'

'And that's good because . . .?' Dwayne asked.

'Because it suggests to me, Dwayne, that the gravel is perhaps manmade.'

'And that's good because . . .?' Dwayne repeated.

'Because it means the gravel was bought in a shop. And if it was bought in a shop, then we've maybe got a chance of identifying who bought that gravel, and therefore where the car was when it got some of it trapped in its tyres.'

Richard noticed that Camille, Fidel and Dwayne were all still somewhat underwhelmed. What was wrong with his team? Richard thought to himself. Sometimes they seemed to lack any thrill in the hunt. Very well, he decided. It was their loss, not his. He'd pursue the gravel angle without them.

'What have we got on the grey Citroën so far?'

'Well, sir,' Fidel said, picking up his notes. 'It belongs to a local fisherman called Michel Branet. I've spoken to him, and he says he doesn't use his car much, but he thought it was still in the car park behind the main harbour. After I asked him to go check, he called back a few minutes later and said his car was missing.'

'Can his testimony be trusted?'

'He's an old boy I've known for years,' Dwayne said. 'And I wouldn't trust him to keep his boat ship-shape or safe, but he's not a criminal, and there's no reason to think he's lying.'

'So it's not possible he set the car on fire himself to claim the insurance?'

'I asked him that, sir,' Fidel said. 'And he said it was such an old car, he didn't have any insurance. And we've no record of him calling in the car as missing, so it doesn't feel like a scam to me.'

'Then remind me, Fidel,' Richard said. 'Is the car park behind the harbour in any way gravelled?'

'I don't think so, sir. It's just dirt.'

'That's right, it's just dirt!' Richard pronounced, and headed back to the office's whiteboard. 'So we still can't explain how our mystery gravel got into the wheels of Michel's car.'

As Richard wrote up the words 'Mystery Gravel' on the board, he called back to Camille.

'So what have you been doing, Camille?'

'Well sir,' Camille said, happy to get the conversation off the subject of gravel, 'I've been running checks on Stefan Morgan, just to see if his story checks out.'

'Good thinking.'

'And I reckon it does. He only owns one car, and it's a white Nissan, just like he said. But more importantly, I rang the General hospital on Guadeloupe, and he really was having an MRI scan when Conrad's boat exploded. In fact, he was having a forty-minute scan, it started at 10.30am and finished at 11.10am.'

'Which is ten minutes after the boat exploded. Is there any way he could have made a call while he was receiving the scan?'

'I asked, and the scan is one of those machines you get slid into lying down and wearing only a gown. If he'd had any kind of mobile phone on him – or any electronic device, apparently – it would have shown up on the scan.'

'So he's in the clear. Whatever beef he has with Pierre Charpentier, he wasn't involved in killing Conrad. Pierre remains our number one suspect. Has anyone made any progress in tracking him down?'

Richard's team shook their heads and answered that they hadn't.

'I'm pushing my contacts as hard as I can,' Dwayne said. 'But it's like the whole island has forgotten about him.'

Richard remembered that he'd put in a call to the only person who had visited Pierre in prison.

'Have there been any calls from that priest? What was his name?' Richard went to his desk and checked his notes. 'That's right. Any message from Father Luc Durant?'

'Nothing yet,' Camille said with a shrug.

'Better late than never, then,' a friendly voice said from the doorway. Richard looked over and saw a thick-set man wearing a black shirt, black suit, black shoes, and a little white dog collar around his neck. The man looked to be about seventy years old, and had the puffy face and laugh lines of someone who lived life well.

'Are you Father Luc Durant?'

'Guilty as charged,' Luc said with a warm chuckle, and offered his hand for Richard to shake. It felt soft to the touch, Richard noted.

'I've been meaning to call you back, but I was passing, so I thought I'd visit in person to tell you what I know about Pierre face to face. Although I'm not sure what a humble parish priest can do to help the Police.'

'Well, let's see about that,' Richard said, and then suggested they move to the veranda outside.

'Of course,' Father Luc said.

Once they were outside, Camille joined them.

'Ah, Camille. How's your mother?' Luc asked.

'Very well, Father. But I'm sorry to say, she won't be coming back to church any time soon.'

Father Luc smiled easily, and Richard wondered what Father Luc had done to offend Camille's mother, Catherine. He then realised what a foolish question this was. Camille's mother was both French and female, so really there'd have been any number of ways she might have taken or caused offence.

As for Father Luc, he smiled.

'Don't worry,' he said. 'The church is never in any rush to get its sheep back. They all seem to wander back of their own accord in the end.' He then gently clasped his hands together in front of his swelling belly. 'Now, how can I help you?'

'I understand you're the visitor at the Central Prison?'

'That's right.'

'So you visited a prisoner there called Pierre Charpentier?'

'Oh yes. I even helped Pierre prepare for his parole board. So I'm slightly worried that the Police would be asking about him so soon after his release.'

'Well, his name's come up in conjunction with another case. So we just wondered. Can you tell us what you can about him? According to Pierre's file, you saw him every two or three months?'

'That's right. I try and visit all the prisoners once a month or so. And I have to admit Pierre seemed like a typical prisoner. When he was transferred to Saint-Marie from the UK, he was sullen and suspicious. Particularly of me. They're like wounded animals, prisoners, I always think. You have to gain their trust. It takes time. So I'd sit with Pierre and talk to him about whatever was going on in his life. Work in the laundry room. Or sewing mail bags. Anyway, over a number of months, I saw him settle into prison life, and I could see him find his place.'

'Did he join any of the gangs?' Richard asked.

'Oh no, he wasn't that sort of a person. In fact, he wasn't interested in making friends at all. Not even with me. I just got the impression that he was keeping his head down until he could make parole. But I have to say, that wasn't to say he didn't have anger in him. I always felt with Pierre that he was giving me the "best" version of himself, and there was actually quite a lot of emotion going on under the surface.'

'And that emotion was anger?'

'You see it in a lot of prisoners. There's a ferocity to them sometimes. Like a coiled spring. After all, they're locked up all day. And that's what I felt with Pierre. That he had a whole load of energy just waiting to burst out. And not good energy. Anyway, as I say, this is all quite normal for a man who's spent the best part of two decades in prison.'

'Would you say he was an intelligent man?'

Father Luc was surprised by the question.

'I'd say so, I suppose. He had that sort of brooding intelligence. Although, now you mention it, I never saw him with a book in his cell. But there was a way he'd look at you, like he was working you out.'

'Did you like him?' Camille asked.

Father Luc pursed his lips as he thought.

'I'm not sure that I did, if that's not an uncharitable thing to say about another human being. After all, it's very hard to like the people who are inside for murder. I always show them kindness, of course. And sympathy. But I don't have to like someone after they've taken another person's life.'

'But I see you recommended that he be released early on parole.'

'Of course. Everyone deserves a second chance whether I like them or not. And he'd not been violent at any time in the twenty years he was inside. Not as far as I knew.'

'Did he ever talk about the reason why he was in prison?'

'He did, actually. Just the once. He told me he wasn't the man he'd been then.'

'When was this?'

'Last year. I think I'd started to talk to him about his upcoming parole.'

'And that's when he finally spoke about what he was in for?'

'He didn't talk about it all that much. He just said he wasn't the man he'd been when he'd been sent to prison. He said he'd learned his lesson.'

'Which is why you recommended him for parole.'

'Admission of guilt is a big part of the parole process.'

'Did you believe him?'

'Maybe. Sometimes you just have to trust that human nature is good after all.'

Father Luc pulled a smartphone from his inside jacket pocket and checked the time on it.

'Now, if you'll excuse me, I have an evening service to prepare for. There really is no rest for the wicked.'

'Of course, but could I just ask you about Conrad Gardiner?'

'I'm sorry. What's that?'

'Did you know Conrad Gardiner?'

'I know most people on the island, so of course I knew Conrad. And I must say, I was just as shocked as everyone else when I heard what happened to him.'

'Was he a member of your congregation?'

'I don't believe he was a member of anyone's,' Father Luc said sadly. 'He suffered from the same illness as Camille's mother here. Atheism.'

'Then what about his wife? Is she a member of your congregation?'

'Look, you really must excuse me, but I can't be late for my service,' Father Luc said, doing up the buttons on his jacket.

'But how well do you know the family?'

'I barely know Conrad, but we hardly moved in the same circles. As for his wife, now you mention it, she comes to church regularly. And I've got to know her a little over the years. She's a very good woman, if you ask me. And I don't think she deserved to be married to a man as lazy as Conrad was. There, I've said it. Is that what you wanted to hear? That I thought he was lazy?'

'Actually, that's not what I wanted you to say.'

'Then I can only apologise—'

'Because what I wanted you to say was, "what has Conrad's death got to do with Pierre Charpentier's?"'

'I'm sorry?'

'You see, I just jumped from talking about Pierre Charpentier to talking about Conrad Gardiner and you didn't stop for one second to ask what the connection was.'

'Forgive me,' Father Luc said, unable to keep a note of annoyance out of his voice. 'I also have no idea why you're asking about Pierre Charpentier, but I answered your questions like a good citizen. And it's the same for Conrad Gardiner. You ask, and I answer. Now, I'm sorry I can't be of more help, but I really have to return to my flock. If you have any further questions,' Father Luc said, already leaving the veranda, 'you know where to find me. My door is always open to the Police, but I really must go.'

Richard and Camille watched Father Luc beetle away down the steps from the Police Station.

'Now I don't know about you,' Richard said to his partner, 'but did we just rattle Father Durant's cage?'

'It's how it felt to me.'

'But why? What's his connection to Conrad?'

Richard returned to the main office deep in thought, and saw that Fidel was taking a phonecall.

'Now, don't worry,' Fidel said calmly into the receiver while waving to get the attention of everyone else. 'You stay right there, miss. I'm hanging up now, and we'll call an ambulance on the way, but you'll have the Saint-Marie Police Force at your house in a matter of minutes.'

Fidel slammed the phone down into its cradle.

'Sir, that was a woman called Blaise Frost. She says she's just discovered her husband's body at her house. Someone's shot him dead!'

As the Police jeep screeched to a halt, Richard and Camille jumped out, and Richard saw that Dwayne's bike had arrived before them, and Dwayne and Fidel were already dismounting. As for where they were, Richard had no idea. He'd had his eyes closed and his hands gripped to the passenger door for most of the journey. Not that Camille was a bad driver. Far from it. She was just fearless, and that's what put the fear of God into Richard.

As Richard and his team strode to the door, he saw that the house they'd arrived at was grand, but not in a typical Saint-Marie style. It was all jet-black cladding and large sheets of geometrically shaped glass.

The front door opened as they arrived to reveal a tall, willowy woman who was wearing a deep red silk dressing gown over a tight exercise outfit in electric blue, and who appeared to be even taller because she had a cascade of brown hair that rose out of a pair of chopsticks.

'Are you the Police?' she asked in a broad Cockney accent, her eyes red-rimmed with tears.

Richard couldn't work out who else they could have looked like, but he knew that shock affected different people differently, so he decided to make things as simple as possible.

'Detective Inspector Richard Poole of the Saint-Marie Police,' he said, pulling out his warrant card and holding it up for inspection. 'I understand there's been a fatality.'

'It's my husband!' the woman blurted. 'Someone's shot him. Shot him dead.'

'Then can you please take us to him at once.'

As the woman led them inside, Richard briefly wondered what a Cockney woman was doing in the Caribbean, but he was soon distracted by the house's decor. It was all extremely expensive-looking, but it was devoid of colour. The floors, wall, ceilings and all of the furniture were shades of white, grey, brown and black, and there wasn't a single picture on the wall or personal photo in a frame. The whole house felt like an antiseptic show home that hadn't been sold yet.

The woman led them from the cool of the house onto a sun deck that contained an infinity pool as flat and still as a sheet of glass, and which overlooked the wide Caribbean sea beyond. Richard briefly startled at how bright the sunshine reflecting off the swimming pool was, but he cupped his hand above his eyes so he could see against the glare. The woman continued to lead them away from the house towards a separate building a little way away in the garden that was also constructed from black timber and glass. As she reached it, she stopped on the threshold, her hand clutched to her chest.

'He's in there, but I can't go in,' she said, shaking her head. 'Not again.'

'Of course not,' Camille said.

'My Detective Sergeant will stay with you,' Richard said, and carried on to the sliding glass door that led into what he could see was a little office. The door was already open, so Richard stepped inside and found his feet disappearing into a lush white carpet. Once again he noticed that there was only the minimal amount of furnishings, and the whole room was dominated by a large desk that was covered in a shiny black veneer.

There were no signs of a break-in that Richard could immediately see, and nor was there any indication of there having been a struggle. As for where the woman's husband was, that became apparent as Richard moved around the desk.

A man was lying on the floor in his pyjamas, and every inch of his upper torso and head was thick with clotted and drying blood. There was blood on his pyjamas, on his hands, in his hair and on his face, and to make the scene all the more macabre, the white carpet was smeared with streaks of blood where the poor man had clearly tried to escape as he expired.

As Dwayne and Fidel entered, Richard held up his hand for them to pause because there were a few things he wanted to check first.

Bending down to the body, Richard saw that there were a couple of bullet wounds to the man's torso, a third bullet wound in the man's back, but there was also what appeared to be the 'killing shot' that had entered above the left ear and gone straight into the brain.

That made four bullets that had been fired into the body.

Richard touched the edge of the pool of blood on the carpet and could feel that it was already dry. The man had been lying there for some time. He'd have to get the pathologist to estimate the time of death. But as much as Richard was aware of what he could see, the one thing he *couldn't* see troubled him the most.

Richard looked at the man's desk. There was a monitor, a keyboard and a couple of pens in a little tray, but what Richard was looking for wasn't there.

Where was it?

Richard bent down to the body again and this time noticed that the man's mouth was ever so slightly open, as though there was something inside it.

With one hand he gently prised the jaws open. They were already stiff with *rigor mortis*, but he was able to slip the finger and thumb of his other hand into the man's mouth to locate what he was looking for.

He found it immediately.

Richard pulled it out and held it up.

It was a bright red ruby just like the one that had been left at the scene after Conrad Gardiner's murder.

Dwayne saw the ruby from across the room.

'No way,' he said, amazed.

Richard looked at the ruby, his mind awhirl with appalled possibilities, but there was one thing he was now sure of.

Pierre Charpentier had struck again.

I was disappointed he didn't beg when I pulled the gun. I thought he would, but I don't think he thought I'd see it through. He thought I was joking. That after all this time, I wouldn't have the courage. He always was so arrogant. So full of himself. Instead, he asked me where I'd got the gun from and I just laughed and shot him in the shoulder. It was everything I hoped. To put a bullet in him. On an island like Saint-Marie you can get anything, I told him. An unmarked handgun. An untraceable mobile phone. Or two. If I'm honest I don't think he heard a word I said. Not after I shot him in the other shoulder. It was a nice carpet. Expensive. And the blood came in little spurts through his fingers as he tried to stop the bleeding. That's when he tried to get away. I had to stifle a laugh as I watched him try to crawl to the door. The third bullet went

straight into his back, and his body dropped to
the floor, just like that. I bent down. He was
still breathing. Just. Thin breaths. The thinnest
of thin breaths. His eyes looked at me, and I
could see he finally got it. He was going to die.
I smiled, put the gun to his temple and blew his
brains out.

CHAPTER NINE

While Dwayne and Fidel started working the murder scene, Richard and Camille interviewed the woman who'd let them into the house. She told the Police her name was Blaise, and she'd been married to Jimmy Frost – the man who'd been shot dead – for the last eighteen years.

'So how did you and Jimmy meet?' Camille asked, more as a way of keeping Blaise focused on simple matters than because she needed to know.

'We met in London,' Blaise said, briefly transported by the memory. 'At a nightclub. Just gone twenty years ago.'

'You met in London twenty years ago?' Richard asked.

Blaise didn't seem to pick up on Richard's interest.

'That's right. I'm from Woodford in East London, so me and my mates would go up West on a Friday night. That's what we always did. And this really sexy guy came up to me with this amazing Caribbean accent and asked me if I'd ever had a Ti'punch before. Well, I'd not even heard of it, and the barman hadn't, either. So Jimmy got behind the bar and made it himself. He was amazing. And when he came back to Saint-Marie, I came with him. I've not been back to the UK since.'

'You haven't?'

'No.'

'Why not?'

'Well, I think I was a bit grand when I first married Jimmy. You know, to my family. Having all this money for the first time. I thought I was a cut above, and we lost touch. So no, I've not been back to the UK, and I've not spoken to my family in years. Anyway. You make your bed, you lie in it.'

'And this was twenty years ago?'

'Just over.'

'Then can you tell me what your husband was doing in the UK when you met him?'

'Well, he was setting up his first big property deal. So he was only in London for a few weeks. But he explained it all to me. He was going to "strike it big", and then he was going to come back to Saint-Marie. I found that all very exciting.'

'Did you find out what the property deal was?'

'No. All he told me was that he had three partners, and if the deal came off, it would set him up for life.'

Richard and Camille shared a glance, knowing full well that if there'd been any doubt that Jimmy had been one of the original jewellery thieves before, there wasn't now.

'So what happened when you returned to Saint-Marie with Jimmy?' Richard asked. 'I take it the big deal worked out?'

'You can say that again. He was cock of the walk. The deal had gone even better than expected. That's what he told me. So it was party time for the next few weeks. For the next few months, if I'm honest. I met all his friends. And then, a few months later, the money from the deal started to come through, and he was wealthy overnight. Or so he seemed to me. But he didn't want to spend it all on parties, he told me. So with that money, he bought a plot of land by the cemetery just outside Honoré and built some flats on it. And it was when he sold that first block of flats that the money *really* started to flow and he hasn't looked back since.'

'So is that what he does?'

'How do you mean?'

'Your husband's a property developer?' Richard asked.

'You don't know him?'

'No,' Richard said.

'He's Jimmy Frost, of Frost Property Services.'

Richard and Camille both heard a note of scorn in Blaise's voice.

'I see,' Richard said. 'Then can I ask, what happened today?'

'I don't really know,' Blaise said.

'Perhaps you can tell us the last time you saw your husband?'

'Well, that's easy. It was last night.'

'At what time?'

'I don't know. At about 9pm. We'd had dinner, and he said he was just going to the office to finish up the day's work.'

'Was that unusual?' Richard asked.

'Oh no. He liked to check in on his work before bed most nights.'

'So he went to his office outside at about 9pm?'

'That's right.'

'And what did you do?'

'Well, I don't really know. I tried to find something to watch on TV, but there was nothing, so I went to bed. I checked my phone for a bit, and turned my lights off at about ten, I suppose.'

'You went to sleep at about 10pm?'

Blaise nodded.

'And what time did your husband come to bed?'

'I don't know. If I'm already asleep, he gets into bed without waking me up. So I don't always know what time he comes to bed. And this morning, when I woke up, it looked to me like his side of the bed hadn't been slept in at all. I wasn't worried at first. I just thought he'd maybe worked late and slept on the sofa in his office. He's got this little sofa there, and he sometimes sleeps on it if he doesn't want to come back to the house.'

'So what did you do next?'

'Well, I just got on with my day. I reckoned he'd turn up at some point.'

'You didn't check on him in his office?'

'No-one checked up on Jimmy. He didn't like it. And when he still hadn't turned up by lunchtime, I just thought he must have gone out. Maybe some time in the night. You know, in his car.'

'You thought your husband had "gone somewhere in the night"?' Richard asked sceptically.

'That's what I thought.'

'And was that normal?'

'No, but it's the sort of thing he'd do. You know, if there's a problem, Jimmy has to sort it out there and then.'

'So you didn't see him all morning, and nor did you see him at lunch. What did you do for all that time?'

'I stayed in the house. Reading. Watching TV. Just hanging out. That's what I do.'

Richard and Camille detected a note of bitterness in Blaise's voice.

'And you really never thought to check up on him in his office?'

'I've said. By this stage, I thought he'd gone out.'

'So when did you realise he hadn't?'

'Well, just before I called the Police station. I was getting a bit fed up, if I'm honest. You know, I'd rung him a few times, but his phone was going through to voicemail. And then I decided to go to the gym. Just to have something to do. And when I went to the front of the house, I saw his car was still there. I couldn't understand why. Because if his car was there all along, and my car was also there, then he couldn't have gone out, could he? That's when I went to his office to see if he'd maybe left me a note, and that's when I . . . found him.'

'Can you talk us through what happened?' Camille asked.

Blaise took a deep breath to steady herself.

'Okay,' she said when she was ready. 'I went to his office. His door was open. That's what puzzled me. He always has to have the air conditioning on inside, so why was the door open? But I went in, and he was just lying there. Behind the desk. And the blood . . . it was everywhere. That's when I phoned you.'

'Thank you,' Camille said, wanting to bring Blaise's testimony to an end. 'You don't need to continue.'

Blaise looked at the Police officer gratefully.

'I see,' Richard said, but it was clear from his tone that he wasn't entirely happy with what he'd just heard.

He turned his notebook over to a fresh page.

'Mrs Frost, has anyone visited the house since 9pm last night?'

'No. No-one visited at all yesterday. It was just Jimmy and me.'

'Then perhaps you heard someone else go to your husband's office at some stage? Either last night or maybe this morning?'

'But I didn't. And if someone did, I wouldn't have heard. Jimmy's office isn't that near the house.'

'Then perhaps you heard gunshots at some point after 9pm and before you found his body?'

'That's the thing. I didn't hear anything. That's what I'm saying. It must have happened while I was asleep.'

'So you didn't hear anything or see anything suspicious at all?'

'I didn't.'

'Mrs Frost, did you kill your husband?'

'What? No! How dare you! I may have not liked the man, but I wouldn't ever kill him.'

Realising what she'd just said, Blaise put her hand to her mouth in embarrassment.

'I shouldn't have said that,' she said.

'What do you mean, you didn't like him?'

'Does it matter? I had nothing to do with his death.'

'We still need to know about your relationship with him,' Richard said sternly.

'Alright. I'm innocent. I've got nothing to fear. So yes, since you're asking, I didn't much like my husband.'

'And why was that?' Richard asked.

'Where do you want me to start? He was controlling. He wouldn't let me be myself. I mean, look at this house, do you think it's how I'd do it up? I hate it.'

Looking at Blaise's bright red dressing gown and almost fluorescent blue gym clothes, Richard had to concede that Blaise was the only spot of colour in the entire room.

'But Jimmy said he was the one who earned the money, he was the one who got to spend it. So he chose *everything* about this house. Can you imagine what that's like for me? Even putting aside how horrible his taste is, I mean, I'm his wife. And I don't even get to choose how the place looks that I've got to live in. This house is like a prison. It's even in the colours of a prison. And if you think the decor inside the house is cold, it's nothing compared to how cold Jimmy was inside. His surname was right. He's frosty. And uncaring.

Since you're asking. He just did what he wanted and didn't care about anyone else. And I'm sorry you have to hear it, but I could cope with him doing his own thing, or working every hour of the day – or for keeping such frightening company – but what I couldn't cope with was the women.'

'The women?' Camille asked.

'He's one of those men who thinks he has to bed every woman he meets.'

'He was adulterous?'

'The whole time. And then he wouldn't have sex with me.'

Richard covered his sudden embarrassment by discovering he had a frog in his throat that he had to clear with a few coughs.

'There, that's better,' he said, once he'd regathered what he hoped was a degree of gravitas. 'Can I pick you up on something? You said your husband kept "frightening" company. What did you mean by that?'

'He really doesn't know?' Blaise said to Camille, and Camille smiled sympathetically.

'Mr Frost was known to have links to the criminal underworld,' she told her boss.

'I thought you said he was a property developer?'

'He was a gangster,' Blaise said, all of her anger suddenly spitting out of her. 'Not that any of your lot ever caught him. He was too clever for that. But he was involved with rackets, with casinos, and I think he only ran his property business as a way of laundering money. For himself and other people. But what could I do? I'd married him, I was thousands of miles away from home, and let me tell you, even with him working so hard, and doing what he did, I look about myself here and think I've got it better here than I did back at home. So if you want to know who shot my husband dead, you'd better start asking his business partners and the people they worked for. Because in Jimmy's world, when things go wrong, you don't always survive.'

'You think one of his business associates did this to him?'

'Or someone he crossed. It could have been anyone. But if I were you, I'd start working out what he was up to professionally. Because I bet there are plenty of people out there who'd be capable of committing murder.'

Richard got the distinct impression that Blaise was beginning to enjoy sticking the knife into her deceased husband.

'And what about you?'

'How do you mean?'

'Are you involved in your husband's work life?'

'No way. I know what side my bread's buttered. As I say, it's not been a perfect life with him, but I'm not short of anything financially, if you see what I mean. And, before you ask, I don't have any *proof* he was a crook. But I was his wife, so I can tell you he was a crook as far as I could tell. And the person who's done this to him is someone from his world. It's obvious.'

'Okay,' Richard said, and realised that he could possibly pin down whether Jimmy had been one of the people who'd visited Conrad on the day he was released from prison. 'Can I ask, do you remember your husband's movements last Monday?'

Pierre had been released from prison on the Monday of the week before.

'I'm not sure I know.'

'Did he perhaps leave the house in the morning? Before 10am, let's say?'

'You know what, he did. This is last Monday? Yes, I remember, he left in his car at about nine in the morning, and didn't come back until about 11pm that night.'

'He was gone all day?'

'That's right, I'd been in bed for an hour or so when he got back, and he was blind drunk. He made such a racket as he got changed.'

'Do you know where he'd been?'

'It's like I said. I never asked, but I guessed he'd not been with a woman. I can normally smell perfume on his clothes when he's been with a woman.'

'And how was his mood that day? Or in the few days beforehand?'

'He was fine. Mind you, he's been in a funk ever since then. You know, snappy. I just thought he was under pressure at work – but maybe you're right,' Blaise said with sudden enthusiasm. 'Maybe whatever was worrying him since last Monday is the reason why someone shot him dead?'

'You think it's a possibility?'

'I think it's a very definite possibility. I'm surprised I didn't make the connection sooner.'

'Then can I ask, did you or your husband know Conrad Gardiner?'

'Who?'

'Conrad Gardiner.'

Blaise thought for a moment, and then she realised something.

'That was the poor man who died last week.'

'That's right.'

'Why are you asking? Was his death connected?'

'If you could just answer the question?'

'Of course. And no, I'd never heard that name before his accident. But if his death is connected to my husband's, then you should look into Conrad Gardiner's background, because I bet you it's dodgy as hell. He'll be some hoodlum or something.'

Richard looked at Blaise and realised that she was looking far more assured than she'd been at the beginning of the interview. It was almost as if previously she'd been nervous of taking a test, but now she felt as if she'd passed it with flying colours.

'Can I ask you one final question? Do you have any idea why we found a plastic ruby at the scene of your husband's death?'

'A ruby?' Blaise said, nonplussed.

'That's right. A fake ruby.'

'Well, it's not one of mine, I can tell you that much. All my jewels are real.'

'You really have no idea why the person who did this would have left behind a ruby?'

'Of course not. Why would anyone do that?'

It seemed a fair enough response, so, thanking Blaise for her time, Richard and Camille left the house and returned to the Police station.

'Well, I can't say that Blaise Frost is your typical grieving widow,' Richard said as he wrote the words 'Jimmy Frost' and 'Blaise Frost' on the whiteboard.

'You can say that again,' Camille agreed. 'But you know what, if she was involved in her husband's death, I think she'd have bothered to get herself an alibi. And I'm not sure she'd so happily admit to hating her husband.'

'The same thing occurred to me,' Richard said, a bit miffed that Camille was stealing his investigative thunder.

'But seeing as she's the wife, I'm sure she benefits directly from her husband's death. He was a very wealthy man.'

'Yes, I was going to say that as well, you know.'

'So if she has a motive and the opportunity—'

'Did she have the means?' Richard said, jumping in. 'Although, it's not that hard to get yourself a gun on the island.'

'If you know where to go, and who to ask. And if your husband is a crook, I bet she knows where to go and who to ask.'

'So – theoretically – we're saying we could make a case against her for killing her husband. But the ruby we found at the scene suggests that Mr Frost's murder is related to Conrad's. In fact, it suggests very strongly to me that Pierre Charpentier has indeed struck again. He killed Conrad, and now he's killed Jimmy.'

'But how can we prove that Jimmy was a member of Pierre's gang?'

'Well, Blaise told us she met Jimmy when he visited London twenty years ago – which is when we know the robbery happened.'

'And he told her there were four of them in on the deal, didn't she?'

'Indeed. Just as there were four members of the gang.'

'We'll just have to hope Fidel or Dwayne can find something at the murder scene that links Jimmy to Pierre.'

'Indeed. But in the meantime, I'd like you to start digging into Jimmy's background, and see if you can definitively prove whether or not he was a member of Pierre's gang twenty years ago. And while you're doing that, I'll check on Blaise Frost. To make sure she really is as innocent as she claims.'

Richard went to his desk and started working, but he was soon frustrated. There seemed to be very little information on Blaise Frost that he could establish. She'd not held down a job or ever filed taxes for the whole time she'd been on the island. As for her bank accounts, she received a regular income from her husband. It was sizeable, and there were also a number of credit and store cards, but she paid off her debts every month. Money clearly wasn't an issue. As for her lifestyle, Richard saw from her bank statements that she spent most of her time at the Saint-Marie Country Club, and most of her money on clothes and shopping. It was all somewhat vacuous, but hardly criminal.

And yet Richard couldn't shake the feeling that Blaise

should have been more upset about her husband's death. There was no doubting she'd been upset to start off with, but as the interview with the Police had continued, she'd very obviously relaxed. Why was that?

As for proving whether or not Jimmy had been part of the original gang who had stolen the jewels, while Richard waited for Camille to finish her own research, he realised that there was someone on the island who might know the answer.

Richard picked up the phone and dialled the number for Conrad's widow, Natasha. After all, she'd told the Police how her husband had confessed everything to her. And although she claimed she didn't know who the other members of the gang were, maybe she'd change her tune if he named Jimmy Frost?

'I'm sorry?' Natasha said on the other end of the line when Richard asked her if she knew Jimmy or Blaise Frost.

'I don't know her,' Natasha said after Richard had repeated his question, 'but Jimmy was a friend of Conrad's. Why are you asking?'

'Can you please tell me about Mr Frost's relationship with your husband?'

'I don't know what it was, but I didn't like it. They'd see each other from time to time. For a drink. Or a game of poker.'

'Why didn't you like it?'

'Everyone knows Jimmy Frost is a crook. I didn't like him spending any time with Conrad. Why are you asking?'

'Is it possible Jimmy Frost was one of the original gang who robbed the jewellery store?'

'*Jimmy?*' Natasha sounded shocked. 'I don't think so. Why would he need to rob a jewellery store? He's rich.'

'He's rich now. But maybe he wasn't in the past.'

'Well, I'm sorry, I wouldn't know about that. I've barely met the man. But can I ask, why all this sudden interest in Jimmy Frost?'

Richard explained how Jimmy had just been found shot dead.

'But he can't be dead!' Natasha blurted, and Richard's instincts spiked.

'What makes you say that?'

There was another pause on the phone, and Richard got the impression that Natasha was thinking fast. When the silence had lasted a good ten seconds or so, Richard repeated the question.

'Was there a ruby found by his body?' Natasha asked.

'I'm afraid I can't possibly comment.'

'But there was a ruby, wasn't there?' Natasha said, her voice rising in panic. 'Are you saying Pierre killed him as well?'

'It's still early days,' Richard said, but Natasha interrupted him.

'I'm sorry, I can't continue this call, this is all too upsetting. I'm going to hang up now, and please don't call again.'

Natasha hung up, and Richard found himself wondering what exactly it was about Jimmy's death that Natasha had found so upsetting. After all, if she hardly knew him, it shouldn't have been that shocking. Richard wanted to interrogate this thought further, but he was interrupted by the return to the Police station of Dwayne and Fidel. They were each carrying cardboard boxes full of Jimmy's personal effects.

'Okay, Chief, we've finished at the Frost house,' Dwayne said.

'And what did you find?' Richard asked.

'Well, sir, the glass to the sliding door was covered in fingerprints,' Fidel said. 'And I picked up a fingerprint on the fake ruby you found in the deceased's mouth.'

'You did?' Richard asked.

'I'll see if it matches the prints we've got on record for Pierre Charpentier.'

'Please do. Although, seeing as we didn't find his fingerprint on the first ruby, I'd imagine it's not his print on the second.'

'Let me see what I can find.'

'Then what about you, Dwayne? What have you got in the boxes?'

'Whatever files, keys, bank statements and so on we could find. And the deceased's laptop and mobile phone. Although I can tell you already, this man has dozens of bank accounts. And with a lot of cash in them all. He's seriously wealthy.'

'But you've got his mobile phone?'

'I have.'

'Does Jimmy have his email account on his phone?'

'Sure does, Chief,' Dwayne said, getting out Jimmy's phone. 'It's got everything. A calendar, his emails, everything. It's synchronised to his main computer as far as I can tell.'

'Good,' Richard said. 'Can you do a search on Jimmy's

phone for the name Conrad Gardiner? Maybe they've been in touch.'

'No problem,' Dwayne said as he started typing into the phone. Not long after, he shook his head. 'Nothing's coming up.'

'Then search for "Natasha",' Richard said, remembering how Natasha's reaction to the news that Conrad had died had seemed a touch off.

Dwayne typed again, and again shook his head.

'He's not emailed or texted anyone called Natasha. Or received any messages from anyone called Natasha, either.'

Richard harrumphed at this news, but he didn't want to give in. There had to be something incriminating in his emails.

'Then what about Pierre Charpentier?'

Dwayne typed again, and this time he didn't look up from the phone.

'Oh, okay, that was the right call,' he said, as he started to scroll up and down on the screen with his finger.

'What is it? What have you got?' Richard asked.

'He's not been in touch with him, not as far as I can tell, but his web history over the last week has been full of hits for Pierre Charpentier. He's been looking up the old newspaper reports on the robbery in London. And would you believe it, he also did an internet search, "Pierre Charpentier Saint-Marie Prison" on the morning that Pierre was released. It took him to the Justice Department's website, and the list of what prisoners are leaving at what date.'

'He's one of Pierre's gang members, isn't he?' Fidel said.

'It's what it looks like to me,' Dwayne agreed.

'And, sir,' Camille said, 'that would fit with what I'm getting on him, because his company Frost Property Services was founded twenty years ago. Just under six months after the original jewel robbery. And it had seed capital of three hundred thousand dollars.'

'That came from the robbery, didn't it?' Richard said.

'Just like Conrad set up his record label with his money,' Camille said.

'But whereas Conrad's business failed, Jimmy's went from strength to strength. So we now know the identity of three members of the gang of four. Pierre Charpentier, Conrad Gardiner, and Jimmy Frost.'

'And, sir,' Fidel said, looking up from his desk, 'you should know, I've been checking the fingerprint on the fake ruby you found in Jimmy's mouth, and it belongs to Pierre Charpentier.'

'Hang on,' Richard said, stunned. 'Pierre left his print on the ruby this time?'

'He did.'

'Why would he do that?' Dwayne asked.

'It's obvious,' Richard said. 'He knows we're onto him, doesn't he? And he's letting us know he doesn't care.'

'But why leave his print at the scene?'

'He really doesn't think we're capable of finding him, does he?'

Richard decided that the time for half measures was over.

He took his jacket off. He then realised he felt all wrong, so he put his jacket back on and did the front button up as he went to look at the whiteboard.

'He thinks he's one step ahead of us,' he said. 'So he's taunting us. Letting us know that whatever clues we process and leads we follow, he's always going to be one step ahead of us. You know what?' Richard said, a dangerous thought beginning to form in his mind. 'If Pierre thinks we're just the local Plod, why don't we do the last thing he'd expect?'

'And what's that, sir?' Camille asked.

'I don't know. But I want to shake his sense of superiority.'

'Well, sir,' Camille said, joining her boss at the whiteboard, 'I agree with you. There's an arrogance to Pierre. And it's all because he thinks he can pick off all the members of the gang before we can stop him.'

'Agreed.'

'So how about we get to the fourth member of the gang before he does?'

'But how can we do that?'

'Well, there's one way I can think of. Let's go to the Saint-Marie *Times*, give them everything we've got, and make front page news. How Pierre's on the loose. How he's a suspected killer. How he's already killed two of the members of his gang, and the last member of the gang's life is now in grave danger. And either this fourth person takes his chances on his own, or he presents himself to the Police. And we might be able to save him.'

'That's a brilliant idea,' Fidel said.

'I agree,' Dwayne said. 'And while we're doing that, how about we get Pierre's mugshot printed up? You know, if we're going to throw a grenade into the room, let's *really* throw a grenade – with pictures of Pierre's face plastered on every street corner and lamppost on the island. You know, proper old-fashioned "Wanted" posters.'

'Great idea!' Camille agreed. 'Because someone must have seen Pierre since he left his halfway house. Let's use the whole island to flush him out, sir.'

Richard looked at his team and had a fleeting epiphany – squashed by his conscious mind even as his subconscious suggested it – that this was why he loved policing: to be part of a team that was purely focused on bringing criminals to justice.

Mind you, he thought to himself as he returned to the safety of his desk, what Camille was suggesting went against all known Police protocol. It just wasn't the done thing to reveal your hand to the killer like this.

And yet, Pierre was laughing at them. There was no denying it. And Richard *really* didn't like the idea that a double killer felt that he was superior to him.

Richard looked at his team and made his decision.

He took off his jacket and hung it on the back of his chair after all.

'Let's do it,' he said. 'Let's do it all.'

CHAPTER TEN

The following day, the headline in the Saint-Marie *Times* screamed 'Serial Killer on the Loose'. Even so, Richard wasn't entirely happy, although this was mainly because of the picture of him that accompanied the article. Did he really look that old? So pasty? And so very . . . sweaty?

But then, it was fair to say that the hastily arranged press conference hadn't gone quite how he'd expected from the start. Richard was used to dedicated meeting rooms and Constabulary signage being used at similar events in the UK. Here, on Saint-Marie, the press conference had actually been one man called Francois visiting the Police station when he got off from his day shift as a tourist guide in the rum museum.

But for all that Francois was old and wheezing, he got the gist of what Richard needed right from the get-go. In his article, he made it clear that the Police urgently wanted to interview Pierre Charpentier in connection with the murders of Conrad Gardiner and Jimmy Frost. And that there were four gang members who had carried out a robbery twenty years before, and now the fourth member of the gang's life was in danger if he didn't present himself to the Police.

Putting aside his feelings about his photo, the article was everything Richard had hoped it would be. And if it wasn't enough to put a pep in his step, Richard had also made what he considered to be a major breakthrough in the case.

'So I've just been to the Bricolage,' he announced to his team as he strode into the station.

'You have, sir?' Fidel asked.

Richard could see that Fidel had a host of fingerprint cards on his desk. He'd clearly been working through the remaining prints they'd been able to lift from the scene of Mr Frost's murder. But Richard could also see that while Camille was at her own desk, Dwayne hadn't yet arrived for work.

'I have,' Richard said, 'and I think I've got something. Because it turns out that the little pieces of gravel we found in the tread of the Citroën CX aren't just generic, they're actually five-millimetre bleached pea shingle.'

Richard announced this fact in the same way that a magician might announce 'was this indeed your card?', but he was surprised to discover that neither Camille nor Fidel seemed that interested.

'What's that, sir?' Camille asked, barely looking up from her monitor.

'I said, the pebbles we found in the tyre of the Citroën CX aren't just any common-or-garden shingle. I've been able to check them against the gravel that's for sale at the

Bricolage, and I can tell you that they're a perfect match for the five-millimetre bleached pea shingle they sell.'

Again, this didn't seem to land as he'd expected.

'I'll do this,' Camille said to Fidel. 'But why is that of interest?'

'Well, it's of interest,' Richard said, 'because it's a specific brand of pea shingle, and I got the manager at the Bricolage to check his records. They're the only shop on the whole island that sells this particular brand. But it gets even better than that, because he showed me some of the five-millimetre shingle he'd got on an area of driveway outside, and it was seriously discoloured. It wasn't anything like the perfect samples we found in the grey Citroën's tyre treads. Which suggests to me that the gravel that was picked up in the tyres of the Citroën must have been bought recently because it was still bright white.'

Camille and Fidel were impressed, despite themselves.

'You've worked out the exact shop where the gravel came from?' Camille asked, once again privately marvelling at how obsessive her boss could be.

'And it gets better than *that*, because I got the manager to give me a record of every sale he's made in the last six months, and guess what, he's only sold the stuff on seventeen different occasions. So, seeing as I can see that Fidel is working hard on identifying fingerprints, Camille, I'd like you to go through the list of all of the people and companies who've bought bleached five-millimetre shingle in the last six months.' With a flourish, Richard pulled a printout from his inside jacket pocket and handed it over to his Detective Sergeant. 'Contact each person on this list and ask them if they saw a grey Citroën parked on their shingle on the day Pierre was released.'

Camille took the piece of paper.

'Okay, sir.'

'Now where's Dwayne?' Richard asked, heading over to his desk.

'It's a Thursday, sir,' Fidel said. 'So he's at home studying for his sergeant's exam.'

'And we know that that's definitely what he's doing?'

'Of course, sir. If he has Thursday morning off for studying, then that's what he'll be doing. I'm sure.'

'We'll see about that,' Richard said, picking up the phone. He dialled Dwayne's home phone number, and heard the call start ringing at the other end.

Dwayne didn't pick up.

After it had continued to ring for a good minute, Richard slammed the phone back down on its cradle.

'Typical! He's with his new girlfriend, isn't he?'

'No, sir, he'll be studying,' Fidel said, but Richard could see that even Fidel didn't believe what he was saying.

'That's it, he's had his last warning. He's going to be getting an official caution the moment he walks in here!'

'What's that, sir?' Dwayne said as he ambled into the station.

'Where have you been?' Richard all but squawked.

'Well, I know I'm supposed to be studying this morning,

but I reckoned we needed to hit the ground running with the article appearing in the *Times* this morning. So I got up at 4am, and I've spent every second since then putting up our "Wanted" posters for Pierre Charpentier. And I reckon they're now on every lamppost, bus stop, community noticeboard, road sign and bench I could find within five miles of Honoré. Why are you asking?'

'You've been working?'

'I know, Chief, and I'm sorry, but I can make up the study time over the weekend. I won't get behind.'

'I don't think that's what the Detective Inspector meant,' Camille said.

'Oh? Then what did you mean?' Dwayne asked.

'Nothing,' Richard said, and turned back to his computer monitor. He started typing to make it look as though he was in the middle of writing a report.

'Sir,' Fidel said, 'your computer's not turned on.'

Richard paused in his typing.

Very carefully he reached out, turned his machine on and then waited for it to make its start-up chime. As he waited, he grumbled to himself about how it was just bloody typical that Dwayne would be lackadaisical every second of his working life, but on the one occasion that Richard called him out on it, it turned out that he was being extra diligent. But this didn't change anything, Richard told himself. Dwayne was still flaky, self-absorbed, and there was no doubting that he'd become even more unreliable since he hooked up with this new girlfriend. Amy McDiarmid. A woman who was prepared to answer the door to a complete stranger wearing almost no clothes. And who, in case anyone forgot, had clearly stopped Dwayne from studying for his sergeant's exam at least once.

Richard looked up and saw that Camille was staring straight at him, her right eyebrow raised. He shrugged as if to say, 'what are you staring at me for?' and then he got back to his work, which he was able to do now that his computer had finally booted up. But he couldn't quite shake the feeling that Camille felt that it was him who'd somehow overstepped a mark, not Dwayne. Life was so unfair sometimes.

'Okay, I think I've got something, sir,' Fidel said from his desk.

'You have?' Richard asked.

'I have,' Fidel said. 'I've been processing the fingerprints we were able to lift from the glass sliding door that led into Mr Frost's study. And they all belong to Mr Frost or his wife. As you'd expect. But there were three prints we lifted that didn't match either of them.'

'Maybe they belong to a cleaner or maid?' Dwayne offered.

'That's what I thought, but I reckoned I'd better check them against the exclusion prints we've already taken, and the thing is, I've got a match.'

'You have?' Camille asked. 'Do they belong to Pierre Charpentier?'

'No – that's the thing. Pierre was the first person I checked.'

'Then who does the fingerprint belong to?'

'Natasha Gardiner.'

'What?'

'She's left three fingerprints on the door to Jimmy Frost's study.'

'A man she very specifically told me on the phone she didn't know,' Richard said in quiet fury.

Richard had to resist the urge to bang his fist on his desk in frustration.

'Camille,' he said, 'give Mrs Gardiner a ring, and tell her we'd like to interview her, but this time I'd like her to come into the station.'

'Yes, sir,' Camille said, all thoughts of points scoring about Dwayne long forgotten as she picked up her phone to make the call.

Ten minutes later, Natasha walked through the door.

'You wanted to see me?' she asked, and Richard saw that she was nervously holding a little clutch bag in front of her.

'If you'd please sit here,' Richard said, indicating the chair he'd already set in front of his desk.

Natasha crossed the room and sat down in the chair.

'You see, I've got a problem,' Richard said by way of an opening. 'Because we have clear evidence that your husband was murdered by Pierre Charpentier. And just as clear evidence that Pierre went on to murder Jimmy Frost. But I have no hope of getting to the bottom of your husband's murder if you continue to lie to us.'

As Richard said this, Natasha fumbled with her clutch bag and it dropped to the floor.

'Oh sorry,' she said, and bent down to pick it up. It took

her a few moments to gather it and when she straightened up she was unable to hide the look of fear on her face.

'I haven't lied,' she said.

'You have, and you know it. You knew Jimmy Frost.'

'I didn't.'

'We've found your fingerprints on the door to his outside office.'

This brought Natasha up short.

'You have?' she asked in a small voice.

'If you don't want us to arrest you for his murder, I suggest you start telling us the truth. And now.'

Richard pulled out his notebook and put it down on his desk with a little slap.

He clicked his retractable pencil and looked unflinchingly at Natasha.

Natasha's eyes lowered. She couldn't meet the Police officer's gaze.

'I'm so sorry,' she said. 'But you have to believe me, I couldn't murder Jimmy. You see . . . I loved him.'

'I'm sorry?' Richard asked.

'Or I thought I did,' she said in a voice steeped in shame. 'For a spell.'

'So you're admitting you knew him?'

Natasha nodded.

'And therefore lied to us before?'

Natasha nodded again.

'Very well. How did you meet?'

'He came to the house. About six months ago. As I said to

you, I didn't like him being friends with Conrad, but we'd not met before. I'd always stayed out of his way.'

'Why did he visit that day?'

'He said he wanted to see Conrad. I told him he was out on his boat. Jimmy laughed, and said he was happy to wait. I felt awkward, so I invited him in and offered him a coffee. But he wasn't like I expected him to be. He seemed so charming. So interested in me and Conrad, and he wanted to know all about our daughter, Jessica. How she was getting on in St Lucia. And then he told me . . .'

Natasha gulped, summoning the courage to carry on with her story.

'Yes, he told you . . .?'

'That Jessica was attractive, but then it was no surprise as she had such an attractive mother. He meant me.'

'So what did you say?'

'Oh, I just blushed. I was so embarrassed, but Jimmy didn't seem bothered at all. He told me I was beautiful. And normally I'd have been so offended, but he was so matter of fact about the way he said it. And I could see that he was being sincere. Or I thought he was being sincere. And I can't deny it was quite something to have a man take an interest in me. Conrad . . . well, I can't remember the last time he paid me a compliment or said I looked pretty. And he spent all his time on his boat. It's not like I even saw him, so I couldn't help but feel a flutter of excitement that *something* was happening in my life that was a little exciting. But I had no idea. No idea at all.'

'How do you mean?'

'As he left, Jimmy told me that he owned the Presidential Suite at the Fort Royal Hotel. And then he said to me, like it was all acceptable and above board, that if I wanted to go there tomorrow, I could collect the key to the suite from reception. All I had to do was say that I was with Mr Snow and the key was mine. And then I could use whatever spa facilities I wanted. Get a haircut. Have a facial. Whatever I wanted. I should make myself as pretty on the outside as I was on the inside. And then, if I wanted, he'd come to the suite at 4pm. If I wasn't interested in being there for him, that would be fine, too. He wanted me to have a good time. But if I wanted more, no strings attached, all I had to do was be in the suite at 4pm. And then with a smile, he left. I didn't know what to think. I was so shocked. Offended that he thought he could pick me up so easily.'

Richard couldn't quite equate the extraordinary story he was hearing with the dowdy woman sitting in front of him.

'What did you do?'

'That's the thing, I did nothing. But when Conrad finally got home, I didn't tell him that Jimmy had come to the house. I think that was my first act of rebellion. Or the first time that I realised I was maybe thinking about going to the suite. And this isn't like me, you have to believe me. I'm a good, church-going woman, you just ask Father Luc. I've never done anything like this before. But everyone has a right to some happiness, don't they? And I was so flattered, I can't deny that that was part of it as well. So I didn't tell Jimmy, and then Conrad announced that he and some friends were going away for a couple of days for a big fishing trip. Just like that. Like I wasn't even part of his plans. Which I realised I wasn't.

'So the next day, I woke up as Conrad was packing for his trip. And he was being such an idiot. Forgetting the cool bag, and leaving his wallet behind. And I found him so irritating that after he'd gone, I began thinking about the Fort Royal. I mean, it's the best hotel on the whole island. I'd never even been inside it. And all I had to do was go to the reception, and I could spend the day pampering myself? It was such an exciting thought. And I believed Jimmy when he'd said that I could leave before 4pm and it would all be alright. Or I convinced myself I believed him. So I went. Said the codeword Mr Snow to the receptionist. She gave me a key and I went to the suite at the top of the hotel. It was amazing. Huge. And there was a jacuzzi on a balcony overlooking the sea. But I was just there for the spa. And for a bit of pampering. That's what I told myself. But it kept popping into my mind. That he'd be turning up at 4pm. As he knew it would. After I'd had lunch and a swim, I realised I'd better leave. So I went up to the suite for a quick rooftop jacuzzi, and I had every intention of getting dressed and leaving before 4pm.

'I don't know when I decided I was going to stay after all. I'm not sure I even quite made a decision, but I was still in the jacuzzi at 4pm when Jimmy stepped out onto the balcony holding a bottle of champagne and two glasses.'

It was clear from Natasha's demeanour that modesty prevented her from continuing the story.

'And . . .?' Richard asked, his pencil poised.

'And I didn't leave until the next morning.'

'Oh, I see.'

'I had one of the best nights of my life.'

Richard realised that he didn't quite know what his next question was, so he threw a look at Camille, hoping she'd help him out.

'Did you see him again?' she asked as she got up from her desk and came over.

'Three times,' Natasha said. 'Three more times I went to the Presidential Suite, but Conrad got suspicious. He found a bracelet Jimmy had bought me. I said I'd bought it for myself, but he guessed I was seeing someone. And threatened to leave me, can you believe it? Conrad had countless affairs over the years, he spends all his time on his boat, and then when the stupid man notices I've found someone else, he's shocked.'

'He threatened to leave you?' Richard asked.

'That's what he said. But he wasn't going anywhere. He didn't have the money to leave me. And anyway, I stopped seeing Jimmy.'

'Why was that?'

'He told me he'd had his fun, he was moving on.'

'Just like that?'

'Just like that,' Natasha said sadly.

'That must have hurt,' Camille said.

'It did. But I always knew it was going to end. After all, a man who beds other women while still being married isn't ever going to be faithful, is he?'

'And yet you said you loved him,' Camille said innocently enough, but Richard could see that Camille didn't feel that Natasha's story quite added up.

'I did. I do. For the time we spent together.'

'When did your relationship with Mr Frost end?' Richard asked.

'Only a few weeks after it started. About five months ago.'

'So how come we found your fingerprints on the glass door to his office?'

Natasha looked uncomfortable.

'I . . . had a moment of weakness.'

'You went to see him?' Camille asked.

Natasha nodded.

'When was this?'

'A couple of weeks ago. Conrad was out on his boat, of course, and I realised how alone I was. So I drove up to Jimmy's house and waited until I could see his wife leaving. I was shocked to see her, I can tell you. She's so beautiful. I couldn't understand what Jimmy saw in me. It didn't make sense. But when she drove off, I went to the front door. It was locked, but Jimmy had told me he worked in an office in the garden, so I went around, and that's where I found him. In his office. He wasn't happy to see me, I'm afraid.'

'He wasn't?'

'He was furious I was at his house. He said surely I knew he was married, and the thing is, I realised how stupid I was being almost immediately. He was right. He *was* married. We'd had our fun, and now we both had to move on. I apologised so much, but it didn't seem to make any difference, he was just so very angry with me. So I fled, and when I got back to my car, I just burst into tears. I felt so stupid. Why did I have to ruin everything?'

'Did you see him after that?'

'No. That was the last time. I promise you. And I have no idea why he died, or who did it, or how it was done.'

'I see,' Richard said, and turned the pages of his notes. As he did so, he once again marvelled at how humans seemed hard-wired to lie. After all, if Natasha had just told them all this immediately, she wouldn't have ended up looking so guilty.

Richard's eye caught one of the first notes he'd made.

'You mentioned how the first time Mr Frost came to your house, he was wanting to see your husband?'

'That's right.'

'Did you ever find out what that was about?'

'I don't think I did.'

'Then perhaps Jimmy met Conrad at some other time?'

'He didn't come to the house again. I don't think. Not after that time.'

'Then did Conrad mention Jimmy? Or give any indication as to why he'd perhaps want to see him?'

'No.'

'Very well,' Richard said. 'Then I'm going to ask you one more question, and I want you to answer it truthfully.'

'I'll tell you the truth, I promise you. I've got nothing to hide.'

'Mrs Gardiner, where is Pierre Charpentier?'

Natasha didn't seem to understand the question.

'I'm sorry?'

'I believe you know where he is.'

'I don't! I hate that man. For what he did to Conrad.'

'But you and your husband didn't get on,' Richard said.

'So? Didn't mean I wanted him to die.'

'And now the man who had an affair with you and then broke your heart is dead at his hand as well.'

'His death had nothing to do with me. Why won't you believe me? I'm grateful for everything Jimmy gave me.'

Richard looked at Natasha, and he saw a mixture of confusion, guilt and fear in her face. But had they finally got the truth out of her? That was the question.

Richard dismissed Natasha and then tried to sift through what he'd learned, because there was no doubting that she had a motive to kill both her husband and Jimmy Frost. Conrad for being a bad husband, Jimmy for being the lover who dumped her. And yet, Richard knew, everything about the case suggested that Natasha had nothing to do with either murder. After all, they only happened after Pierre had left prison and learned that there was no money for him. And the fake rubies and physical evidence that bore Pierre's prints made it clear that he was the person behind both murders.

It was possible, Richard supposed, that Natasha was perhaps in cahoots with Pierre, but that didn't seem very likely, did it?

'Okay, team,' Richard barked. 'Update me on where we've got to with Pierre Charpentier.'

Richard listened to his team's reports, but it didn't even begin to improve his mood. Pierre's name had been put on the Watch List for the airports and the ports, but he hadn't tried to leave the island. Neither had he tried to set up any bank accounts. Nor had continuing checks at an ever-widening list of hotels, hostels and B&Bs revealed his location. And no-one had yet called in with a positive ID of Pierre, having seen the posters that Dwayne had put up that morning. As for Pierre's known associates, Dwayne had been to the prison on more than one occasion and tried to lean on the few inmates who'd been closest to Pierre, but they'd had no idea where he was as well.

Increasingly, Richard was sure that someone must be helping Pierre. Someone out there was helping to house, feed and water him. But who could it be?

Richard banged his fist on his desk in frustration, and the sudden pain reminded him of two things: firstly, he shouldn't bang things with his hand, it really hurt. And secondly, the physical pain perfectly mirrored the pain he was feeling at failing to track down an ex-con who had no resources to his name, and yet had managed to commit two murders so far under the Police's nose without them picking up a single useful lead.

Just where the hell was Pierre Charpentier?

CHAPTER ELEVEN

Richard told his team they weren't leaving the office until they'd found at least one concrete lead that might reveal the hiding place of Pierre. This was something of a mistake because, as the hours passed, and the afternoon sun warmed them all to boiling point, it became harder and harder to concentrate. Tempers were getting frayed.

Richard grabbed his hankie to wipe the sweat from his brow, but the hankie was already so drenched with sweat that he felt he was actually putting sweat back onto his forehead. Before he could stop himself, he wiped his brow with his woollen sleeve, and then looked about himself nervously, hoping no-one else had seen his sudden drop in sartorial standards. As penance, Richard tightened the knot on his tie.

The problem was, there just weren't any meaningful leads to follow.

Jimmy Frost's various business dealings were clearly corrupt, but after spending a few hours working through the thicket of his finances, Dwayne gave it up as a bad job, parcelled up all the paperwork he could find, and bagged it for sending to Guadeloupe to be analysed by a forensic accountant. It would take someone far better trained than him to work out where the money was coming from in Jimmy's empire and where it was going to. For the moment, though, all that mattered was that Dwayne hadn't been able to find any obvious links between Jimmy and Conrad, or Jimmy and Pierre.

There were also no incriminating texts. No emails. No payments. Nothing. There was just Jimmy's web history in his browser that made it clear that he'd been following Pierre's release from prison closely.

As for Jimmy's relationship with Natasha, Richard emailed a photo of Natasha to the concierge at the Fort Royal Hotel, asking if he recognised her face. Richard's desk phone rang only moments later, and, once Richard allayed the concierge's fears that he wasn't breaching client confidentially, the man said that he was happy to admit he recognised Mrs Gardiner as someone who'd been to the hotel as a guest of Mr Snow. As the hotel prided itself on the bespoke service it offered, he also had a record of the exact days and nights she'd stayed in the Presidential Suite.

Richard was surprised to learn that Natasha had stayed at the hotel with Jimmy on seven different occasions – meaning, she'd not told them the truth when she said she'd only gone there four times, but Richard found it hard to read too much of significance into this lie. After all, the timings of the visits broadly fitted with what she'd told them. They'd all taken place over a five-week period, six months ago.

'And you're sure Mrs Gardiner hasn't stayed at the hotel since then?' Richard asked.

'Quite sure,' the man replied smoothly.

'Then can I ask, do you by any chance have a Pierre Charpentier staying with you at the moment?'

It was something of a punt on Richard's part, and he was unsurprised when the concierge reported that they didn't. In fact, they'd never had a Pierre Charpentier stay at the Fort Royal.

It was another dead end, and Richard was increasingly regretting his threat that he and his team weren't allowed to leave until they'd found a proper lead.

However, Fidel came to all their rescue when, just after 6pm, he announced that he'd found something.

'What is it?' Richard asked eagerly.

'Well, I don't know exactly,' Fidel said, not sure how to begin.

'Don't worry about that,' Richard said, 'just tell us what you've got.'

'Okay, well, I've been looking at Conrad Gardiner's bank statements, seeing as he not only burnt through his share of the robbery spoils, but also Pierre's as well.'

'What have you got?' Camille asked as she, Richard and Dwayne all converged on Fidel's desk.

'Well, I've got his bank records going back fifteen years. It's taken some time for the bank to get the documents to me, but they arrived this morning. And in those first bank statements, he's got over two hundred thousand dollars in his main business account, and quite a few thousand in his personal account. It all looks above board until you notice he's spending thousands more each month than he's earning. But it's not immediately obvious because there are also these cash payments coming into the account every month or so.'

As Fidel said this, he pointed at some payments he'd high-lighted in yellow. Each one of these was a cash credit for a figure in the region of five thousand dollars.

'So he was topping up his bank account with cash?' Camille asked.

'But his business wasn't successful, so where was he getting the cash from?' Dwayne said.

'Are you sure he wasn't selling records or CDs?'

'One hundred per cent,' Dwayne said. 'No shops ever stocked his bands' music. He sold what he could online. And I don't think that was very successful. He had a stall at the market once a week so he could sell to unsuspecting tourists. But there's no way the market stall would generate that sort of income.'

'So he had a secret supply of cash he could tap into. Which was no doubt Pierre's share of the robbery. Just like Natasha told us.'

'How much cash did he pump into the business?' Richard asked.

'I added up all these one-off cash payments,' Fidel said, 'and they span seven years and come to just under three hundred thousand dollars.'

'Which is about the same sum of money as Jimmy and Conrad both used to set up their businesses,' Camille said.

'So that's the proof,' Richard said. 'Conrad was supposed to look after Pierre's three hundred thousand dollars, but he embezzled it for himself and used it to prop up his failing business.'

'And the cash top-ups stop eleven years ago,' Fidel said, flicking through the pages of the bank statements so he could show everyone. 'And from that moment on, the business goes into pretty rapid decline.'

Richard could see that the bank statements comprised a long list of debits with next to no credits. And then Fidel pointed to an 'ACCOUNT CLOSED' entry. That was just under ten years ago.

'So he closed down his business ten years ago.'

'He did,' Fidel agreed. 'But that's not the big news, because then we come to his personal bank statements, and they make *very* interesting reading. You see, for years after his business folded it's pretty clear Conrad struggled to keep body and soul together. But there are quite a few one-off credits to his bank account – all from local people.'

'That's right,' Richard said. 'Stefan Morgan told us he'd employed Conrad to build a store room for him.'

'Exactly, sir. It's bits of money here and there. And as far as I can tell, he also did a spell taking tourists out fishing on his boat, although that dried up a few years ago. But check this out.'

As Fidel said this, he turned to the most recent bank statement and pointed at some text that once again said 'ACCOUNT CLOSED'. But it wasn't just that, Richard could also see that there had been just over eight hundred dollars in the account at the time, and Conrad had also taken all of that out as cash.

The date for this transaction was the day before Pierre left prison.

'He cleaned out his account.' Dwayne said.

'And then closed it down.' Camille said.

'The day *before* Pierre left prison.'

'Why?' Dwayne asked.

'If you ask me, it suggests he was up to something,' Fidel said.

'I'd agree with you there, Fidel,' Richard said. 'Dwayne, did any of your contacts give you any indication that Conrad was behaving at all suspiciously before he died?'

'No,' Dwayne said. 'I didn't hear anything.'

'Okay. Good work, Fidel. Now, I know I said we couldn't leave before we had a decent lead, but now we've got one, how about we all take half an hour to try and find out what Conrad was up to?'

As Richard returned to his desk, he wondered where he could start. After all, what sort of traces did a man who spent most of his time on a fishing boat leave? Richard pulled everything they had on Conrad from the case file, but everything in his recent life seemed above board. His car was insured, he had no traffic offences, and although he didn't pay anywhere near as much tax as he should, he always filed his tax returns on time. He also didn't seem to have any share holdings, company directorships, or any connection to any kind of business. Whatever surprising financial behaviour Conrad was getting up to before he died, it seemed to be entirely confined to his personal bank account.

As for his boat, despite how decrepit it had been, it was correctly registered to Honoré harbour, its ownership history was without blemish, and he paid all his mooring fees on time.

So what had he been up to?

Richard had of course checked Conrad's presence on the Police Computer Network as part of his initial enquiries. There hadn't been a hit for him. But now, almost on a whim, Richard decided to see if that was also true of Conrad's criminal record in Britain. After all, Conrad had committed a crime on British soil twenty years ago – what if he'd been back since then? It was something of a longshot, but Richard went to the web portal for ACRO, the British Police's Criminal Records Office. He was then able to log on and make a basic search through the database for Conrad Gardiner. There were twelve hits, but none of them were for people even close to Conrad's age.

As Richard considered what to do next, he was distracted by Dwayne yawning loudly.

'Dwayne, do you mind?' he said.

'Sorry, Chief. Getting up early to put all those posters up sure's caught up with me. Although, if I'm honest, it's not like I've been getting many early nights, either.'

'What?' Richard asked, puzzled.

'I've not been getting many early nights, either,' Dwayne said, and smiled suggestively.

Understanding came slowly to Richard.

'Are you talking about your *girlfriend*?'

'Go on,' Camille said in a way, Richard knew, that was designed to irritate him. 'Tell us all about her.'

'Tell you about Amy?' Dwayne asked, already transported by the thought. 'Well, what do you want to know?'

As Camille started asking questions – again, just to irritate him, Richard was sure of it – and Dwayne started rhapsodising about how great he and Amy were together, how they liked the same music and food, and how she loved partying just as much as he did, Richard hunkered down behind his monitor. What was it with his team? Why were they so tolerant of this woman coming into their lives and spoiling everything? They still didn't know who she was, or whether she'd be right for Dwayne – which Richard very seriously doubted – and it was as Richard considered this point that a somewhat wicked thought popped into his head.

He wouldn't act on it, though, he knew that much. Or so he told himself, but as Fidel started asking what star sign Amy was, Richard's irritation flamed, so he turned back to his computer, typed Amy McDiarmid into the search field of the ACRO portal, and saw that there were at least fifty people called Amy McDiarmid who'd been called in for questioning by the Police – or charged – or convicted – in the last thirty years. This pleased Richard very much, as it proved to him that there was indeed a link between people being called Amy McDiarmid and that person being a wrong'un.

But as Richard idly scanned the list, his Police brain

couldn't help noticing that nearly everyone on the list was the wrong age to be the Amy who was currently going out with Dwayne. Pity, Richard thought to himself. It would perhaps have been good if Dwayne's new girlfriend were a hardened criminal. But you couldn't win every time.

Richard was just about to close down the window when he noticed that fifteen years ago, an Amy McDiarmid had been convicted of dealing drugs and fencing stolen goods, and her birth year seemed to fit with Dwayne's new girlfriend. What was more, this particular Amy McDiarmid lived in Edinburgh, just as Dwayne's girlfriend did. Richard considered the name on the screen, and then decided that it was actually no surprise that one of the fifty names seemed to fit the basic biometrics of the Amy that Dwayne was dating. In fact, he decided, with a surname as Scottish as McDiarmid, it would be odd if one of the fifty or so names *didn't* appear to have the same birth year and Edinburgh location.

Richard clicked on the name anyway.

What he saw made him jump up from his chair like he'd been shot.

'What is it, sir?' Fidel asked, and Richard could see that his whole team were looking at him.

'What is it?' Richard parroted back, his mouth trying to buy himself time while his mind tried to comprehend what he'd just seen.

'You look like you've had a shock, I'll tell you that much,' Dwayne said with a smirk.

'Me?' Richard said, trying to look insouciant. 'I've not

had a shock. Just a spasm. A back spasm. Oh, that's better. It's gone.'

Trying to ignore the puzzled looks from his team, Richard lowered himself back into his chair and dared to look at his monitor again. It was still showing the same criminal record for the woman who'd spent two years in prison for dealing drugs and fencing stolen goods.

And the mugshot of the prisoner was very clearly a fifteen-year-old photo of Dwayne's girlfriend.

Dwayne was dating an ex-con.

'That wasn't your back, sir,' Camille said from her desk. 'You've got something, haven't you? What is it?'

Richard pulled the power cable from the back of his monitor and it went off with a bang of electricity.

No-one spoke.

'Sorry,' Richard eventually said. 'Didn't mean to do that. Anyway, don't you all have work to get on with?'

Richard looked fiercely at his team and was gratified to see them return to their work, albeit reluctantly.

But once he knew they weren't looking at him, he plugged the cable back into his monitor and watched the screen light up again. Then, making sure the monitor was turned away from his team, he started to read the case notes in more detail, a cold sense of dread clutching at his heart as he did so.

It turned out that when Amy McDiarmid was in her early twenties, she'd been a drug dealer. She mostly dealt to her friends and acquaintances, but the Edinburgh Police were trying a zero-tolerance policy to all drugs dealing, so they raided her flat on South Bridge Street. Inside, they found marijuana, cocaine, speed and ecstasy, and Richard's heart sank as he saw that the Police also found a small quantity of heroin. Even worse for Amy, the Police then found a book of antique stamps that had been reported stolen weeks before.

When the Police investigated, it turned out that the book of stamps was worth nearly five thousand pounds.

In her interview, Amy told the Police that the guy she got her drugs from had asked her to look after the book of stamps, but she refused to give up his identity – if only because, as she said, he really wasn't a nice man, and she didn't want to cross him.

Scrolling through the document, Richard saw that, at her trial, Amy pleaded guilty, and because she had no previous convictions, the judge had been as lenient as he could be, but he still had to impose a custodial sentence.

Bloody hell, Richard thought to himself. What the hell had Dwayne got himself into? Richard was about to start taking notes from his screen, but he saw Camille head over, so he closed the window at speed.

Camille looked concerned.

'Sir? Could I have a word?'

'Of course,' Richard said, worried about the look on his partner's face. It wasn't like her to look with sympathy at him.

'In private.'

'Oh, you want a word in private?' Richard said. 'Then why didn't you say?'

Richard got up from his desk and clacked through a colourful bead curtain to the cells at the back of the office.

'Are you alright?' Camille asked as soon as they were alone.

'Me, Camille? Why wouldn't I be alright?'

'Only, I just saw you pull the cable out from your computer.'

'Oh, that?'

'And then you refused to tell us what you were doing.'

Richard went back to the bead curtain and lifted a few strands so he could look at Dwayne. He was happily working at his desk, so Richard returned to Camille. After all, she had as much of a right to know that Dwayne was consorting with a known criminal as he did.

'Okay, you're right,' Richard whispered. 'I've found something out.'

'About the case?'

'Not exactly.'

'Then what about?'

'Dwayne. Or rather his girlfriend.'

'What?' Camille hissed.

'No wait, hear me out, because the thing is, I was on the ACRO portal – checking to see if Conrad Gardiner had done anything dodgy in the UK – considering how he and Pierre and the gang were in London all those years ago. You know, it was a long shot, but you know me, Camille, I can't leave any job undone. You've got to dot the "i"s and cross the "t"s. And the interesting thing is, Conrad doesn't have any kind of a criminal record in the UK. He's not even listed as someone who was brought in to assist the Police with their enquiries.'

'Why won't you come to the point?'

'I looked Amy McDiarmid up.'

'I'm sorry?'

'I looked Amy McDiarmid up. Dwayne's girlfriend. Just to check. On the off chance. And lucky I did, Camille. Because she's done time. A two-year stretch. For dealing drugs and fencing a book of antique stamps.'

Richard was gratified to see that his partner looked suitably outraged.

'You did *what*?'

'I know, and Dwayne's got no idea, does he?' Richard said, before he realised that Camille hadn't quite said what he'd expected her to. 'Hang on. What did you say?'

'You looked up Dwayne's girlfriend *on the Police Computer Network*?'

'You make it sound bad.'

'Sir, it's insane. Who looks up a colleague's girlfriend on the Police Computer Network?'

Now it was Richard's turn to be shocked.

'She's a known felon, Camille.'

'But you aren't supposed to know that.'

'I'm a Police officer, I think you'll find it's my job to know who's got a criminal record and who hasn't.'

'Yes, when you're investigating a case, sir, but not in your real life outside that. And you know what? And I'm amazed you're making me say this, sir, but it's unethical to use the Police database for your own personal use.'

Richard was outraged.

But he also knew he had to make sure Dwayne didn't hear him, so he hissed back at Camille, 'Oh, well, that's rich coming from you.'

'I'm sorry?'

'I don't need lectures on ethics from someone who doesn't fill in her weekly time sheets even remotely on time. Yes, that's right, Camille. I know you backdate them.'

Camille's mouth opened, but she couldn't quite form a sentence.

'Exactly. I've known about that scam for a long time. And as far as I'm concerned, if Amy is a criminal, then we have to tell Dwayne at once.'

'What's that?' Dwayne asked, as he pushed aside the bead curtain with a clatter and stuck his head into the room.

'Nothing, Dwayne,' Camille said quickly.

'That's not true, Camille,' Richard said, cross that she'd attempted to change the subject. 'It's to do with you, Dwayne. And I think you and I need to have a bit of a chat.'

'That's as maybe, Chief,' Dwayne said. 'But all this will have to wait. There's someone here to see you. And I think you'll want to see him right now.'

'Why? Who is it?'

'You'd better come through.'

Richard and Camille shared a glance – what was this

about? – but they followed Dwayne through the bead curtain. Who was it who wanted to see them?

As Richard entered the main office, he saw Father Luc Durant standing in the middle of the room. He was holding a copy of the Saint-Marie *Times* in his hands. It was that morning's edition that announced that Pierre Charpentier was on the loose and was suspected of killing his old gang members one by one.

'Father, can we help you?' Camille asked kindly.

'I don't know, but I came here to tell you . . . I think I know who Pierre Charpentier's going to kill next.'

'And how do you know that?'

'Because I know who the fourth member of his gang is.'

Richard could see that Father Luc was looking deeply distressed.

'Then I think you'd better pull up a chair, and tell us everything.'

CHAPTER TWELVE

'You must understand, I'm in a difficult position,' Father Luc said, once Camille had settled him in a chair in front of Richard's desk. 'You see, the fourth member of Pierre's gang is a criminal, isn't he?'

'How do you mean?' Richard said.

'Well, he robbed a jewellery store.'

'That's right.'

'But that means that once you find out who that fourth member is, you'll arrest him for robbery, won't you? Even though his crime was committed all those years ago.'

'Of course. A crime is still a crime.'

As Richard said this, all the life seemed to go out of Father Luc. It was as if he were at the doctor's, had been fearing bad news, and had indeed just received a terminal diagnosis.

'You know,' he said, a tear forming in his eye that he wiped away with the back of his hand. 'You live in hope of redemption. You hope and pray that a life devoted solely to the service of others will be enough to wipe the slate clean. But He has other plans, doesn't He?'

As Father Luc spoke, Richard and Camille both realised the same thing at the same time. Father Luc was the fourth member of the gang, wasn't he? That's why, when they'd last talked to him, he'd not questioned the link between Conrad's death and Pierre's release from prison. He'd known they were linked right from the start. But this realisation, exciting though it was, also put Richard on his guard. After all, Father Luc had been prepared to lie to them before. How would they know if he was lying to them now?

'Father Luc,' Camille said, 'can I ask you a question? You weren't always a priest, were you?'

'I wasn't.'

'And maybe you had different . . . values before you trained as a Priest?'

Father Luc nodded.

'But perhaps something very specific happened in your life that made you decide to train as a priest?'

'That's it exactly. Something happened.'

'And did this thing happen twenty years ago?'

Father Luc made eye contact with Camille and they both knew the subtext of the question she was asking him.

'It did. And I was so ashamed of what I did that I joined a seminary three weeks later. The guilt I felt. What I'd seen. And done.'

'Then can you tell us about the money?' Richard said, somewhat spoiling the confessional mood.

'The money?'

'This event you're talking about, I think it resulted in you getting your hands on a considerable amount of money, didn't it? So I was just wondering, if you really were repentant, what did you do with all of the cash you got?'

'I couldn't possibly comment on whether I came into any money that year, but I trained at St Michael's Seminary on Martinique. If you check their records, I think you'll find they received an anonymous donation of some considerable size the day before I joined.'

'I see,' Richard said, making a mental note to follow up on this, but he also realised he was reappraising Father Luc. He was still the same roly-poly man he'd been when first they'd met, of course, but, as he sat in front of the Police, his hands folded in his lap, Richard could see how weary he was.

'So what would you like to tell us?'

'The truth,' Father Luc said. 'But I can't. Because the fourth member of Pierre's gang is frightened of what a prison sentence would do to him.'

'If you helped with our enquiries—' Camille said, but Father Luc interrupted her.

'There's no statute of limitations on armed robbery. I've looked into it. Especially when the money's not recovered. So I can't ever tell you the name of this fourth person. You can draw your own conclusions, but I won't ever tell you who it is I'm talking about.'

'You may have to in a court of law,' Richard said, not entirely kindly.

'But what if I told you this fourth member of the gang told me his story in the Confessional? Because I can't break the Seal of the Confessional, even if you put me in a court of law.'

Richard realised how cleverly Father Luc had finessed the situation.

'So you're saying this fourth member of the gang is some person other than you? A member of your congregation, in fact. And you'll tell us what he told you, but you won't tell us his name.'

'That's the deal I'm offering.'

'Then we accept it,' Camille said before her boss could disagree. 'Because all we really want to know – in the short term, at least – is where Pierre Charpentier is hiding.'

'I'm sorry to say, I really don't know where he is. Or rather,' Father Luc said, hastily correcting himself, 'I don't think the fourth member of the gang knows where Pierre's hiding.'

Camille inclined her head, acknowledging and accepting the obfuscation.

'But you must have some idea,' Richard said.

'I really don't, but you can imagine that I'm keen for you to find him before . . . well, before Pierre finds the fourth member of the gang.'

As Father Luc said this, he put the Saint-Marie *Times* on the desk, with the page turned over to the article that said that the murders of Conrad Gardiner and Jimmy Frost were carried out by the same person, and they wished to talk to the ex-convict Pierre Charpentier in relation to their enquiries.

'Very well,' Richard said. 'Then can you tell us, was Jimmy Frost one of Pierre Charpentier's gang who robbed the jewellery store twenty years ago?'

Father Luc took a moment to steady himself. It was obvious to Richard and Camille that he understood that what he was about to say next could start a chain of events that could land him in prison.

Father Luc came to his decision.

'He was,' he said. 'The original gang was put together by Pierre Charpentier, and it consisted of Conrad Gardiner, Jimmy Frost and this fourth other person whose name I can't tell you.'

'Understood,' Richard said in a rush of excitement as he realised that he was finally going to get a first-hand testimony about Pierre's past. 'But you can tell us about the original robbery, can't you? Why was it in London? Why not just steal some jewels from a shop on Saint-Marie?'

'That had been the plan,' Father Luc said. 'Originally. You see, there was a young man Pierre had come to know called André Morgan, and he was going to help.'

'André knew Pierre?'

'That's right.'

'And you're saying it was an inside job? André told Pierre about when and how the jewels were going to be delivered to the store?'

Father Luc nodded, and Richard felt a thrill as he realised that this chimed with the facts that André's father Stefan had told them. André had become insolent in the last few months he'd been on the island. But while Stefan had associated this change in behaviour with André getting a new girlfriend, it was clear that it was at least partly because André had fallen under the spell of Pierre Charpentier.

'And this was the same André Morgan who was later shot dead by Pierre in London?'

Father Luc frowned. This was something that still haunted him.

'It was. And I can't tell you how shocking it was. The robbery was supposed to be a victimless crime. That's how Pierre pitched it. He wanted to steal from a large chain of jewellers, because who would even notice if they suffered a robbery? Especially seeing as they were insured against theft.'

'Then can you tell me, how did Pierre meet André? Do you know?'

'I'm sorry, I don't. Pierre just said he'd cultivated a guy who worked at a jewellery shop in Honoré. And for a price, he was prepared to tell him when the next delivery of jewels was going to be. As Pierre explained it, it's always the weakest part of any security on a jewellery shop – the fact that there's always a few seconds after any new delivery of jewels has to leave the security van, and before it's possible to lock them in the shop's safe. But, apparently, just after André agreed to help Pierre in Honoré, he discovered he had a chance of getting a more senior job in the London branch. The head office. And Pierre loved it as a plan. You see, the head office would be taking delivery of jewels of a far higher quality and value. And André said he knew that if he took up this new post in London, he'd be the person who organised the delivery of all new jewels to the shop.

'And if the heist was pulled off in London, it also solved another problem, which was how were the gang going to get away with it? You see, you rob a jewellery shop in your home town, you risk someone you know identifying you. Or someone catching wind of what you did and then telling the Police. But by carrying out the crime on foreign soil, it made it possible to get in there, rob the store, and then get out again. And then afterwards, assuming it had all gone to plan, why would the Police even think to come looking on Saint-Marie for the robbers?'

'I see. So you're saying André was the fifth member of the gang?'

'Not quite. I don't know what the deal was supposed to be with him. Pierre worked all that out. But he wasn't really at risk anyway. All he had to do was give Pierre the date and time of the next big consignment of jewels. But the thing is, there'd been some change in management at the company, or something like that, and after André arrived in London, the shop didn't take delivery of any new stock for some time. Or maybe André didn't have such ready access to delivery dates in his new role as he'd said. I don't know. But there was no chance to rob the store for months. And Pierre was getting really worried. In fact, the whole gang were.'

'Were the gang in London by this stage?'

'No. Pierre said everyone had to wait on Saint-Marie until he knew the exact timings. And then, after a few months of this, Pierre suddenly announced that he'd had the nod from André. Pierre, Conrad, Jimmy and . . . this fourth member of the gang all went to London. Once there the gang stayed with some friends of Pierre near a place called Whitechapel. And that's when the final plans were made, the motorbike leathers were bought and so on. And, I hesitate to add, some baseball bats. But the idea was to be loud, smash up the shop and look so violent that the staff handed over the jewels even quicker.'

'What happened on the day?' Richard asked.

'I . . .' Father Luc said, before correcting himself. 'My *parishioner* said that Conrad and Jimmy stole two motorbikes the day before. They were the getaway drivers. It was Pierre and this fourth member of the gang who had the baseball bats and had to go into the jewellery shop.'

Father Luc drifted off into his memories.

'I'll never forget that day,' he said quietly, and Richard was about to correct the Priest's use of his personal pronoun when he saw the warning glance from Camille. He kept quiet.

After a few more seconds of introspection, Father Luc carried on with his story.

'The feeling in my stomach as we drove up onto the pavement. The terror I felt. I wanted to be sick. But I followed Pierre into the shop. He had no fear, that man; it's like he was built differently to the rest of us. And he started shouting at the security guards, and waving his baseball bat in the air. I started smashing the glass in the displays.

'That poor security guard. He had a set of handcuffs

attaching his briefcase to his wrist, and he couldn't get them off quick enough. He handed his briefcase over in a matter of seconds, and then I shouted to Pierre something like, "let's get out of here," and turned to leave, but Pierre wasn't done yet. He chucked the briefcase of jewels at me to catch and pulled a gun. I had no idea he had a gun on him. He'd never mentioned it before. It wasn't any part of the plan. But Pierre shouted at me to get out, and as I left, I saw him point the gun at the crowd of customers and staff and fire once. I was already leaving, the adrenaline was pushing me through that door whatever happened, but I just had time to see the person he'd shot slump to the floor. It was André Morgan. Our inside man. He just fell to his knees and toppled over.

'And then Pierre had me by the arm and was pulling me through the door. I got onto Conrad's bike, Pierre got on Jimmy's, and then we drove off. I don't know how I held on to the briefcase. Or Conrad. We were driving so fast, weaving in and out of the traffic, and I just felt terrified. When we pulled into an underground car park about half a mile away, I ripped off my helmet and was sick on the ground.'

'So it was definitely Pierre who killed André Morgan?'

Father Luc was briefly puzzled by the question.

'Of course. He shot him dead. Inside the jewellery shop.'

'And when did he realise he'd dropped his gun at the scene?'

'He knew immediately. The gun had knocked on his knee as he got onto the bike and fell to the floor. But Pierre hadn't been able to stop Jimmy from driving away. That's what he told us.'

'But why did Pierre shoot André?'

'I've no idea. I've never known.'

'How did Pierre explain it to you at the time?'

'He said André wasn't to be trusted. He had to be neutral-ised. That's the word he used,' Father Luc said with a shiver. '"Neutralised."'

'Okay, so you've got away and are now in this underground car park. What happened next?'

'There was already a car waiting. So we ditched our bikes and drove back to our flat in Whitechapel. It was easy. By that afternoon, Pierre had handed the briefcase over to his contact in the jewellery trade, and that was the end of it as far as we were concerned. It was up to Pierre's contact to get everything sold off, melted down or recut. He gave us each ten thousand dollars as a downpayment there and then. I felt ill getting it, knowing that a young life had been taken. For no reason as far as I could tell. I didn't even take the paper band off my money. I slipped it into my bag and then the four of us caught a plane back to Saint-Marie the day after.'

'But was it just the four of you?' Richard asked, remember-ing what Blaise Frost had told them.

'You're right,' Father Luc said. 'Somehow, Pierre had picked up a girlfriend in London. A woman called Blaise. She was on the same flight.'

'Then what happened? When the gang returned to Saint-Marie?'

'Jimmy, Conrad and Pierre went crazy with their cash. Jimmy had his new girlfriend Blaise, Conrad had his wife

Natasha and his daughter Jessica, and it was party time the whole time for all of them. You have to understand, they were young men, and they had a heap of spending money.'

'But you didn't spend yours?'

'I couldn't. I imagined the blood that was on each note. So no, it just sat in a drawer, and I went to church. I felt so guilty. For what I'd done. And I prayed for forgiveness. How could I ever put what I'd done behind me? If I hadn't agreed to the plan, André would still be alive. I was sure of it. And the more time I spent in church, the more I discovered that it was only in prayer that I could find any kind of peace from my demons.

'I spoke to my priest about it. Not the specifics. But about the burden of guilt I felt. How it weighed on me. And how it seemed to lift when I was in church, and he suggested I go to a seminary. It was such a stupid idea, or that's what I thought at first, but I couldn't quite shake it. And then Pierre was arrested three weeks after we got back. Some anonymous woman had phoned in a tip-off to the Police that they should match the fingerprints they'd found on the gun Pierre left at the scene to known criminals on Saint-Marie.

'After Pierre was arrested and taken back to the UK for trial, Jimmy, Conrad and I met up. We were all terrified. Because all Pierre had to do was give our names to the Police and we'd be arrested. I realised that if I was going to save myself, I'd have to act, and act fast. So I went to Church, knelt before the altar and made my promise to God. I'd serve him in whatever capacity I could for the rest of my life, and in return I asked only that I be forgiven for my sins. I didn't want to go to prison.

'By the time Pierre stood trial in London, I'd left Saint-Marie, given away all of the money, and enrolled in the St Michael Seminary. And it was the best decision I ever made. Don't get me wrong, none of this makes up for my part in André's murder, but I know I've done the best I could with my life since that day. And if I was implicated in the death of one man, I've saved many lives since then. It's at least something to redress the balance.'

'I see,' Richard said. He was desperate to point out to Father Luc that, irrespective of whatever he'd said about his 'parishioner' being the person who this had all happened to, he'd subsequently given what was quite clearly a first-person confession. He could arrest him right now.

Sensing that her boss was about to ruin the interview again, Camille stepped in.

'So Pierre never told the authorities who the rest of the gang were?'

'He didn't.'

'And why was that, do you think?'

'I don't know. Although, his defence in his trial was that he'd never even been near the jewellery shop that day. He kept saying to the judge he was being set up. And, because he refused to plead guilty, he couldn't very well offer up the names of the rest of the gang. But the thing is, Conrad told me he'd got a message to Pierre just after he was found guilty, but before he received his sentence. I don't know how Conrad did it, but he told me that his message to Pierre was that he'd keep his share of the cash safe. He'd make sure it would be waiting for him when he got out at the end of the sentence. I didn't want to know any of this. I felt sick even thinking about Pierre getting all that money when he left prison.'

'You didn't think it was right?' Richard asked.

'It was wrong at such a deep level. Pierre had committed murder, and he was still going to get a massive pay-off at the end of it all? It sickened me to my heart. But it just stiffened my resolve to give the rest of my life to the service of God.'

'And did it work?'

'How do you mean?'

'When you trained as a priest, were you able to leave your old life behind?'

'You want the truth?'

'Yes.'

'Then you have to promise me some form of amnesty.'

'I'm sorry?'

'Or maybe there's a witness protection programme or something.'

'You think I can cut you a deal?'

'I don't know, but I'm too old to go to prison.'

'Look,' Camille said kindly, 'why don't you tell us what happened next. And if you're as helpful as you can be, I'm sure we can take that into consideration. After all, you *are* a priest.'

'Alright. I'll tell you what happened after Pierre went to prison.'

'You'll tell us everything?' Camille asked.

'Everything,' Father Luc said. 'For the first few years after the robbery, all was fine. For the three of us who weren't Pierre, at least. Although Jimmy wasn't so interested in seeing me any more. He didn't like me taking Holy Orders. It didn't fit with his new status as a hotshot property developer.'

'It wasn't just property he was into, was it?' Richard asked.

'You're right there. He remained crooked, not that I could complain. But his legitimate property deals also made him a lot of money. So he soon turned his cash from the robbery into a serious amount of money. I get the impression he hasn't looked back since. I don't know for sure. I've not seen him for years. As for Conrad, I stayed in touch with him. He was so enthused with his recording studio. So convinced it would be successful. His enthusiasm was infectious. And he loved how I'd become a priest. He thought it was funny. But as the years passed, Conrad got quieter and quieter. Then, after about ten years, his business failed, and that's when Conrad really started to withdraw. If you ask me, I think he was riddled with guilt. In fact, I remember Conrad saying to me a few years later that he'd wished he'd done what I'd done. Turned his back on it all. In fact, he said the money had ruined his life. Ruined his relationship with his wife. His daughter. He'd do anything to get away. But that wasn't to be for him, was it?'

'No,' Richard agreed. 'So what was it *really* like visiting Pierre in prison?'

'I didn't tell you the half of it,' Father Luc said with a sigh. 'Don't get me wrong, I visit a lot of prisoners. It's a decision

I made very soon after I was ordained. I should visit as many prisoners as possible as part of my penance. But Pierre was by some distance the most angry and bitter of any prisoner I ever got to spend time with. He refused to take responsibility for what he'd done. He even tried to claim at one point that it was me who'd shot André,' Father Luc said in amazement. 'He was seriously unstable and angry.'

'So if he was so dangerous, why did you recommend him for parole?'

Father Luc looked ashamed.

'He told me that that unless I supported his application to leave prison early, he'd tell the authorities about my role in the original robbery.'

'He blackmailed you?'

Father Luc nodded.

'And you let him get away with it?'

'What choice did I have?'

'So you lied to the parole board, and told them that Pierre was mentally fit to leave prison when you knew he wasn't.'

'I know what you're suggesting, and you're right. At some level, Conrad's death is all my fault. As is Jimmy's. If I hadn't supported Pierre's application for parole, he would still be in prison now. He wouldn't have been able to murder anyone.'

'And do you know why he's done what he's done?'

'I do. Because about the only thing that stopped Pierre going over the edge during his time in prison was the belief that he was going to get his share of the money we made from the robbery. Jimmy and I thought that too. And Conrad had always told us that he had Pierre's money safe and sound. We had no idea that he'd spent it years ago. Well, we didn't know until we were driving over to Pierre's halfway house on the day he was released from prison.'

'Conrad confessed to you?'

'On the car journey over to see Pierre. That's how late he left it. But he told us the truth, and I couldn't believe it. I had that feeling, you know, where the bottom just falls out of your stomach. Because I was the only person who'd stayed in touch with Pierre. I was the only one of the three of us who knew how desperate he was for this money. How much it had been a beacon for him. I was all for cancelling our visit to Pierre, but Jimmy insisted we had to go through with it. Jimmy always was Pierre's loyal lieutenant. So Jimmy made us all continue, and when we saw Pierre, there was an energy about him that was real scary. He was happy to be out of prison at last, but there was anger as well. An anger that we'd had our liberty all this time when he hadn't. And then Conrad told him outright that his share of the money was gone, and I'll never forget how still Pierre became. It was like, in that moment, his soul cracked. And then he just exploded and went crazy. We had to hold him off from attacking Conrad. But he was shouting at Conrad – at Jimmy and me as well – and threatening to pull Conrad limb from limb. And Jimmy and me as well.'

'He threatened you all?'

'He said we were all to blame. I couldn't disagree with him. And then he said we all deserved to die for what we'd done. Again, I could see his point. Then he said our days were numbered, he was going to come for us one by one and finish us off.'

'He said he was going to kill you all?'

'He did. We just fled as soon as he started shouting that at us.'

'And then what did the three of you do?'

'We were seriously shaken. So we went to a bar in Honoré. I had my first glass of rum in twenty years. And that's when Jimmy went for Conrad for what he'd done. He said if Pierre didn't kill him, he'd kill him first.'

'And you?' Richard asked.

'How do you mean?'

'Would you have happily killed Conrad for spending Pierre's money?'

'No. Of course not.'

'So what did you think when Conrad had his boat accident three days later?'

'I was shocked.'

'Did you think it was murder?'

'Not at first, no.'

'You *didn't* think Pierre had killed him?'

'That's right. I just thought it was a terrible accident. Or maybe Conrad was up to something on his boat and it had gone wrong?'

'I'm sorry but I don't believe you. Conrad spent all of Pierre's money. Pierre told Conrad he'd murder him. And then a few days later, Conrad goes up in an explosion on his boat. Are you really telling me you didn't put two and two together?'

Father Luc was too hangdog to reply immediately.

'Well?' Richard asked again.

'I was too scared.'

'What?'

'This was my punishment, I was sure of it. This was the divine retribution I'd been expecting for the last twenty years. After all, I'd become a priest, I'd given myself over to the service of Christ, but I always knew in my heart that it wouldn't be enough. That at some point, God would want more from me. So that's what I thought was happening. *This* was my punishment. Pierre was going to kill Conrad and I was going to be too cowardly to do anything about it. That's how I felt after Conrad died, that I was a coward,' Father Luc said, his voice rising as he spoke, and Richard could see that panic was beginning to take hold of the old man. 'But if I was worried before, it was nothing compared to how I felt after I heard what had happened to Jimmy. That's when I realised Pierre hadn't been making a hollow boast when he said he'd kill us all. He was doing just that, and I'd be next. When I saw your article in the paper, I realised that you were right. You were the only possible safe haven open to me. That's when I decided I had to turn myself in. Even if I risked being jailed. I had to tell you the truth.'

'Where's Pierre now?' Richard asked, his pencil poised above his notepad.

'I said at the start. I don't know.'

'But you must have some idea. You knew him best.'

'I promise you, I don't. He's got no family on the island as far as I know, and I was the only person who ever visited him in prison. And I know he hasn't got any money, he made that clear when he shouted at us the afternoon he left prison. So you have to believe me, I've no idea where he is, that's why I'm so worried!'

'I think you'd better stay in our cells overnight,' Richard said.

'What? No!'

'For your safety.'

'I'm not staying in your cells. I've got somewhere safe to go.' Father Luc said, pulling an old iron key from his jacket pocket and holding it up. 'There's a small cottage that belongs to the diocese on the other side of the island. It's a tiny retreat, and almost nobody knows of its existence, but it's for clergy when they're having a crisis. So I spoke to the Bishop, and he's letting me stay there for the next few days. Until you catch Pierre. Not that that's why I told him I needed to disappear.'

'What's the address of this place?'

Father Luc told the Police, and Richard wrote it down.

'That's where I'm going. And you can believe me. I'm a priest. I'll be in the retreat. You have my word.'

'I don't think I can let you go.'

'But I can't stay in your cells. Have some mercy. And I can't stay at home, either. It's not safe there. Pierre knows where I live. And the thing is, someone burgled my house a few weeks ago.'

'What's that?'

'There was a break-in to my property.'

'When exactly was this?'

'Five weeks ago.'

'You mean, three weeks *before* Pierre was released?'

'I didn't think it was connected. You see, nothing was taken.'

'Hold on. Your house was burgled, but nothing was stolen?'

'It was pretty unsettling, I can tell you.'

'Did you report it to the Police at the time?'

'No. Seeing as nothing was taken. I just tried to put it out of my mind. But now Pierre is on the loose, I don't like the fact that someone's been in my house recently.'

'But it couldn't have been Pierre who broke in. Not if it happened before he left prison.'

'I don't care, I still don't like it. So I'm going to the retreat. To think, to pray and to decide what I have to do next.'

'You could make a full confession.'

'I've told you what I can.'

'But you should make a formal statement.'

Father Luc looked at Richard, and a rigidity came into his demeanour.

'Give me time. I need to think. And pray. For the minute, just be grateful I was prepared to tell you what I was told in the confessional by one of my parishioners.'

'But Father, you can't really expect us to believe—'

'It was one of my parishioners who robbed the jewellery store, not me,' Father Luc said, cutting in on Richard. 'And if, from time to time, I slipped up and used the word "I" when I meant "he", then that's because I'm still so upset. And I can't ever be expected to break the Seal of the Confessional. I've already said too much.'

'Father—' Camille said, but the old priest scraped back his chair and stood up.

'I've told you all I can about Pierre, which is my civic duty. And I've told you where I'm staying for the next few days. Which is also my civic duty. But that's all I can give you for the moment. Please. If you need to speak to me, you know where to find me.'

Father Luc turned and left the Police station.

No-one spoke for a few seconds.

'Wow,' Dwayne finally pronounced.

'Wow indeed,' Camille agreed.

Richard was biting his lip. He'd found the whole encounter troubling, if only because he knew that he'd just allowed a self-confessed criminal to walk free from his Police station. He couldn't work out if this was just sensible policing, or if he was perhaps letting his standards slip. Either way, Richard couldn't help noticing that although Father Luc had apparently just made a full confession, he'd not given them a single clue that helped identify where Pierre Charpentier was hiding. Was this because Father Luc genuinely didn't know, or was it because he was protecting Pierre? But why on earth would Father Luc ever want to protect a murderer like Pierre Charpentier?

CHAPTER THIRTEEN

'Dwayne,' Richard called across the room, 'I want you to find out everything you can about Father Luc Durant. What he earns, where he goes, how good he is at his job, I want it all.'

'Yes, Chief.'

'And Camille? Have you worked out where the bleached pea shingle came from?'

'What's that, sir?'

'The white pea shingle we found in the tyres of the burnt Citroën. Have you chased up the sales of it over the last six months?'

Camille realised that Richard was trying to keep her busy so she didn't talk to him about Dwayne's girlfriend Amy, so she decided to provoke maximum irritation in her boss by smiling sweetly.

'Of course, sir. I'll get on to that right now.'

'Please do. We can't let any of this slip, team.'

Within the hour, Dwayne was able to report back.

'Okay,' he said, always happy to take centre stage, 'so this is what I've found. Luc Durant entered the St Michael Seminary twenty years ago. I spoke to the registrar there, and he said he remembered Father Luc being a troubled man when he arrived, but he found happiness with each passing month. He was "a good man and servant of Christ" by the time he left.'

'Then what about his apparent donation to the Seminary just before he arrived?'

'I got the registrar to check. It took him a bit of time to dig it out, but it looks like Father Luc was telling the truth about that as well. In the same month that he joined, there was an anonymous donation of three hundred thousand dollars.'

Richard remembered how this was the same sum of money that Jimmy and Conrad had received – and which Conrad had also spent in cash over the years as he embezzled Pierre's share of the heist.

'As for Father Luc's character since then,' Dwayne said, 'I've just had a long chat with a guy who's the Chaplain to the Bishop, and he told me that Father Luc is one of the most popular priests on the island. He's honest, hard-working, conscientious, and he "lives entirely for the benefit of others" – those were his exact words.'

'So he's the perfect parish priest?'

'That's it in a nutshell. In fact, according to my source, he's tipped to replace the current Bishop when he retires.'

'Which is hardly the typical profile of a murderer, is it?'

Richard was frustrated that Dwayne hadn't been able to dig up anything of use on Father Luc. But then, he thought to himself, he'd been frustrated since the very first murder. How did you catch a killer when you didn't know where he was?

However, Richard had to concede that in Father Luc they'd finally developed an active lead, and as it was now after 10pm, he told his team that they were finally allowed to go home.

'Oh Chief,' Dwayne said, as he shut his computer down, 'before Father Luc came in, you wanted to say something to me?'

'I did?' Richard said, before remembering the bombshell he'd learned about Amy.

Richard looked over at Camille and saw her staring fiercely at him. It was clear she expected him to drop the subject.

As Richard considered what he should do, Camille shook her head.

'What is it?' Dwayne asked, now looking somewhat worried.

'Nothing,' Camille said with finality.

Richard sighed. Maybe Camille was right? After all, she tended to be right when it came to human-to-human interactions.

'Don't worry,' Richard said. 'It's nothing.'

'Oh, okay,' Dwayne said breezily, happy to move on. He finished tidying his desk, put his Police cap on and started to stroll out of the station.

'Your girlfriend's a convicted felon,' Richard said.

Richard couldn't help himself. He didn't mean to – although he did, really. It was just, having let Father Luc walk out of the office without his situation being resolved, Richard had suddenly realised that he couldn't let Dwayne do the same.

Dwayne stopped in the doorway, his back to the office.

'What?' he said without turning around.

'Oh, okay, I'm leaving,' Camille said. 'And you're coming with me, Fidel.'

'Why?' Fidel asked, but Camille was already bundling him out of the office. As she went, she passed Richard and said, 'Well, good luck with this, sir. I'll see you tomorrow. Or what's left of you after Dwayne's torn you limb from limb.'

As for Dwayne, he turned slowly to face his boss.

'Did I hear that right?'

'You did,' Richard said. 'I mean, I'm sorry to be the bearer of bad news, but we can't hide from the truth. Even if it's uncomfortable. And in this instance, the truth is that your current girlfriend has done time.'

'Okay,' Dwayne said in a voice so calm that Richard realised he was suddenly very scared. 'What do you know?'

'Well, Dwayne,' Richard said, noticing how hot it had become in the station, 'I looked Amy McDiarmid up on the Police Computer Network.'

Dwayne took one step towards his boss. His boss took one step back.

'You did *what*?'

'I looked her up on the computer. And discovered she had a record. I'm very sorry, but you should know. She's a convicted drug dealer who spent two years in prison.'

'You found that out, did you?'

'I did.'

'Then what about the stamps?'

'I'm sorry?'

'Wasn't she also put inside for fencing a book of stolen stamps?'

Now it was Richard's turn to be surprised.

'You *know* about that?'

'Yes. I know she spent two years in prison. Assuming that she's been telling me the truth. I didn't check up on her.'

'She told you about her record?'

'Yes.'

'Then why on earth are you going out with her?'

'I'm sorry?'

'Then how can you go out with her?'

'Chief, have you any idea how relationships work?'

'How do you mean?'

'Look, when we started going out with each other, she didn't tell me about her past. Not at first. And anyway, it's none of my business.'

'But you're a Police officer.'

'I was talking.'

There was a tone to Dwayne's voice that brooked no disagreement.

'Sorry. You were saying.'

'So she didn't tell me about her secret. Not at first. But after a few weeks, we both realised that what we had was pretty special. And that's when she got a bit worried. I could tell. I even had to think if it was me who'd done something wrong, crazy though that sounds. But there was no doubting it. She had something on her mind. And then she told me. If we were to date, she said, considering what I did for a living, she'd have to tell me about her past. So she did. The whole thing. About how she came from this posh background. How her parents expected her to be perfect, and put all this pressure on her to pass exams and do everything right. But she flunked her exams. She said it was her only way of taking control of her life. Then she fell in with a bad crowd after she left school. And got into drugs. And dealing them. It was how she could afford to move out of her parents' home. And then she was asked by her dealer to look after an old book of stamps. She had no idea what they were worth, or that they were stolen, but that's what the Police found when they broke into her flat.'

'She told you all that?'

'And that she'd done her time. She'd learned her lesson. Although she said she'd understand if I wanted to end the relationship now I knew. Considering how I was a Police officer. But I said that as long as her time in prison was over, it didn't matter what her past was. Anyway, we've all got a past, so I told her a bit about mine and we were back on track – but more so, if you see what I mean.'

'You've got a past?'

'It's like I said. Everyone's got a past, Chief.'

'I haven't.'

'Well, everyone normal.'

'No, I don't believe this,' Richard said, still confused. 'Are you telling me I've been worrying about telling you about your girlfriend's Police record, and you've known about it for some time?'

'I just said, didn't I? And seriously, Chief, you need to get over your obsession with my girlfriend.'

'I'm not obsessed with her.'

'You reckon? First you were caught spying on her with binoculars, and now you're stalking her online.'

'I'm not stalking anyone. And I wasn't spying on her.'

'Are you jealous, is that it?'

'*What*?'

'I get it. I'm the older guy here, and I've got a girl who's clever and hot, and you've got no-one. You're jealous.'

'I'm not jealous.'

'It's the only thing that makes sense.'

Richard had no idea how he'd so completely lost control of the conversation so quickly.

'Tell you what,' Dwayne said, an idea occurring to him, 'how about you meet her? Because I reckon, if you met her properly, and talked, then maybe you'd get over your fixation with her. You'd see how normal she is. And how she's not on the market. She and me, we're an item.'

'Please stop saying I'm obsessed with your girlfriend.'

'No, this is a good idea. She can tell you how into me she is. And I know she will, because she *really* is.'

'Please, Dwayne, you have to believe me. I really don't want to spend any time with one of your girlfriends telling me how great you are.'

'No, I think this is the only way we're going to cure you.'

'I don't need curing!'

'And you know what? Now I'm thinking about it, I reckon you'll just have to do as I say. Because you wouldn't want the Commissioner finding out you'd used Police resources for your own personal research, would you?'

'Are you *blackmailing* me?'

'Blackmail?' Dwayne said in mock outrage. 'Who said anything about blackmail? But here's what I'm thinking. I think it's time you had a good long chat with Amy. And then you'll be able to move on.'

'But I don't want to talk to her.'

'I'll be honest, Chief. I don't reckon Amy will want to spend any time with you either. But here's the thing. Talk to her. Ask her about herself. And listen to her answers. Maybe you'll realise she's more than her criminal record.'

Richard racked his brain and realised how precarious his situation was. Because Dwayne was right. He'd used Police resources for his own personal use. And if the Commissioner ever found out, he'd be in hot water.

With a sinking heart, Richard realised there was only one thing he could say.

'Okay.'

And with that, Dwayne's face broke into a broad grin.

'That's the spirit, Chief. I'll set it up. And I'm telling you, you'll like her once you get to know her. Everyone likes Amy.'

Richard smiled as best he could, but he already had the deepest suspicion that if everyone liked Amy, he'd be the exception that proved the rule.

The next morning, Richard arrived at the Police station and found a package already waiting for him on his desk. It was about the size of a shoe box, it was wrapped in brown paper, and Richard's name and address were laser printed onto a label that was stuck to the outside.

'When did this get here?' Richard asked.

'A courier brought it just before you got here,' Fidel said.

'Any indication who sent it?' Richard asked, picking the parcel up and looking to see if the sender's name was anywhere to be found. It wasn't. So he got a pair of scissors from his desk drawer and sliced through the brown wrapping paper. As it fell away, he discovered that the reason the parcel had been the shape and size of a shoe box was because it was a shoe box. But it didn't contain shoes. It was too light for that. Richard popped the lid and looked inside.

The box was full of documents and photos.

He picked up a photo and saw that it showed Blaise standing by a boat in Honoré harbour. There was a tattooed man taking a small package from her, and from the way that he was looking about himself, it was a clandestine transaction of some sort. But then, as Richard picked up some more photos of the same event, Richard could tell that the whole thing was clandestine, as the photos had been taken with a telephoto lens from quite a distance.

So who was the man, and what was in the package that Blaise was giving to him?

As Camille joined her boss at his desk, Richard started picking through the other documents. They were legal contracts of some sort. They looked like shell companies that were being used to move money into an offshore account in the Cayman Islands. But what united each contract were the signatures at the bottom of each document. They all belonged to Blaise Frost.

'Sir,' Camille said. 'I know this man in the photos. He's muscle for one of the island's illegal bookmakers.'

'Blaise hangs out with illegal bookmakers?' Fidel asked, amazed.

'Or one of their enforcers,' Camille said, inspecting the photo carefully. 'She seems to be giving him something. I don't imagine it's legal, whatever it is.'

'And not just that,' Richard said, laying the contracts out on his desk. 'These documents seem to suggest that she's also been laundering hundreds of thousands of dollars into a secret offshore account.'

Richard and Camille looked at each other, both of them trying to equate the box of new evidence with the woman they'd met after her husband was shot dead.

'She's a criminal?'

'It would seem so, Camille,' Richard said, returning his attention to the front of the shoe box. 'Although that's not the question I want answered. Because what I really want to know is, who just sent all of this in to us? It's obviously an attempt to discredit Blaise, but where has it come from, and why did it arrive this morning? Fidel, can you dust all this for fingerprints? In particular, I want you to know if Pierre Charpentier's prints are on the box or evidence anywhere.'

'Yes, sir,' Fidel said.

While Fidel started working on the box, Richard and Camille drove up to Blaise's house.

They found her sunbathing by her pool – like all grieving widows, Richard thought to himself drily as he and Camille approached.

'Oh hello, what are you doing here?' she asked, lowering her sunglasses.

'We just wanted to know why a box of incriminating evidence has just arrived at the station.'

'How do you mean . . . incriminating?'

'It seems to be a fair amount of paperwork proving that you've been siphoning funds offshore. And there are photos of you handing over a package to a man we know has con-nections to illegal bookmakers on the island.'

Blaise looked at the Police expectantly, and when they didn't say any more, she seemed disappointed.

'That's it?' she said.

'What do you mean, "that's it"?'

After a moment, Blaise clapped her hands together, threw back her head and laughed, although Richard couldn't help but notice that her amusement was shot through with a degree of hysteria.

'Some incriminating photos and some contracts I signed?' Blaise asked again.

'Why's that so funny?'

'I'll tell you why that's so funny,' Blaise said. 'Because I told Jimmy earlier this year I wanted to leave him. Since you're asking. And what was more, I told him I was going to take him to the cleaners financially. As is my right. I've given that man my life and all he's done is bed every tart he can find. And when I went to see a divorce lawyer, he agreed with me. I'd been with Jimmy from before he started building up his business, so I had every right to half his entire estate. So I could leave my husband, and take quite a few million dollars with me. But I didn't dare tell Jimmy for a spell after that. Even though I was desperate to get away from him. I was so scared of how he'd react. And I'd tell myself every day that this was the day I was going to tell him. It was all over. I was leaving. Anyway, I knew he had some new woman, because I caught him going to the Fort Royal Hotel a few times, and I know that's where he beds his bits on the side.'

'Do you remember when this was?'

'I don't know. It was something like six months ago.'

Richard realised that this probably meant that the 'bit on the side' that had precipitated Blaise's actions was almost certainly Natasha Gardiner.

'And I realised I could take no more,' Blaise said. 'So I packed a suitcase, took out a wodge of cash from the house safe, and confronted Jimmy in his office. After I'd told him that he'd been unfaithful for too long, and that I was leaving him and starting divorce proceedings, he didn't say anything. Not for a bit. But there was a smirk on his face. Like he was pleased or something. And then he told me that he was happy for me to walk out on him. Even though it was my duty to stay. As his wife. I couldn't believe it. He managed to make it all about him. How I'd be letting him down. He took no responsibility for his part in all of this. But I didn't care, I just wanted out. And that's when he told me what would happen if I left him. You see, he'd been preparing for this moment for years, he said.

'And he was so pleased with himself when he explained it all to me. He said he'd made me sign a number of documents over the years that made it look as though I was a crook. And while I was reeling from that little revelation, he reminded me of the time he asked me to deliver a package to a bloke in Honoré harbour. I'd had no idea what was in the package, but Jimmy told me it had been a package of fake passports, and he'd hired a private investigator to follow and record the whole exchange.

'So that's why I laughed just now. Because Jimmy told me he had loads more evidence against me like that, and if I ever tried to leave him, he'd make sure it landed in the Police's hands. I had to stay with him or I'd go to jail.'

'He blackmailed you into staying with him?' Camille asked.

Richard felt a little uncomfortable hearing of Blaise's blackmail so soon after his own brush with the dark art the night before with Dwayne.

'That's exactly what he was doing,' Blaise said. 'I didn't know what to do. And a man like Jimmy feeds on fear. As soon as he saw I wasn't sure any more, he started acting like he'd won and I wouldn't leave him. And he was so confident. I sort of believed he must be right. I couldn't leave him. Ever. Because of the incriminating evidence he'd lodged with his solicitor.'

'He said it was with his solicitor?'

'That's right. He'd left a package, he said, and if I ever tried to leave him, his solicitor was instructed to release the information to the Police.'

'Then what if he died?' Richard asked.

'How do you mean?'

'Did your husband instruct your solicitor to release the information if he died? Maybe in suspicious circumstances?'

Blaise was shocked by the idea.

'I don't think so. That's pretty warped.'

'You really didn't know we'd receive the package?' Richard asked, wanting to be sure that Blaise had been entirely clear in her answer.

Blaise seemed to understand the importance of the question.

'I didn't. And you should know, I've never done anything wrong. Or, the only thing I've done wrong is sign a bunch of documents that Jimmy told me I should sign. I didn't know what they were about. He just told me it was to make our money more tax efficient. So I signed.'

'Without reading the document?'

'Of course not. Who reads financial documents? They're

boring. And as for that package I delivered to Honoré harbour, I had no idea what was inside it. Jimmy was away, and he asked me to go to his office and get the package from the safe and take it to a contact of his in Honoré.'

'But you must have guessed the contents weren't entirely legal?'

'Okay, maybe I guessed they weren't quite legit. But I didn't care. As far as I was concerned, I didn't know what was inside, so I was just doing as Jimmy asked me. That was all. And the thing is,' Blaise said, sliding her shades back on and leaning into the cushions of her sun lounger, 'you can try as hard as you like, but I wasn't a crook. So I know you won't be able to dig up anything that's really incriminating. It will only be evidence that Jimmy planted to discredit me.'

Richard looked at Blaise and realised that if she was going to deny everything and blame her husband instead, then it was possible they'd never be able to make any kind of case against her, seeing as her husband was no longer alive to give his side of the story. And as he thought this, Richard couldn't help noticing that things had turned out very well for Blaise. The man she hated was dead, and she'd just inherited his fortune.

Yes, things had turned out very well for Blaise indeed.

As he and Camille left the house, Richard felt a deep sense of anger bubbling up inside him. He'd never known a case where they'd spent so long getting nowhere. They hadn't even managed to identify where their killer was hiding, for heaven's sake. And how could they ever arrest Pierre if they didn't know where he was?

The rest of the day didn't improve Richard's mood. Camille was able to speak to Jimmy Frost's solicitor, and he confirmed that he'd sent in the cardboard box of information to the Police. He insisted that he had no knowledge of what was inside, he was just following the instructions that he'd been left by his client. He was to send the box to the Police if Blaise left his client, or if he died in suspicious circumstances. The man was also able to confirm that Blaise was the sole beneficiary of her husband's estate.

As for the list of people who'd bought white pea shingle from the Bricolage over the last six months, Richard learned that Camille had so far only had time to ring a few of the names, so he reassigned the job to Fidel.

And all day long, Richard had a creeping sense of dread. This was because Dwayne had informed him that Amy was happy to meet him for a drink at Catherine's bar that night. Or rather, as Dwayne explained to his boss, she didn't much want to have a drink with Richard, but she was going to go through with it for Dwayne's sake. Since he'd asked.

Richard hadn't known what to say to Dwayne when he heard that Amy was just as doubtful of the whole endeavour as he was – other than that maybe she was more sensible than he'd first thought. After all, what on earth could they talk about? Dwayne? That didn't even seem possible. But Richard also knew that he couldn't wriggle out of the encounter, so he found himself, just as the sun was setting, sitting in Catherine's bar at a table for one. Amy wasn't due to arrive for a little while, so he decided to get some work done while he had his evening meal.

'Well, hello there,' the flamboyantly dressed Catherine said as Richard took his usual seat at one of the few tables that was inside the bar rather than outside in the sunshine.

'Hello, Catherine,' Richard said, pulling out the notes he'd got on the case and starting to spread them out on the little table to make it clear to Catherine that he didn't want to make small talk.

As for Catherine, she could see that Richard was pretending to be busy, but, like her daughter, she'd decided long ago that it was her duty to 'warm him up' into a functioning human being, so she pretended she hadn't noticed.

'How was your day?'

'It was terrible, thank you for asking. Now, could I have my usual, please?'

'And why was it so terrible?' Catherine said, sitting down in the other chair at Richard's table.

Richard looked up from his notebook. Seeing as Catherine was Camille's mother – and, more importantly, the owner of the nearest bar to the Police station – he couldn't help but bump into her every day or so. But every time they talked, she had the annoying habit of always wanting to discuss his feelings. Richard would have stayed away from her entirely, but, in one of the great tragedies of his life, Catherine made the only decent cup of tea on the whole island, and she could even rustle up a halfway decent fried egg and chips. This was the meal that Richard had been referring to when he'd asked for his 'usual'.

'Why was my day so terrible?' Richard replied, happy at least that the conversation wasn't yet in any way 'touchy feely'. 'Well, for a simple reason, really. I'm trying to solve a double murder before a third murder is carried out, and I can't even find where our prime suspect is hiding.'

'You mean Pierre Charpentier?'

'You know him?'

'Oh no. But the whole island's talking about him. Since your article in the paper.'

'The whole island?'

'The whole island. It's frightening. Knowing a killer is out there. We're all worried. And looking out for him.'

Catherine indicated one of the 'Wanted' posters that Dwayne had put up on the wall of her bar. It showed the head and shoulders of Pierre Charpentier.

'And I've had a good think myself, and I bet I know where he is,' Catherine said.

'You do?'

'I do. It's obvious.'

'Then where is he?'

'Not on the island at all.'

'I'm sorry? How can he not be on the island?'

'Think about it! You know how it is on Saint-Marie. Everyone knows everybody. You can't do anything without someone seeing you, or commenting to their neighbour.'

Richard agreed with Catherine's analysis. The whole island was a hotbed of gossip as far as he could tell.

'So it's not possible that this killer is anywhere near Honoré. Someone would have seen him. Or seen a house that was suddenly occupied when the owner is supposed to be away. So what I've been thinking is, what if he's not here?'

'So where would he be?'

'Out there,' Catherine said pointing in the general direction of the bay and the sea beyond. 'On a boat. I mean, he could be miles out at sea, and then come in to a secluded bay, slip onto the island, commit murder, and then return to his boat and go back out to sea. You wouldn't know where he was.'

As much as Richard wanted to dismiss the idea on the grounds that it was Catherine who was suggesting it, he could see that there was some logic to it. Although, if Pierre was hiding out at sea, then that suggested that he had access to a boat. This seemed unlikely in the extreme, considering how Pierre had had next to no money when he left prison. So how had he bought a boat? Richard decided that he'd get Fidel or Dwayne to ask around and see if any seaworthy boats had been stolen since Pierre had left jail.

'You agree?' Catherine said as she realised that Richard was giving her suggestion some thought.

'You know what, Catherine? That's quite a good idea.'

'It is, isn't it?' she said, and then she stood up again. 'Now, let me get you your "usual".'

As Catherine left, Richard decided to go back to the very

beginning of his notes. This was something he did when he felt stuck in a case. He started reading, and was deep into the case when Catherine returned with a plate of food in one hand, and a cup of tea in the other.

'Here you are,' she said proudly. 'Fried eggs with all the trimmings.'

'Ah, perfect, Catherine, thank you,' Richard said, and, as he looked at the chips and fried eggs with the edges of the whites crisped 'just so', he really meant it. The next few minutes were going to be the highlight of his day.

'You know,' Catherine said. 'I saw Dwayne's new girlfriend Amy outside.'

'You did?' Richard said, already panicking. She wasn't due to turn up for half an hour.

'So I told her you were here.'

Richard was appalled. What sort of traitor would allow some stranger to interrupt an Englishman just as he was tucking into his egg and chips?

'Hello,' a woman's voice said.

Richard looked over and saw Amy standing in the doorway. She was holding a bottle of beer.

'Well, I'll let you two chat,' Catherine said with a smile, and returned to the bar.

'Sorry I'm early,' Amy said.

'No, no worries at all,' Richard lied.

'I thought I'd get a drink in first. For Dutch courage.'

'You'd better sit down,' Richard said, not entirely kindly. He refused to believe that he was the only person who'd noticed that in front of him was a plate of delicious hot food and a steaming cup of tea that was getting cold.

'Thanks,' Amy said, and sat down.

Oh, Richard thought to himself. He was the only one.

'Dwayne said we should talk,' Amy said. 'Although I'm not sure why.'

'Yes. He said the same to me.'

An awkward silence grew, and Richard began to wonder if he could perhaps eat one of his chips.

'Although I do kind of know, I suppose,' Amy said with a sigh. 'You found out about my record.'

'Yes,' Richard said, and he removed his hand from where it had been hovering over his fork.

'Even though it was fifteen years ago. And I haven't been that person for a long time.'

'You still served time,' Richard said distractedly, his eyes once again drifting down to his plate of food.

'Please don't judge me. Can I at least tell you what happened?'

Richard realised he hadn't quite been listening, and he looked up from his egg and chips.

'What's that?'

'So I'm from Edinburgh. Do you know it?'

'Edinburgh? Not really. Although, the tins of shortbread biscuits I get sent over from the UK have Edinburgh castle on them.'

'Well, Edinburgh's a bit more than the castle. And the bit of it I come from is probably the most conventional place in the world. It's all families living in sensible houses and doing sensible jobs. Can you imagine being a teenager in that environment?'

Richard could. It sounded idyllic.

'It was so boring. So conventional. Saturday night dinner parties, everyone sending their kids to the same schools, wearing the same clothes, having the same values. I wanted to scream. I felt trapped. So when I was a teenager and came across drugs, I couldn't get enough. I was desperate to escape. To rebel. But then, my dad's a doctor, and my mum's a housewife. I think I just wanted to shock them out of their complacency.'

'Well, I imagine you did that.'

'The more outraged they got, the more outrageous I tried to be.'

'And is that why you started dealing drugs as well as buying them?'

'I left school at eighteen with no qualifications, and all I wanted to do was leave home. I had to get away, and it was my way of funding my own flat. That's why I started dealing. And it was the biggest mistake of my life. Because that's when I lost control. When I really started hanging out with some seriously dangerous people. I'm ashamed of how arrogant, how full of myself I was. I thought I was untouchable.'

'And then one day the Police arrived.'

'That's the moment I'll never forget. Answering the door to two men in uniform and them pushing past me into my flat. I just stood there, and it was like my whole body froze. My insides drained away. I was terrified.'

'They found the book of stamps.'

Amy started picking at the paper label on her empty beer bottle.

'They found the book of stamps,' she agreed.

'And you went to prison.'

'And I went to prison. Although, afterwards was much worse.'

'Leaving prison was worse than being in prison?'

'And prison was bad, don't get me wrong. But after I left, I was "Amy, who'd been in prison". Even to people like my mum and my sisters. They never even visited me, can you imagine that? My dad did a few times, but he was too ashamed to come that often. And when I finally got out, I wasn't welcome back home, that much was made clear to me. But I'd decided in prison that that was it, I wouldn't break the law again. I was going to get back on track. On my own.

'And it's the hardest thing I've done in my life. After prison, I was on benefits. I was in debt. But I wouldn't break the law, that was my only rule. And slowly, over the years, I clawed my way back. And then the year before last, I finally got a proper job at this posh department store on Princes Street. I'm at least ten years older than all the other assistants. They all think I'm this weirdo, and the customers are the worst. Talking down to me just because I'm a shop assistant. But I can handle it. Just about. Because when I'm standing on the shop floor, I know I got there on my own. I did it all on my own.'

Against his better nature, Richard found himself warming

to Amy, just as Dwayne had said would happen. But it wasn't because he'd finally come to accept that she was Dwayne's girlfriend and was therefore 'off the market', it was because Richard was beginning to realise how hard Amy must have worked to put her life back together. Although he also found that her story prompted an obvious question.

'So what brought you to Saint-Marie?'

'It was a promise I made myself when I left prison. You see, I came here when I was nineteen. Just after I started dealing drugs, and could afford a proper holiday abroad. And I had such a great time, this island really is the best place in the world. Don't you think?'

Richard decided that now was not the time to get sidetracked by his opinions of Saint-Marie.

'That certainly seems to be the consensus,' he said.

'So when I got out of prison I vowed that one day I was going to go on another holiday to Saint-Marie. But this time I'd do it with money I'd earned legally. So it's always been the prize at the end of the tunnel for me. What I've been aiming for. It's how I've put up with working in a department store. And when I'd saved enough money, I told my floor manager I was quitting and going on the holiday of a lifetime. She knew something of my story – you know, that I'd been to prison – and she's basically the nicest person in the world, so she told me I could rejoin her team when I got back. If I wanted to. I was kind of amazed. But that's what I've noticed over the years. If you have a positive outlook, positive things start to happen to you. Like meeting Dwayne.'

'Like meeting Dwayne,' Richard said, but a lot less enthusiastically.

'I met him the first night I was on the island, did you know? We just hit it off at once. And best of all, he didn't want to know about my past, or even what I was up to now. He just wanted to dance and party, and I can't tell you how amazing that's been for me. Just being with someone who's always so happy. And who accepts me for who I am. Because you should know, I'm not really the sort of girl who normally answers the door to strangers wearing only a towel. It's just the spirit of the island, and how Dwayne makes me feel, that lets me be this relaxed. I love him.'

Richard really didn't know what to say to this impossible-to-believe statement, but luckily for him, Amy carried on with her story.

'That's what I realised real fast. I love him. And it made me sad because I knew there couldn't be any secrets between us. But I was worried how he'd react if I told him I'd been to prison. I mean, he's a Police officer. An upstanding member of the community. But I couldn't lie to him, either. So, one day, I just told him straight up. I'd done time. For dealing drugs and fencing stolen goods. It was terrible, I could feel our whole relationship ending with every word I said. But when I was done, he asked me if I'd broken the law since I'd got out of prison. I told him I hadn't, and he just said that he didn't care about my past. Everyone deserved a second chance.'

'He said all that?' Richard asked, but what he really wanted to ask was, 'You think Dwayne's an upstanding member of the community?!'

'He did. But it's one thing for Dwayne to know about my past, it's another to know that everyone else does as well.'

'No-one else knows.'

'But you know.'

'I haven't told anyone. Apart from Camille,' Richard couldn't help adding.

'You *have* told someone?'

'Only my Detective Sergeant. And I'm sure she won't have told anyone else.'

Amy looked so very forlorn that Richard felt the briefest stab of guilt.

'You're just like everyone else,' she said, and Richard could see that her eyes had filled with tears. 'When you look at me, you just see someone who's been in prison. Don't you?'

Richard didn't know what to say, because it was true. Amy *had* been in prison. He couldn't help that.

Amy stood up.

'When you see Dwayne,' she said, 'tell him I've gone back to my B&B. I don't think I want to see anyone tonight.'

And with that, Amy walked out of the bar. As Richard watched her leave, he tried to tell himself that he'd done nothing wrong. That he was in fact in no way implicated in Amy's sense of hurt and disappointment. After all, he was a Police officer. It was his duty to check that everyone was 'above board'.

But as he replayed the conversation to himself, a deeper

truth seemed to settle within him. He *was* to blame. Somehow. In ways he didn't fully understand. But his actions had made a young woman unhappy and had potentially put a wedge between her and her boyfriend, even though that person was Dwayne. And, as Richard realised how very ungallant he'd been, an even more fundamental realisation came to him.

He was going to have to make it up to Amy, wasn't he?

But how could he possibly even begin to do that?

Richard Poole picked up his knife and fork and took a first mouthful of egg and chips.

Like his relationship with Amy – and the murder case for that matter, Richard realised – it was cold.

CHAPTER FOURTEEN

It was a brooding Richard who arrived at work the following morning. This wasn't just because of Amy's words the night before, it was also because of what had happened following her exit from Catherine's, because Dwayne had arrived soon after and Richard had had to tell him that Amy didn't want to see him that night. Dwayne had been puzzled at first, but as soon as he realised that it was Richard's presence at the bar that had driven his girlfriend away, he'd got antsy with his boss and left.

And then, to put the tin lid on it, Camille had turned up to see her mother, discovered Richard sitting on his own, and had then given him an earful about interfering in Dwayne's love life, and how he had to stop trying to control everyone. When Catherine came past a few minutes later and saw that Richard had barely touched his meal, she tutted loudly and whisked the plate away in disapproval.

Richard had had to go home hungry, just to get away from everyone in Honoré who seemed to feel he'd let them down.

And, as was so often the case with Richard, he decided to displace his feelings of confusion by throwing himself into his work. After all, he still had his notes with him, so he spent the night closely studying the case – and that had been the greatest frustration of all.

After all this time, what had they really learned?

Pierre Charpentier left prison after serving a twenty-year term for robbery and murder. He then met up with his three fellow gang members, Conrad Gardiner, Jimmy Frost and Father Luc Durant, and learned that Conrad had spent the money he should have been keeping safe. Because of that, Pierre threatened to kill Conrad and the other members of the gang. And then, one of the gang returned in a grey Citroën and drove off with Pierre.

After that, what exactly had happened?

It was hard to say. All that was known for sure was that someone – Richard could only presume it was Pierre – had later set fire to the grey Citroën. But why exactly? And why exactly in that part of the jungle?

As for Conrad's murder three days later, Richard found himself drawn time and again to the fact that Pierre had left a paste ruby behind on Conrad's desk. In fact, it was this detail that irritated Richard the most. Because, although he'd not told his team yet, the existence of the fake rubies suggested a degree of pre-meditation that seemed entirely at odds with Richard's belief that Pierre had only decided to commit murder after he'd left prison and learned that his cash had been spent. After all, if Dwayne – with all of his contacts – had spent days trying to find a shop on Saint-Marie that sold fake rubies with no success, where had Pierre got his supply from?

Richard couldn't shake the feeling that Pierre must have bought the rubies in advance of his release.

As for Jimmy Frost's murder, this had offered up even fewer clues than Conrad's. Assuming that Blaise could be believed, Jimmy had gone to his office that night, and had then been shot dead at some point before the next morning. There were no witnesses. And, apart from the ruby that was found in Jimmy's mouth which had Pierre's fingerprint on, and the fingerprints of Natasha they found at the scene, they'd not been able to identify anything else that was incriminating.

As for where the gun might have come from that was used to kill Jimmy, Richard imagined that Pierre had got them from a similar source to the hooky mobile phones. As Dwayne was so fond of saying, anyone could lay their hands on an unregistered handgun on the island if they knew who to ask. And, once again, an ex-con who was fresh out of prison would know who to ask.

And yet, Catherine had also been right, Richard knew. If Pierre was hiding on the island, following the publicity of the case in the newspaper and the posters going up all around Honoré, surely someone would have seen him by now?

It was possible, of course, just as Catherine suggested, that he was hiding on a boat. So Richard rang the harbour master, and learned two things. The first was that, to his knowledge, there'd been no boat sales in Honoré since Pierre had left prison. And the second was that the harbour master really didn't like being woken up so early in the morning.

When Richard checked the Police Computer Network, it confirmed that no boats had been reported as stolen on Saint-Marie in the last few weeks.

Richard was wondering what to do next when he noticed a single sheet of A4 paper in his in-tray. He picked it up and saw that it was a page of Fidel's handwriting. As he checked it over, he realised that it was all of Fidel's research into the people who'd bought the bleached gravel from the Bricolage.

Richard could see that all of the purchases had been to businesses of one sort or another, and only one of them seemed to have any possible link to the case: Honoré cemetery had bought three tonnes of bleached pea shingle three months ago, and Richard recalled that André Morgan – the man who'd been shot dead in the original robbery – was buried in Honoré cemetery. As Richard remembered this fact, he also remembered that Stefan Morgan, André's father, had admitted to driving to Honoré cemetery to visit the family crypt immediately after he'd seen Pierre leave prison. He'd said he'd parked up, gone to the family crypt, but hadn't gone inside. But then, Richard also remembered how Stefan drove a white Nissan car, so how come they found the bleached gravel in the tyre treads of a grey Citroën CX that had been stolen?

Richard got a box of drawing pins from his desk drawer and went to the large map that was pinned to the wall behind him. Taking out a golden pin, he stuck it in the map at the location of the harbour car park where the grey Citroën CX had been before it was taken. He next found Philippe's halfway house on the map and stuck a pin in that. Lastly, he found the location where the car had later been discovered burnt out, and put a pin in there as well.

He then went back to his desk and pulled out a ball of string. Wrapping it around the first pin, he connected the string to the second and third pins to show the rough journey that the car might have taken that day.

And as he did that, Richard saw something on the map that made his heart race. But he squashed any feelings of excitement, and decided that he had to be methodical. He got Fidel's list of businesses that had bought the bleached shingle and he worked through the names one by one. First he used the internet to establish their addresses, and next he put a pin in the map of Saint-Marie to see where the businesses was located.

By the time he'd located most of them on the map, he could see that not one of these new pins lay anywhere near the string that marked the rough possible route of the grey Citroën on the day Pierre disappeared.

However, Richard had left one business until last.

It was Honoré cemetery. And Richard didn't need to look up its location – he already knew where it was – and he also knew that he'd have to move the string a bit to get the pin in, because that's what Richard had first seen: the cemetery lay on the road that linked Pierre's halfway house to the jungle where the car was later found.

In other words, in order for the grey Citroën to have driven from the halfway house to the jungle location where it was later set on fire, it would have had to have passed the cemetery.

And that's why Richard's mind had raced. Because, all of this time they'd been trying to work out where Pierre could have been hiding, but there was one place they'd never considered.

Honoré cemetery.

It seemed a touch macabre to imagine Pierre hiding out from the Police in a cemetery, but there was no doubting it would contain dozens of old crypts where Pierre could have hidden himself in some degree of comfort. If he could handle his spooky neighbours, of course.

Richard left the Police station and got into the Police jeep. As he drove onto the main road out of Honoré, he phoned Camille and told her to meet him at Honoré cemetery.

She was already waiting for him as he pulled up in the jeep ten minutes later and parked on the gravelled parking area just outside the cemetery's walls.

As Richard got out of the jeep, he bent down and hungrily grabbed up a handful of the gravel. It was exactly the same pea shingle as they'd found stuck in the wheels of the grey Citroën.

'I think it's the gravel we've been looking for,' Richard said.

'But how did you work it out?' Camille asked, quietly amazed. 'And does that mean the grey Citroën came here before it got torched?'

'I think so. But let's see if we can find out for sure.'

Richard directed Camille to the old iron gate that led through the whitewashed wall. 'But I should point out there's a possibility that Pierre's hiding somewhere in here.'

'You really think so?'

'I think it's a distinct possibility.'

Stepping through the gate, Richard stopped, somewhat assaulted by the hundreds of apparently haphazard crypts, all tiled in black and white squares, and all arranged around a loose network of dusty paths. None of the crypts was in any way the same as its neighbours, so they were all different sizes and shapes, and to make the visual jumble of structures even more unsettling for someone of Richard's organised mind, there were mirrors, brightly coloured candles, handmade statues, gaudy plastic flowers and other random artefacts and keepsakes perched on every spare surface or hanging from tiled roofs and windows.

'Now, how can we tell if any of the buildings are currently occupied?' Richard said.

'Occupied by the living rather than the dead,' Camille whispered back at him.

Richard ignored his partner as he started to head up the central avenue. 'There'll be obvious signs of habitation. We just need to look for them.'

'You're no fun sometimes, you know that?' Camille said as she followed.

For the next few minutes, Richard and Camille wandered among the crypts, although Richard was getting increasingly

irritated by the way Camille kept stopping to read the enam-
elled plaques and painted wooden boards that detailed the
virtues of those who had died.

Richard was relieved to see that most structures weren't
actually large enough for someone to be hiding inside, and
those that were had been bricked up or sealed in such a way
that it was pretty clear no-one had opened them recently.

As he headed up the hill, Richard made sure he didn't
wander too far from the central avenue because there was
one building he was keen to inspect, and that was the crypt
that belonged to Stefan Morgan's family.

Richard had already identified that there was one structure in
the whole cemetery that was grander than all of the others, and it
was just off the main avenue. As he approached, he couldn't help
but feel that – finally – here was a building that looked as though
it might pass muster with the local building authority inspector
with only the smallest of bribes and a nudge and wink. The crypt
had two floors and a pitched roof – and together with the outside
staircase, arched openings on the first floor, and alternating black
and white tiles plastered to every inch of the structure, the whole
thing looked like a crazy Escher drawing made real.

Richard saw a narrow staircase that led down to an iron-
grilled door that had ancient plaques screwed to the wall all
around the frame. Heading down the steps, Richard saw that
most of the plaques were dedicated to various members of the
Morgan family. So this was it, Richard thought to himself,
impressed. The Morgan family crypt was by some distance
the grandest in the immediate vicinity.

As Camille joined Richard, he looked for the freshest-looking plaque, and saw it at once. It was deep blue, and it had white writing on it announcing that 'André Morgan, whose life was ripped from us too soon' was interred inside. Richard could see that the plaque was dusty, so he pulled his hankie and wiped it clean. There. That was a bit better.

'Sir?' Camille said, as she looked at the doorway.

'What is it?'

'I think someone's opened this door recently.'

'What's that?'

'Look at the ground under the hinges,' Camille said, indicating the thinnest scattering of rust on the tiled floor directly beneath the hinges of the barred gate.

'You're right,' Richard said as he inspected the hinges, and he could see a brightness to the metal where the rust had recently rubbed away. 'So who's been in here?'

Richard peered into the main body of the crypt, but it was shrouded in darkness. He took hold of the iron bars of the gate and tried to pull or push it open, but it wouldn't budge.

'It's locked,' Camille said.

Richard looked at the old lock that was keeping the door secured. It was decades old – and didn't look very strong – but it was very definitely locked shut.

Richard tried to remember what Stefan had told them about the key to the family crypt. He had the only key to the crypt. Although that wasn't quite right, was it? Richard also remembered that André had got a copy made so he could meet his girlfriend down here just before he got his job in London. But that had been over twenty years ago.

'Wait here,' Richard said, stepping back to the main avenue and pulling his notebook and phone as he went.

Richard phoned the bakery in Honoré and was soon speaking to Stefan Morgan. He explained that he wanted Stefan to confirm that he'd not gone into the family crypt after he'd seen Pierre.

There was a shocked silence at the other end of the line.

'I'm sorry?' Stefan eventually asked.

'I just wanted you to confirm. Did you go inside your family crypt after you saw Pierre?'

'No, I told you. I visited, but I stood outside. There's a plaque to André on the wall. That's as close as I got.'

'Then can you tell me, do you currently have the key to the crypt to hand?'

'I'd imagine so. I don't know.'

'Can you check that you still have it?'

'I keep it in my desk drawer here,' Stefan said, and Richard heard a thud as the phone was put down. This was followed by the sound of someone rummaging in a drawer.

'Here it is,' Stefan said, picking up the phone again.

'You have the key with you?' Richard asked.

'I do. But why are you asking?'

'Do you know, apart from the copy your son made twenty years ago, have there been any other copies of the key made?'

'Absolutely not. That's why it was so shocking André made his copy. There's only supposed to be the one key, and it stays in the possession of the most senior member of the family. That's me, and it's a point of pride that I'm allowed to look after it.'

'Then can you tell me the last time you opened the family crypt?'

'What is this?' Stefan asked, warily.

'When did you last go into your crypt?'

'Why do you want to know?'

'Just please tell me the answer.'

'It was years ago.'

'Really?'

'At least three years, I'd say. Maybe four.'

'Thank you,' Richard said, hanging up the call.

It didn't make sense. If the crypt hadn't been opened in years, why had they just found fresh rust on the ground under the hinges? Richard tried to imagine that the Morgan crypt was where Pierre had been hiding, but that didn't quite add up, either. How could Pierre have been coming and going if Stefan was still in possession of his key?

'Sir,' Camille called from the gate to the crypt, 'I've had a bit of an accident.'

'What's that?' Richard said, returning to his partner, but he stopped dead in his tracks as he arrived.

The gate to the crypt was open.

But he could see that it had been wrenched open on the side where the hinges were – or rather, as Richard looked more closely, where the hinges had been.

'Camille, what have you done?'

'I don't know how it happened,' she said in fake innocence.

'I was just inspecting the door with this iron rod, and the whole gate popped open.'

Camille held up an old iron rod that Richard guessed had fallen from the bannisters on the veranda above.

'Sir, if we think a crime's being carried out, or is about to be carried out, we don't need a warrant.'

'And what crime do you think is about to be carried out? The occupants in there are all dead.'

'That's the thing, sir. We won't know, unless we go inside. And I don't have to remind you, a killer's on the loose. So if Pierre's been hiding here, there'll be evidence through that door. We just have to go in and see for ourselves.'

Richard looked at his subordinate and for once he realised he agreed with her. This was too important to wait on a warrant.

'Alright,' Richard said. 'Follow me.'

'And I'll just keep hold of this bar if that's okay,' Camille said, and Richard saw her grip the iron rod with both hands like a baseball bat.

'Okay,' he said as he stepped down into the dusty darkness.

Inside the crypt, the air was musty, and there was a strange smell. It was sort of sweet and sickly. Richard pulled his hankie out and put it over his nose. As his eyes became accustomed to the gloom, he could see that the far wall was covered in little metal doors that were rusting and dented. He guessed that this was where the family coffins were placed.

There were also two truly ancient stone sarcophagi on the floor, one to each side of the room. They were very plain, very dusty, and the stone lids didn't look like they fitted very well.

Looking around, Richard couldn't see any evidence that the crypt had been used as a temporary camp for Pierre. There were no provisions, no sleeping bag, no candles – no anything, really. Just dust and dry leaves.

But there was something Richard could discern, just on the edge of his consciousness. What was it?

'Shh,' he said to Camille.

'I wasn't talking.'

'Be quiet.'

Richard stood stock still and tried to open up all of his senses to his environment. What was it that he was responding to?

And then he realised.

There was a buzzing noise. Barely discernible, but it was there, he was sure of it.

'Can you hear that?'

'Hear what?' Camille asked.

Richard took a few steps to the side of the room and stood still again.

Yes, he was right. There was a buzzing noise. So faint he could barely hear it, but it was definitely there.

Richard bent down a little – it felt like it was coming from the floor.

He was wrong.

The noise was coming from the stone coffin on the left-hand side of the room.

A stone coffin that Richard saw had a powdering of stone dust on the floor all around it. Almost as if someone had recently scraped the lid off and then put it back on again.

'Camille, it's coming from *inside* the sarcophagus.'

This got his partner's attention.

'There's something in there. Here, we'll need to get the lid off.'

'We can't do that!'

'We have to. Come on, bring your iron rod with you. We can use it as a crowbar.'

'Okay, you're the boss.'

Camille went to the sarcophagus and managed to jam the iron rod under the rough edge of the lid.

Richard grabbed the other end of the lid and got ready to lift.

'After three?' Camille asked.

Richard gulped. Despite his bravado, he was deeply unsettled opening an old sarcophagus like this. Especially seeing as there was clearly something inside that was making a noise. But then he realised something.

'*After* three, or on three?'

'What?'

'Are we going one, two, three, and then we push on four, or do we push on three?'

'Does it matter?'

'Yes.'

'Then push as soon as I say three.'

Richard nodded. He understood.

Camille briefly looked up to the heavens to give her the strength to deal with her boss, before bracing herself to push.

'Okay. One . . . two . . .'

As Camille said three, a number of things happened that were going to haunt both Police officers for the rest of their lives.

Firstly, the stone lid scraped upward, but as it did so, a cloud of black flies swarmed into the air in a sudden crescendo of buzzing as though released by Satan himself. And secondly, before recoiling violently, both Camille and Richard saw that there was a dead body inside the sarcophagus.

A body that had been dead for some time.

But that wasn't what would stay seared into the Police officers' minds.

And nor was it the single bullet hole that penetrated the dead man's forehead.

As Richard and Camille ran from the crypt into the brightness of day again, flies streaming out of the crypt door behind them, what had shaken them to their core was the dead man's identity.

The dead man was Pierre Charpentier.

And he had a bright red ruby placed over each closed eye.

CHAPTER FIFTEEN

As Camille phoned Fidel and Dwayne and updated them on what they'd just found, Richard tried to keep his spiralling thoughts in check.

It was Pierre who'd been committing the murders, it had to be. And yet, here was his dead body, a bullet hole in his forehead, and bright red rubies placed over each eye. He was a victim, just as Conrad and Jimmy had been.

What was more, considering the swarm of flies that had erupted from the sarcophagus when they'd removed the lid, Richard guessed that Pierre had been dead for some time. In fact, seeing how Pierre hadn't been seen since the day he left prison, it was even possible that he'd been the first victim.

But if Pierre had been the first victim, who on earth had been carrying out the murders? What did this all mean?

It meant, Richard considered, mentally berating himself, that he'd had the case upside down, inside out, and the wrong way round from the start.

'Okay, sir,' Camille said, heading over, 'Dwayne and Fidel are on their way. And so is an ambulance.'

'Camille, tell me I'm not mad,' Richard said, 'but was that really Pierre Charpentier's body in there?'

'It was, sir.'

'With a bullet hole in his forehead?'

'And fake rubies over his eyes, sir. I saw it as well.'

'Then what's he doing there? How can our prime suspect be dead? All the clues have always pointed to him! The fingerprint we found on the SIM card on Conrad's boat. The fingerprint we found on the lump of concrete he smashed Conrad's window with.'

'And don't forget the print we found on the ruby in Jimmy's mouth after he was shot, sir.'

'Exactly!'

Richard looked around for something to kick in frustration, but just as he was lining up an old tin can for a wallop, he realised something.

'They were all fingerprints,' he said.

'Sir?'

'Well, just go with me on this for a second, would you? We know that Pierre was alive when he left prison. Obviously. The taxi driver and Stefan Morgan both saw him. And the half-blind old woman next to his halfway house also said he was alive when he arrived. Again, obviously.'

'And she also said that Pierre was visited by three men.'

'That's right. Father Luc, Conrad Gardiner and Jimmy

Frost – assuming that Natasha and Father Luc are telling us the truth about the members of the original gang.'

'And there's no reason to believe they'd both lie to us about that.'

'Exactly. But after Pierre argued with Conrad about where the money was – again, confirmed by our half-blind neighbour – the three gang members all left.'

'Although one of them returned later on. In a different car.'

'A grey Citroën that this person had stolen from the harbour area of Honoré.'

'That's right.'

'So why did they steal the car?'

'Maybe they didn't own a car and needed one.'

'Maybe. Or maybe they did own a car, but they just wanted to return to the halfway house as secretly as possible. Because of what they had planned for Pierre.'

'You think the person who came back is the person who killed him?'

'At the moment, I don't want to commit to anything, but we know *someone* killed him. So, one of the three gang members comes back and picks Pierre up in the grey Citroën. Later on, we find it pushed off a road in the jungle and torched, but with a very specific pea shingle caught in its tyre tread. That means the grey Citroën must have stopped at the cemetery at some point, and seeing as the cemetery is halfway between the halfway house and where the car was abandoned, it's not too much of a stretch to imagine that Pierre was taken straight to the cemetery from the halfway house.'

'To be killed?'

'It's possible.'

'But why here?'

'Well, it perhaps suggests that this case has more to do with André Morgan's death than we originally thought. Don't you think? After all, it was Pierre who murdered André. And we've just found his dead body a matter of feet from André's last resting place. It can't be a coincidence. And I'll tell you something else. The metal gate to the crypt hadn't been forced, had it? That suggests that whoever took Pierre in there to kill him had a key.'

'Does that make Stefan Morgan the killer? As he's the only person with a key?'

'I don't see how that's even possible, seeing as he was inside an MRI machine on a different island at the precise time that Conrad was killed. But I can't help thinking that there's maybe one other person who might be able to get a key to a locked crypt.'

'And who would that be?'

'A priest.'

'You think Father Luc's the killer?'

'Look at the facts, Camille. Three of the original gang members are all dead, leaving only one of them still alive. Father Luc.'

'But why would he want to kill the other three? He's a priest. It doesn't make sense.'

'And yet, everything we've been thinking about the case has turned out to be wrong, hasn't it? Come on,' Richard said, starting to stride down the hill. 'I think we need to bring Father Luc in for questioning.'

'But sir, we can't leave the crime scene.'

Richard turned on his heels.

'Dwayne and Fidel will be here imminently. And I don't think we have a moment to lose.'

Richard strode off again, and Camille realised she had no choice but to follow.

As it happened, Richard and Camille reached the Police jeep just as Dwayne and Fidel tore up on the Police motor-bike, so Camille was able to fill them in on what they'd found and where they were now going.

'Come on, Camille, we haven't got all day!' Richard called out from the window of the passenger side of the jeep. Camille left Dwayne and Fidel and got into the driver's side. Then, with a spray of bleached pea shingle kicking up behind, she put the vehicle into gear and drove off with sirens blazing and lights flashing.

Camille took the main road to the other side of the island, where Father Luc had said his retreat was. As she drove, Richard fished out his notebook and looked up the exact address Father Luc had given them, and then located it on the maps app of his phone.

'So, Camille,' Richard said, 'you think a man of the cloth isn't capable of committing murder?'

'Of course not, sir. But this is a man who's dedicated his life to God for the last twenty years.'

'Which is very much the nub of the matter, I think.

Because you're right, I agree. Father Luc has dedicated his life to the island since his days as a jewellery thief, but I think that's the problem. I mean, think about it from his point of view. Conrad and Jimmy left Luc to get on with his life, so they'd obviously come to terms with his decision to take Holy Orders years ago. And Luc had visited Pierre as often as he could to keep him on side as well. So as long as Pierre came out of prison and got his money, all would have almost certainly continued to be well in the world for Luc. He could even continue visiting Pierre. After all, what could be more priestly than staying in touch with a poor soul he'd apparently befriended during his prison sentence?

'But then Conrad had to spoil everything by revealing he'd spent all of Pierre's money. At which point, Pierre threatened to kill them all. And I have to confess, it was here that I made the biggest mistake of all. Just because Pierre had issued this threat, I presumed that he'd been the one who'd then carried it out. But, logically, that doesn't necessarily follow, does it? After all, whether or not Pierre makes his threat to kill the other gang members, that doesn't stop someone else from also having the same plan, does it?'

'I suppose not. But are you really saying it was Father Luc who hotwired the grey Citroën?' Camille asked as she changed down a gear, floored the accelerator, overtook an old man on an ancient moped, and then swerved back into the lane just as a massive concrete truck bore down on them coming the other way.

Once Richard had recovered his poise – having grabbed for dear life onto the hand support above the window with both hands – he turned to address Camille again.

'But he was a criminal twenty years ago, Camille, and remember what Dwayne said? The car that was stolen was at least twenty years old, and so a technique from twenty years ago had been used to hotwire it.'

'That could just be a coincidence.'

'Okay, but we know that *someone* came back to pick Pierre up in the grey Citroën, don't we?'

'Sure.'

'Do you really think Pierre would have gone off so happily with this person if it had been Conrad?'

'How do you mean?'

'Neither Pierre's visually impaired neighbour – or the witness you found who saw Pierre get in the Citroën – said Pierre was in any way angry when he left that afternoon. He just got in the car, it did a three-point turn, and then it drove away. So it's unlikely to have been Conrad. Seeing as he was most angry with him.'

'Meaning it was either Jimmy Frost or Father Luc who came back.'

'And of those two, I'd put my money on Pierre trusting Father Luc the most. After all, they'd continued their relationship over the years, hadn't they? And it's like I said, Honoré cemetery has got to have some spare keys to the crypts. If a priest wanted to get into the Morgan crypt, I bet he could find a way.'

'Okay, so maybe Father Luc hotwired the car and then picked up Pierre. Are you then saying that Father Luc drove Pierre to the cemetery, led him to the Morgan family vault, and then shot him dead?'

'At the moment, it's a possibility we can't rule out.'

Without apparently changing speed, Camille spun the wheel, and the Police jeep lurched off the main road and started thumping down a dirt track.

While Richard realised that he'd stopped breathing, Camille said, 'So where does a Priest get a gun from?'

'For the love of God, Camille, would you please slow down?'

'We don't have time to slow down, sir. Where did Father Luc get a handgun from?'

'I don't know!' Richard squeaked as they banged into and out of a pothole. 'But he's a prison visitor. I bet he could get hold of a gun if he tried.'

'Okay, that's a fair point. But why would he kill at all? What's his motive?'

'And that's the easiest part of it. Remember what Dwayne said? Father Luc was being lined up to be the next Bishop of Saint-Marie. And we've got to bear in mind, this isn't your common or garden priest, this is someone who flew all the way to London all those years ago to rob a jewellery shop with baseball bats. Despite his protestations to the contrary, there's violence inside Father Luc, have no doubt about it. And I think, after all these years of sacrifice, of dedicating his life to the church, he wasn't prepared to have the prize of a Bishop's mitre snatched from him.'

With a thud of the suspension hitting the ground, the jeep finally left the sloped track and bombed out onto the flat white sand of the beach. Luckily, the sea was at low tide, so Camille was able to drive on an almost perfectly flat crust of fresh sand.

Richard could see a little cottage a hundred yards away, at the far side of the secluded cove.

The curtains were drawn, but the lights were on.

'Is this it?' Camille asked.

'It's the address Father Luc gave us.'

'Then let's see what he has to say for himself,' Camille said as she slid the jeep to a juddering halt to the side of the cottage.

Richard and Camille banged out of the jeep and each took a side of the house, meeting up on the further side where the front door was.

It was already open.

Richard and Camille were surprised.

'Father Luc?' Richard called out. 'Saint-Marie Police.'

There was no sound that indicated that anyone was inside. In fact, all Richard could hear was the gentle lapping of the sea nearby.

Pushing the door open, Richard stepped into the cottage and found himself in a little room with ochre-coloured tiles, white walls and simple furniture. But he didn't take much of the surroundings in, because all Richard had eyes for was the man who was lying sprawled on the floor.

It was Father Luc Durant.

Camille pushed past Richard and dropped to her knees by the body, putting her fingers to the priest's neck to check for a pulse.

'Sir,' she said. 'He's dead.'

Richard had guessed as much as he'd already seen a bottle of pills on a desk by the door. The pills were sitting next to a half-empty glass of water and a piece of paper with handwriting on it.

Richard bent down to read what was written on the note.

'"It was me",' Richard read out loud. '"Father Luc Durant. I did it. I killed them."'

'It's a suicide note?' Camille asked.

'Can you see a ruby anywhere?'

'I don't think so, sir.'

Richard quickly scanned the room, and there didn't appear to be a ruby anywhere.

'You were right,' Camille said. 'He was the killer all along. And now he's taken his own life. Before we could bring him in.'

'Yes, it's what it looks like, isn't it?'

Richard tried to feel happy that the case was so self-evidently closed. After all, the scene really was presenting as a straight-up-and-down suicide. So much so, in fact, that he couldn't imagine how else it could be interpreted.

And yet, Richard couldn't help feeling that he was being manipulated somehow. It was all too neat, with all the loose ends tied up.

But all four members of the original gang were now dead.

So how could Father Luc's death be anything other than suicide?

I didn't expect Pierre's body to be found. Not that it mattered much. I'd already got that covered. That's why I got Luc Durant to write out a suicide note before he died. And guess what? Luc wasn't even surprised when I walked in on him with my gun. He said he'd never known how it would end for him, and now he did. Mind you, all the pious hypocrisy he was spouting, I was tempted to shoot him dead there and then. But he swallowed the sleeping pills alright. And then he talked. About his life. About his regrets. I didn't listen. Didn't care. I just wanted to watch the moment he slipped into death. In the end it was hard to tell. His breathing became shallower and shallower. I had my face right up against his. Was it actually possible to see the exact moment his soul left him? In the end, I think he'd been dead for a few seconds before

I even realised. There was no change. He was alive. He wasn't. It was all the same. Unlike with Pierre. His death was what made all of this worthwhile. Putting my gun to his forehead and squeezing the trigger. You see, he'd known his life was in danger from the moment we got to the cemetery. That's when I pulled the gun on him. He was weeping by the time I made him get into that old stone coffin. I didn't plan it. It was just there, and it occurred to me. But he was sobbing and begging me to let him live as he opened it up. And he was just telling me how it was his first day of freedom after twenty years in prison when I shot him so he'd shut up. And my beloved André saw it all.

CHAPTER SIXTEEN

'I hear congratulations are in order,' Police Commissioner Selwyn Patterson said as he strolled into the Police Station as if he'd just been passing and wanted to kill a few minutes – which, Richard realised, was very possibly the case.

'Thank you, sir,' Richard said, but he knew the Commissioner of old. His view of the world and Richard's weren't always in alignment. 'And why would congratulations be in order?'

'Our killer has finally been revealed.'

'You mean Father Luc Durant?'

'Obviously. Although I should say, the Bishop has communicated his disappointment to me that you weren't able to arrest him before he took his own life. Or before he'd even committed a single murder. But as I told him, how could you have caught him before he'd even struck?'

Richard observed that only the Commissioner could offer up a compliment that, by the time it arrived, sounded like a criticism.

'Don't worry, sir,' Richard said. 'I'm not sure Father Luc Durant took his own life.'

'You aren't?'

'I'm not.'

'But I understand you've confirmed that the suicide note was written in the priest's own hand.'

'Indeed, sir. It's very definitely his handwriting.'

'And I also understand the sleeping pills that were on the table in the room were also prescribed to him?'

'That's right, sir. I've just spoken to Father Luc's doctor, and he confirmed that he'd been prescribing sleeping pills to Father Luc for a number of years. And the pills he prescribed are the same brand as the pills we found.'

'And as for fingerprints at the scene . . .?' the Commissioner said, turning to Camille as she sat at her desk, the glass, suicide note and bottle of pills from the retreat on the desk in front of her.

'The only prints on the glass belong to Father Luc,' Camille said. 'It's the same with the pill bottle. Only Father Luc touched it. And although we'll need to send the suicide note to the labs to be sure, there's nothing about it so far that raises suspicion.'

'Camille's right,' Richard said. 'It very much looks as though the note was written entirely of Father Luc's free will.'

'Then perhaps there was a sign of a struggle or a fight that suggests that Father Luc was coerced somehow?' the Commissioner asked.

'There wasn't, sir.'

'Then let's see. Who even knew that Father Luc was staying in that particular retreat?'

'That's what I'm struggling with, sir. Because as far as I can tell, the only people who knew where Luc was hiding were the Bishop of Saint-Marie and the people in this room.'

'And I take it you're not suggesting the Bishop of Saint-Marie just murdered one of his priests, are you?'

'No, sir,' Richard said, but his mind had started to turn as he realised that the Commissioner was right. Seeing as the Bishop was unlikely to be a multiple murderer, and the same was true of Richard and his team, Father Luc must have confided the address of where he was hiding to the killer – by mistake or on purpose, there was no way of knowing just yet.

But who would Father Luc have told?

And when you got down to it, Richard realised, with Conrad, Jimmy and Pierre dead, who else did Father Luc even know who was connected to the case that he could confide in?

'Inspector?' the Commissioner said, and Richard snapped out of his reverie.

'Sorry, sir,' he said. 'It's just, I think you're right. If he was killed, then why did Father Luc tell the killer where he was hiding? It doesn't make a whole heap of sense.'

'Father Luc can't have known that the person he told about the retreat wanted him dead.'

'That's my thinking exactly, sir.'

Selwyn looked at his Detective Inspector, and then he sighed.

'You really think it could have been murder?'

'It's the rubies, sir.'

'The rubies?'

'When we discovered the bodies of Conrad, Jimmy and Pierre, we also found large fake rubies at each murder scene.'

'Yes. They were left by the killer.'

'As a message. To the rest of the gang. Or to us. I don't know. But that speaks of a killer who is hugely arrogant, sir. Or seriously unhinged. I mean, how warped do you have to be to leave extra clues behind at a murder scene? It's not normal. You see, Dwayne's checked, and there's not a single shop anywhere on the island that sells fake red rubies. Or any kind of fake jewels at all. So where did our killer get them from?'

'And you don't think this case can be solved until you've worked out where the fake rubies came from?'

'I don't, sir.'

The Commissioner smiled. He couldn't help but admire his lead investigator's dogged determination.

'Then have you considered this? Perhaps Father Luc was already in possession of the rubies? After all, clergy often have various beads and pearls and other bits of haberdashery sewn into their robes, don't they? Why not Father Luc?'

Richard's attention sharpened.

'Say that again, sir?'

'I'm just pointing out that a priest's robes are often ornate. Studded with jewels that I'm sure are plastic. So, maybe the rubies belonged to him and came from wherever priests get their vestments from? What do you think?'

Even though Richard wanted time to work out why his mind had just twitched, he couldn't ignore his boss, so he refocused his attention on the Commissioner.

'It's a possibility, sir,' Richard said. 'But it's not just the rubies. All the evidence seemed to be pointing to Pierre Charpentier being our killer, but now it looks as though he was very possibly killed on the same day he came out of prison. Or so soon after as makes no difference. And that speaks of a degree of pre-meditation on the killer's part. So why would Father Luc have already decided to kill Pierre and the rest of the gang? Unless he already knew that Conrad had spent all of Pierre's cash – which he also knew would send Pierre rogue. What's his motive? And while I'm on the subject, why would Father Luc shoot and hide Pierre in the Morgan family crypt? I mean, I know that that's where André is buried, but I still don't get it.'

'Very well. Then what if Pierre really did murder Conrad? Just like you always suspected. And then he smashed in the window of Conrad's house so he could leave a ruby there. In fact, having killed Conrad, what if Pierre then went on to kill Jimmy Frost next? But having struck twice, Father Luc found out what was going on – that Pierre was killing off the old gang one by one. And again – somehow – he also knew that Pierre was hiding out in Honoré cemetery. So it was a case of kill or be killed, and Father Luc was prepared to kill Pierre if only to save his own life. I mean, look at it from Father Luc's point of view, Inspector. Pierre had killed André Morgan in the past, and now he'd gone on to kill Conrad Gardiner and Jimmy Frost in the present. I could imagine even a man of the cloth believing that Pierre deserved to die for what he'd done. And then, to cover his tracks, all Father Luc had to do was find Pierre's stash of rubies and leave two of them over Pierre's eyes, and *voila!*, we'd think that Pierre's murder was all part of the grander scheme. When, in reality, Father Luc was merely taking down the man who'd just murdered Conrad and Jimmy.'

'Then why did Father Luc need to commit suicide afterwards? With Pierre dead he was in the clear. And why would he also leave a note saying that he'd killed them all? Surely, if he was writing a proper confession, he'd have explained that Pierre had killed Conrad and Jimmy, and now he'd killed Pierre and was taking his own life in remorse.'

'Oh,' the Commissioner said, disappointed. 'Yes. That seems a fair point. In which case, it seems to me that you've got two options. One, Father Luc is the killer. He really did kill them all. Or option two, there is some other person out there who's behind the murders. But think on this, Inspector, because I know how hard you and your team work. Is it really possible for someone to have remained so well hidden from you for all this time?'

Richard was grateful that the Commissioner at least acknowledged how hard they worked. Unlike his boss, he couldn't help noticing, as Selwyn slipped his peaked cap back onto his head, announced that he was late for a drinks party at Government House, and ambled off.

'Father Luc didn't commit suicide,' Richard said, but his

team could see that he was trying to convince himself. 'We interviewed him in this very room. His fear was real. And, if he was already a killer – having killed one person – two – or three, even – why did he confess anything to us first? And why even go to the retreat? If you're about to take your own life, you want to be somewhere familiar. I just don't believe he'd go to the retreat, write out his confession and then take his own life.'

'But sir,' Camille said. 'If it wasn't suicide, how did the killer make it look like it was?

'Oh, I'd say that was the easy part, Camille. Because, when Father Luc came to us he was riddled with guilt, wasn't he? And full of shame for what he'd done in the past. And we know from the murders of Conrad and Jimmy that the killer's got a gun, don't we? All the killer had to do was turn up at the retreat, point their gun at Father Luc, and I imagine they could have pressured him into writing a fake suicide note. After all, I think Father Luc would have felt that he was implicated in all of the deaths already. So there are pressure points the killer could exploit with him. I'm sure of it. And I could imagine the killer offering Father Luc a stark choice. Either write the note and take an overdose of sleeping pills – allowing him the chance of a peaceful death – or the killer would shoot him dead. And if they were suitably sadistic, which I think we can say is true of our killer, they'd point out to Father Luc that they could shoot him somewhere extremely painful like the stomach so he'd bleed to death slowly and in excruciating pain. When faced with such an impossible choice, and knowing the guilt that he was already carrying, I could well imagine Father Luc taking the easy choice and writing the note and swallowing the sleeping pills.'

'Okay. But how did the killer even know that Father Luc had sleeping pills on him?'

'Oh,' Richard said, realising the truth of what Camille was saying. 'Bugger. That's a good point.'

But then Richard remembered something Father Luc had told them, and he scrabbled out his notebook and turned to the relevant page.

'What was it Father Luc said? Here we go,' Richard said, handing his notebook to Camille so she could see for herself. 'There was a burglary in his house five weeks ago, wasn't there?'

'Assuming Father Luc was telling us the truth.'

'But it was a burglary where nothing was stolen. That's what he said. So what if it wasn't a burglary as such, it was really a fact-finding mission by the killer? He breaks in to see what leverage he can get on Father Luc, and he discovers in the man's medicine cabinet that he has a tub of powerful sleeping pills, and that the tub is almost full.'

'But the burglary was weeks before Pierre was released from prison.'

'Which is good news, Camille, because it fits with my theory that there's some other killer out there, and all of these murders were far more premeditated than any of us have hitherto considered.'

As Richard said this, a very exhausted Dwayne and Fidel clumped into the room.

'Ah, Dwayne, Fidel!' Richard called out. 'What did you get from the scene?'

'Which one?' Dwayne said and slumped into his chair. 'Father Luc's? Or Pierre Charpentier's?'

Richard had some sympathy for his subordinates, as he'd certainly never had to process two separate murder scenes on the same day before. However, Richard also knew that sympathy would have to wait.

'If you could just tell me what you've got?'

'Well, sir,' Fidel said, pulling a notebook from the top pocket of his shirt. 'I'm not sure we got anything from either. Or nothing obvious anyway. But starting with Pierre Charpentier, it was a pretty grim process getting his body out of that coffin.'

'Sarcophagus,' Richard couldn't help but correct.

'But you should know, we found the bullet that killed Pierre under his head. It had gone straight through his skull and out the back.'

'Suggesting he was still alive when he got into the sarcophagus,' Dwayne said with raised eyebrows. 'Imagine what that was like. Being held up at gunpoint, being made to get into a stone coffin, lying down, and then you're shot dead.'

'But it fits with the M.O. for Father Luc, doesn't it?' Richard said. 'He was held up at gunpoint and made to do something he didn't want to do as well, wasn't he?'

'Maybe so,' Camille agreed.

'Then what about time of death for Pierre?'

'It wasn't possible to tell. But there was a considerable amount of maggots and pupae on the body, sir. We've alerted the Forensic Entomologist on Guadeloupe. He should be able to work out how many cycles of life the blow flies had been through, and give a rough time of death that way.'

'Good. Then what else did you find?'

'Well, sir, the lock and bars to the crypt were all so rusty, we don't have the right equipment to lift fingerprints. And the same was true inside the crypt. All the surfaces are all so old and rough, we aren't able to dust for prints at all. Mind you, it's possible the latest equipment might be able to help, but we don't have anything like that on the island.'

'So we just sealed the crypt back up,' Dwayne said with the hint of a challenge in his voice. It was clear that he felt that it was all they could do, and he didn't want his boss to start criticising them for sloppy Police work.

As for Richard, he had sympathy with Dwayne's frustration. After all, he'd also been inside the crypt, and he knew that they didn't have anything close to the necessary forensic facilities to process the scene to the highest standards.

'We could try putting in a call to Guadeloupe?' Camille said.

'What's the point?' Richard said. 'Have any of the crime fighting agencies on Guadeloupe ever spared any us any of their manpower or equipment before?'

Richard's team all knew the answer to that question. Unfortunately for them, the Saint-Marie Police Force was considered such a small outpost on such a tiny island, that all of the money and resources of the bigger islands were always focused on fighting crime locally.

'Okay,' Richard said, wanting to move the conversation on. 'Then what about the scene of Father Luc's murder?'

'That's just as professionally clean, if you ask me,' Dwayne said. 'No tracks in the sand outside the house, other than those from the Police jeep. And there aren't even any neighbours to ask if they saw or heard anything.'

'But this is crazy,' Richard said. 'How can we solve any of these murders if the killer's leaving the scenes completely clean?'

'Well, that's easy, Chief,' Dwayne said.

Everyone turned and looked at Dwayne in surprise.

'What?' Dwayne asked, once he realised everyone was looking at him. 'Oh, you want to know how I know we're going to solve it? With logic, Chief. That's how you solve everything. So what's the one thing that's bugging you about this case?'

'Well, that's easy enough. If the four original gang members are dead, who's the killer?'

'No, not that. That's just something you don't know the answer to just yet. What's really *bugging* you?'

'But what do you mean, "bugging me"?'

'What's the thing that makes you go, "but it just doesn't make any sense"?'

As Dwayne spoke, he lifted his arms in a passable impression of an out-of-control marionette. Richard was only dimly aware that Dwayne seemed to be doing an impression of him, because he was already trying to identify the one paradox or inconsistency at the heart of the case that was troubling him more than anything else.

And then he got it.

'Okay,' he said. 'Since you're asking, the one thing that's bugging me right now is how the killer knew where Father Luc was hiding. Because Luc knew his life was in danger, didn't he? That's why he came to see us. And seeing as he knew what danger he was in, I just don't believe he'd inadvertently tell anyone where he was going to hide. And yet the killer knew where to find him. As you say, Dwayne, it doesn't make sense.'

'Then make it make sense.'

'You mean, maybe the Bishop or someone in his office is the killer? Or tipped the real killer off?'

'That doesn't sound very likely, Chief. So rule it out. Be logical. And then ask the question again. How did the killer know?'

'I don't know.'

As Richard said this, he threw his hands up in the air in exasperation, and he had a slow realisation that that's why Dwayne had done his 'drunken marionette' impression.

'Then start again,' Dwayne said, pointing his finger at his boss. 'No matter how crazy or outlandish your theory is, there has to be a way for the killer to have known where Father Luc was going.'

Richard exhaled. It was all very well Dwayne having this

blind faith in his powers of deduction, but some things just never made any sense. 'Unless . . .?' Richard found himself thinking. 'Unless' what? There really was no way the killer could have known where Father Luc had gone into hiding.

'It's impossible,' Richard said. 'And that's what's bugging me.'

As Richard said this, a thought occurred to him.

He dismissed it almost as soon as it arrived.

And yet, if it was correct, it would explain how the killer would have known where Father Luc had gone to hide. And it would also explain a whole host of other anomalies in the case, Richard realised in mounting excitement.

'I think you're right, Dwayne,' Richard said. 'I need to focus on what's bugging me.'

As he said this, Richard opened his top desk drawer and looked inside. What he was looking for wasn't there. So he opened another drawer in his desk, pushed the contents around, and was just as quickly disappointed.

'Sir?' Camille asked.

'Hold on,' Richard said as he pulled all of the drawers of his desk open one by one, rootled around inside, but continued to be foiled. So he stood up from his chair, turned it over and placed it upside down on the floor.

'Sir?' Camille said, now very definitely confused.

'I asked not to be interrupted, Camille.'

Richard picked up his keyboard and looked underneath it. And then he did the same to his computer monitor, his phone – and then he took his pen tidy and spilled all of his pens over the desk.

Camille didn't say another word. How could she? Like Dwayne and Fidel, she was agog. Had their boss just wilfully scattered pens over his desk?

Within a few seconds, the team were looking back on the whole 'pen scattering' episode as a halcyon time of peace and tranquillity, as they watched their boss pick up his 'In', 'Out' and 'Pending' trays from his desk and tip their contents onto the desk – before checking over the tray itself. Finding it disappointing, Richard dropped the whole thing to the floor, and then got on his hands and knees and checked the underside of his desk. He then stood up again and didn't even seem to notice the patches of dust on his knees as he moved to the filing cabinets to the side of the room and started opening drawers. And, having satisfied himself that what he was looking for wasn't inside the filing cabinets either, he started to check through the clutter of the broken office equipment that was heaped on top.

And then Richard stopped dead in his tracks as he looked at an ancient fax machine that was sitting on a filing cabinet. Or rather, his team noticed, their boss wasn't looking at the fax machine. He was looking at a USB charger that was plugged into a wall socket just to the side of the machine.

The USB charger looked entirely unremarkable. It was made of white plastic, and it had two sockets in it that currently had no USB cables plugged into them.

Richard held up his finger for silence, not that any of his team would have dared speak at this point. They could see from their boss's boggle-eyed concentration that the stakes were, for some reason, sky high.

Richard returned to his desk and picked up a graphite puffer from among the detritus he'd tipped from a drawer. His team were surprised. Why did their boss want to start checking for fingerprints now?

Richard returned to the USB plug, held the puffer up to it, gave one clean puff on the plastic bulb and a spray of graphite powder briefly engulfed the USB plug.

Having done this, Richard didn't move. Not for ten seconds. Not for thirty. He just stared transfixed at the USB plug. Just as his team were staring transfixed at him.

'Fidel?' Richard eventually said, his eyes still firmly fixed on the charger. 'We need to fix the ceiling fan.'

This wasn't quite what anyone expected Richard to say.

'What's that, sir?' Fidel said.

'We need to fix the ceiling fan. Don't we?'

Richard's team knew that their boss had been trying to get the wonky ceiling fan mended ever since he'd first arrived on the island. But why would he mention this fact now?

'Er, yes, I suppose that's right.'

'Then get the ladder and make a start, would you?'

'You want me to fix the ceiling fan now?'

'You heard me.'

'. . . Okay.'

'But I suppose the first thing you'll have to do is isolate the circuit.'

'What's that?'

'Dwayne, go and trip the electrics, would you? So it's safe for Fidel to work on the ceiling fan.'

Dwayne didn't move, but Camille's eyes lit up as understanding came to her.

'Yes, go and turn the electricity to the station off,' she said, before turning back to look at her boss. A silent message seemed to pass between them both. They understood each other.

Dwayne shook his head to himself. Sometimes there was no getting 'management'. He went through the bead curtain that led to the cells, found the ancient fuse board to the station and called out that he was about to turn the power off.

The moment Dwayne cut the electricity to the building, Richard yanked the USB plug from its socket, put it on his desk and grabbed up a tiny screwdriver.

'What are you doing, sir?' Fidel asked.

'Not now,' Camille said as she pulled out her phone, turned on the torch function, and pointed the light at the plug so Richard could see better.

'Thanks, Camille,' Richard said as he finished unscrewing the second of the two tiny screws. As it dropped to the desk, Dwayne ambled back through the bead curtain.

'Okay, someone's got to tell me what's going on,' he said.

Richard popped the back from the USB plug and they could all see for themselves.

'You were right, Dwayne,' Richard said. 'I just had to work out what was bugging me.'

Inside the plug were all the usual circuits of a piece of

electronics, but there was also something else that really shouldn't have been there.

It was a SIM card.

The device wasn't just a USB charger.

Someone had been bugging the Police station.

CHAPTER SEVENTEEN

A few minutes later, Richard had noted down the identification numbers for the SIM card, put it back inside the plug and then slotted it back into the wall socket. Then, once Dwayne had turned the electricity to the station back on, he and his team went through a charade of congratulating Fidel for mending the ceiling fan before they all decided that it was probably time to retire to Catherine's bar for an early evening drink.

Once there, Richard's team wanted to know how he'd worked out the USB plug was fake.

'I didn't know for sure,' he said. 'Other than the fact that it was the only thing in the vicinity that wasn't covered in years' worth of dust. And when I sprayed it with graphite powder, I saw it didn't have a single fingerprint on it. That's what clinched it. After all, how is it possible to plug something into a wall socket without leaving a fingerprint on it? But you realise what this means, don't you? I was right. Father Luc's not the killer.'

'How can you be so sure?'

'It's simple. All four of us saw Father Luc every second he was in the Police station, didn't we?'

'I reckon so,' Dwayne said.

'And did he at any time stick a USB plug into the wall?'

'No way.'

'And has he visited the Police station before or since?'

'He hasn't.'

'But, sir,' Fidel said, 'none of the suspects has been in the station apart from Father Luc.'

'But don't you see what this *really* means?' Richard said, interrupting his team. 'All along, that bug's allowed the killer to be one step ahead of us. But now we know about it, we're one step ahead of him.'

'How do you mean?' Fidel asked.

'Because we know that he's listening in on us. But he doesn't know we know.'

'Oh, I see what you mean!' Fidel said excitedly.

'And that means we can finally turn the tables on him. Or her, of course. Because I think the existence of this bug proves categorically that we haven't yet caught our killer.'

'But who could it be?' Fidel asked. 'All the members of the gang are dead.'

'Well, let's not get ahead of ourselves. Whoever it is, they think their job is done, don't they? I mean, all four members of the gang are, as you say, dead. And the killer's even managed to make it look as though Father Luc is responsible for the murders. Job done. Their guard will be down.'

'But how can we use the bug to catch them?' Camille asked.

Richard didn't have a ready answer, so he told his team that he was going to go back to the station to work through all of his case notes. After all, as he saw it, now that he knew that the killer had been listening in on them, he backed himself to find some information – or loose end – that he could use to make the killer reveal himself. Fidel and Camille both offered to accompany Richard, but he wouldn't let them.

'I don't think so, considering the circumstances,' Richard said as he got up from the table. And then, to the general bafflement of his team, he announced that 'loose lips sink ships' and left the bar.

Once back at the station, Richard realised he first had to tidy his desk before he could get any work done. What was more, he'd have to do so silently, as he didn't want the killer hearing that anything out of the ordinary had happened, beyond a bit of routine maintenance on the ceiling fan. So Richard started silently reconstructing his desk, and, as was so often the case when doing displacement activity, he found his mind skipping through the case as he did so.

If the killer wasn't one of the original gang, then that meant that there was a fifth person out there who wanted all four members of the original gang dead. But who could that be?

Seeing as his desk was now covered with a fine powdering of dust, Richard got a bowl of hot soapy water from the kitchenette area. Once he'd returned to his desk, he started wiping it clean, revealing the tired leather underneath. As he did so, Richard tried to imagine all the hundreds – no, thousands – of cases that had been solved at this one desk.

He found the act of cleaning therapeutic, and while he worked, his mind continued to drift over the case. In particular, he found himself remembering how the Commissioner had said something that had seemed to resonate with him. But what was it? Casting his mind back, Richard recalled that he'd had the feeling when Selwyn had talked about where a priest might have bought fake jewels for his robes.

And then, precisely because he wasn't thinking about it too hard, it came to him.

The exact point that had niggled him.

Richard wrung the filthy water out of his dusty cloth, but he was no longer in the Police station, he was a streak of pure thought flashing through the case. And everywhere he alighted to check out his new and incredible theory, it was as though he was seeing the case in Technicolor for the first time.

Everything now made sense.

But how to check if his theory was correct?

Well, that was easy enough, Richard realised.

Richard fired up his computer and looked up a phone number online. He checked his watch, and was pleased to see that it wasn't too late. He then picked up his desk phone and dialled the number on the screen.

A man answered the call, and Richard soon explained who he was and why he was ringing.

'Tell me,' Richard said, knowing that the question he was about to ask would possibly reveal the identity of their killer, 'do you sell fake plastic jewels?'

'Fake plastic jewels?' the man replied, surprised by the question.

'That's right. You know, fake jewels made of plastic. For costumes and so on. To be more specific, do you sell quite large and gaudy plastic rubies?'

There was a pause at the other end of the line, and then the man said, 'As it happens, we do. Would you like to buy some?'

A surge of adrenaline rushed through Richard, but he also knew that he had to be careful – the killer was still listening.

'You don't sell them?' Richard said into his phone.

'I said we did. We've got a number of different jewels. Fake rubies, fake emeralds, fake diamonds and so on.'

'Well, never mind.'

'But I don't understand. I just said we did—'

'Anyway, thanks for your help. I'll just have to see if I can get the rubies elsewhere,' Richard said, hanging up the phone.

He then leant back in his chair and sighed. To anyone listening, it would have sounded like a sigh of frustration, but it was anything but. It was a sigh of deep satisfaction.

'Got you,' Richard thought to himself. '*Got you*.'

The following morning, Richard's team were in place in the station at 8am. As arranged, Richard entered at 8.01am sharp.

'Good morning, sir!' Fidel said

'Good morning, Fidel,' Richard said brightly.

'You seem to be in a good mood, Chief,' Dwayne said.

'I am, Dwayne. Because I've realised our killer has made one terrible mistake.'

In truth, Richard and his team had planned this whole conversation the night before, when Richard had returned to Catherine's bar after working out who the killer was – not that he'd yet told them the murderer's identity. At the time he'd said he had his reasons, although his team guessed that those reasons were basically because their boss was a control freak. But then, if truth be told, they'd been so amazed that he'd solved the case that they'd been happy to go along with everything he then suggested – including creating a charade for the killer's benefit the following morning.

'The killer's made a terrible *mistake*?' Dwayne asked with strange amateur dramatic emphasis, and Richard held up his palms to suggest that Dwayne should dial his performance down.

'I think so.'

'Then what is it?' Camille asked.

'Well, it's obvious,' Richard said. 'They've not considered the teachings of Edmond Locard.'

Now it was Camille's turn to wonder if Richard was perhaps enjoying his moment in the spotlight too much.

'What's that?' Fidel asked.

'Edmond Locard, the French criminologist. He created the very first forensics lab, and he came up with the principle that it was impossible for a criminal to enter and then leave a crime scene without leaving some trace behind, be it DNA, blood, hair, dirt on a shoe, or whatever. And it was impossible for them to leave without taking something of the crime scene with them. That's why it's called the exchange principle.'

'Are you quoting a *Frenchman*?' Camille asked, realising that she was happy to follow her boss into this particular conversational cul-de-sac.

'I know, Camille, but these are dark days and desperate times call for desperate measures.'

'Then tell me more about Edmond Locard, sir. He sounds fascinating.'

'It only occurred to me last night,' Richard said. 'But the first two murder scenes were next to impossible to revisit, even if we'd wanted to. After all, Conrad's boat exploded – which hardly facilitates a deep forensic analysis of the scene, seeing as so much of it is still on the sea bed. And Conrad's study – and Jimmy's office for that matter – are both full of physical evidence from countless numbers of people. It would be next to impossible to separate the known DNA or other clues from all of the other people who'd been in those rooms before. And if forensics found anything that identified the killer, I'm sure he'd have been able to explain it away.'

'So what about the crypt, sir?' Camille said, deciding to move the conversation on.

'Well, that's where it gets more interesting, Camille. Because I remembered last night that Stefan had said that no-one had been inside the crypt for a number of years – and that means that there'd be next to no forensic evidence from other people to confuse the scene. To all intents and purposes, we can say that the crypt is a blank canvas. And that's where our friend Edmond Locard comes in. Because the killer will have left DNA at the scene. A single drop of saliva. Or a strand of hair. Or even a fingerprint, if we're lucky. But he must have left some forensic evidence at the scene. And unlike the other scenes, these slender traces won't be hidden amongst all the other forensic evidence of the other people who'd previously contaminated the scene.'

'But, sir,' Fidel said, knowing that it was his turn to ask the next question. 'We aren't set up for a deep forensic sweep of the crypt. It's like we said yesterday. We don't have the facilities.'

'And that's why I spoke to the Commissioner last night,' Richard said, even though he and everyone else in the room knew this was a lie. 'He then spoke to his counterpart on Guadeloupe and I can inform you all that, for the first time in the history of the island, a crack team of Forensic Analysts are travelling to Saint-Marie this afternoon.'

'They are?' Dwayne said in theatrical amazement.

'And they're going to collect every leaf, speck of dirt and hair from the crypt and take it back to Guadeloupe for fast-track analysis. No expense spared. And once they've discounted the physical evidence we and Pierre left at the scene, I think it's fair to say that whatever is left over will belong to our killer. It's the first concrete evidence we'll have that categorically reveals our killer's identity.'

'But that's brilliant news,' Fidel said.

'It is,' Richard said, putting his finger to his lips as he spoke and silently indicating with his other hand that Fidel and Camille should prepare to leave the station with him. 'This afternoon, after the Forensics team arrive from Guadeloupe, we're going to be able to collect the physical evidence that will ultimately put our killer in jail. I'm sure of it.'

Camille and Fidel got up, careful to be as quiet as possible, and they joined their boss at the station door.

'So I suggest we spend this morning trying to advance the case in whatever way we can. Then, as soon as the Forensics Team arrive from Guadeloupe, we'll take them to the Morgan crypt in the cemetery.'

As Richard said this, Dwayne gave a big thumbs up to them all, wishing them luck.

'Then let's get to work,' Dwayne said.

Richard, Camille and Fidel slipped out of the Police station silently.

And with that, the trap was set.

CHAPTER EIGHTEEN

'Okay sir, so who are we waiting for?' Fidel asked from inside the confined space of the mausoleum opposite the Morgan family crypt.

'Don't worry,' Richard said. 'I believe it will all become clear very soon.'

It had taken only ten minutes for Richard, Camille and Fidel to drive from the Police station, park in a lane near the back of the cemetery, and enter by a side gate. As agreed with Richard the night before, the cemetery groundsman was already waiting for them with the keys he possessed that opened the vaults nearest to the Morgan family crypt. It didn't take Richard long to choose the building directly opposite the Morgans', and he, Camille and Fidel had closed themselves inside it.

As Richard had explained to his team the night before, if they announced that a crack Forensics team from Guadeloupe was coming to sweep the Morgan crypt for evidence the following afternoon, there was no way the killer would be able to resist cleaning or interfering with the scene before then. Exactly how, Richard wasn't sure, but he was convinced they'd be able to catch the killer red-handed.

All they had to do was wait.

'But just to be clear, sir,' Fidel said, still trying to work out exactly what they were doing inside a mausoleum, 'you're saying the killer is still out there?'

For once, Richard didn't mind Fidel's questions. After all, they had nothing better to do.

'Oh yes,' he said. 'The killer is still out there.'

'Then I think I know who it is,' Fidel said.

'You do?' Camille asked.

'It's about who has a motive, isn't it?'

'Always,' Richard said without taking his eyes off the Morgan family crypt.

'And as far as I can tell, there's only one person who has a motive to want all of the original members of Pierre's gang dead.'

'And who's that?'

'Stefan Morgan.'

'Stefan?' Camille said, surprised.

'Think about it. His son would be alive today if the gang hadn't robbed the jewellery store in London.'

'And not just his son,' Richard said. 'His wife as well. She died of pneumonia within the year. Stefan's been on his own since then.'

'And he has cancer, doesn't he? So he might feel he doesn't have anything to lose. He wants Pierre and the rest of the gang dead before he dies himself. And the thing is, sir, he even went to the prison to see Pierre leave that morning. And that's pretty crazed, isn't it? But what if he then followed Pierre in his taxi and found out where he was staying? Stefan could then go back to Honoré and steal the Citroën, return to the halfway house, and get Pierre into his car.'

'All of which makes perfect sense,' Richard agreed. 'Especially when we consider where Pierre was murdered – the Morgan family crypt. After all, it's sweet justice to despatch your son's killer only feet from where his dead body lies. And, just so you know, that is why Pierre was killed here. It's entirely symbolic. But Stefan's not the killer. Because he may have the cleanest motive of all to kill Pierre and his gang, but he has a cast iron alibi for the time of the murder of Conrad. He was on a different island, and having a full body scan. He didn't call the mobile phone that set off the bomb.'

'Oh,' Fidel said, disappointed. And then he brightened up. 'But you agree that Pierre's murder here was important?'

'It was of paramount importance.'

'Then that's a shame.'

'It is?' Camille asked.

'It is. Because, there's one other theory I've got. You know, if the killer isn't Stefan Morgan.'

'What is it?'

'Well, I think you'll laugh.'

'We won't laugh,' Camille said.

'But I feel stupid.'

'You shouldn't. Should he, sir?' Camille asked her boss.

Richard reluctantly drew his eyes from the Morgan family crypt.

'I can't say whether anyone should feel stupid. But you're right, Camille. We're here for the duration. What's your theory, Fidel?'

'Well, sir, it's not really even a theory. It's more an observation.'

'Then what have you observed?'

'Well, the Commissioner was right, wasn't he? We've looked at all of the suspects and realised that they couldn't have been the killer – or, they've ended up being murdered, which kind of proves they weren't the killer.'

'Agreed,' Richard said.

'So maybe the person we're looking for is someone we've never considered.'

'Now that's a very interesting theory,' Richard said. 'Go on.'

'So I was thinking, what if one of the dead people was the killer?'

'I'm sorry?' Camille asked.

'And that's why we'd not considered them. Because we thought they'd been dead all this time. But they weren't dead. They'd faked their death.'

'But who could have faked their own death?'

'Conrad Gardiner.'

Camille looked at her boss, but he was looking out of the grille and had apparently stopped listening.

'Conrad Gardiner?' Camille said. 'You mean, the first person who was murdered?'

'But was he?'

'Okay,' Camille said. 'So how could the first person killed be the killer after all?'

'Well, for starters because he was the only person who knew how much trouble he was in. Wasn't he?'

'How do you mean?'

'Well, Father Luc and Jimmy Frost had no idea that Conrad had spent all of Pierre's cash. But Conrad's known for nearly ten years. That's ten years to worry, but it's also ten years to plan. And all along we've been trying to square an impossible circle. Seeing as the murders could only have been planned *after* Conrad announced he'd spent all of the money, how come the killings always felt like they'd been planned in advance? You know, with the mobile phones, rubies and so on all bought beforehand. And the biggest clue of all that the murders were pre-planned was the robbery that wasn't a robbery at Father Luc's house weeks before Pierre even got out of prison.'

'Okay, I'm listening,' Camille said, surprised that Fidel was making such a cogent case. 'Let's say Conrad was behind the murders.'

'Starting with his own apparent murder.'

'But why would he pretend to kill himself?'

'Because he wanted out. That's what I'm thinking. After all the years of failure. His marriage was over, he'd have known that the moment he discovered his wife was having an affair. He had no job to keep him here. And he knew how angry Pierre would be when he discovered Conrad had spent all of his money. So he decided to do a vanishing act. We know he cleared out his bank account just a few days before his boat exploded. Don't we?'

'That's true.'

'And the thing is, do you remember what he loaded onto his boat on the morning it exploded?'

'No. What?'

'Philippe the harbour master said he helped Conrad get some scuba tanks onto his boat. But, when the Saint-Marie Dive School searched the sea bed directly under the explosion, they couldn't find any scuba tanks anywhere. So how can that be?'

'You think he swam off underwater?'

'It's a possibility, isn't it? And if he did, the whole thing makes sense. All he had to do was smear some of his own blood down the back of the boat before he exploded it – making sure he left his fingerprints in the blood.'

'You think he cut himself?'

'If you're trying to vanish permanently, I think there's a lot you'd be prepared to do. Or maybe Conrad got a nurse or someone to take the blood from him painlessly. After all, he wouldn't have needed much to create that smear on the boat. But once he'd set the scene, all he had to do was cut the fuel line so the engine compartment started to fill with petrol fumes. And then slip into the water wearing his scuba kit and swim off unseen. With a mobile phone in a dry bag of course. But he could then either briefly come to the surface so he could use his phone to set off the bomb, or maybe he just swam to the rocks at the mouth of the harbour. He could have climbed out, got his phone, and watched the explosion from there. Either way, once the boat went up, he could have dived back underwater and swam around the headland to Grand Anse beach next door. And then vanished.'

'But what of his study?' Camille asked.

'How do you mean?'

'If he was swimming off to a new life, how did he also manage to smash in the window of his study and leave a ruby after the boat exploded?'

'Well, that's the thing, what if he didn't do it afterwards? Natasha said she never went into Conrad's study, and we know the window wasn't overlooked in any way. So maybe Conrad trashed the room the day before when Natasha was out, and then he set the scene with the ruby to be discovered after the murder. After all, none of the neighbours heard glass smashing that morning at any time, so maybe it was done before then.'

Despite herself, Camille smiled.

'I like it,' she said.

'But what about the rubies?' Richard asked.

'The rubies, sir?'

'Seeing as we've never been able to find anyone on Saint-Marie who sold those rubies, how do you think Conrad got hold of them?'

'Well, I was thinking about that. Maybe he bought them online.'

'And yet, we found no evidence of Conrad making any online purchases.'

'So maybe he went to another island? Or always owned them.'

'Conrad's not our killer,' Richard pronounced. 'Impressive though your theory is, Fidel. And you've identified another key point. These murders were indeed premeditated. But, despite the fact that we never found his body, I think Conrad was killed in the explosion that day. Although I'm sure you're right when you say the reason he took out all of his money beforehand was because he was worried he'd maybe have to make a run for it once Pierre found out what he'd done. But it was only eight hundred dollars, it was hardly enough to start a new life. And I should add, if no scuba tanks were found on the sea bed after the explosion, well, it's still possible that they're trapped inside the parts of the hull that settled on the sand.'

'But you think the murders were planned before Pierre got out of prison?'

'I proved it yesterday when I spoke on the phone to the person who sold our killer the rubies.'

Camille and Fidel were stunned.

'You know where the rubies came from?' Camille asked.

'But who was it?' Fidel asked. 'Who sold him the rubies?'

'Ah, and that's where you're making a fundamental error,' Richard said. 'No-one sold him the rubies.'

Fidel looked at Camille to check he wasn't mad.

'But sir, you just said that you spoke to the person who sold him the rubies?'

'That's right, I did. But it wasn't a him he sold the rubies to. It was a her.'

'The killer's a woman?' Fidel said.

'Yes.'

'And she's behind all of the murders?'

'She is.'

'But who is it?'

'Wrong question. What you need to ask is, why are we currently staking out the Morgan family crypt?'

'The killings have got something to do with André Morgan's murder,' Fidel said.

'Exactly. In which case, who's the one woman who we know is connected to André Morgan?'

Camille got it first.

'His girlfriend.'

'Exactly,' Richard said. 'André's father never knew her name, did he? In fact, we've never been able to identify her. Other than the fact that she's been on the island somewhere ever since then.'

'So what are we saying?' Camille said, her mind racing. 'Either Natasha or Blaise was André's girlfriend twenty years ago?'

'Very good, Camille,' Richard said, delighted at his partner's acuity.

Before Richard could say any more, they all heard the sound of a car door slamming nearby.

Richard put his fingers to his lips for silence.

In the distance, a figure entered the cemetery.

It was a woman, she seemed to be in a hurry, and she was holding something heavy in her hands.

As the woman approached, it become possible to see who she was and Camille drew her breath in sharply.

Richard flashed Camille a glance to be silent.

As for Fidel, his mouth had parted in slow amazement.

Richard knew who they'd been waiting for, so he wasn't so surprised, although he hadn't been expecting her to be carrying the can of petrol he now saw she was holding.

Without stopping, the woman stepped up to the Morgan family crypt, and then ripped the 'Police – Do Not Cross' tape aside before pulling the remnants of the gate open and going inside.

'Okay, we need to be quick,' Richard said and pushed the door in front of him open.

Richard, Camille and Fidel raced out of the crypt, briefly wincing as their eyes adjusted to the sunshine outside, and then they barrelled down the steps and the three of them entered the darkness of the Morgan family tomb.

Inside, the woman looked up in shock, the petrol can in her hand, the lid already off, and the strong stench of petrol in the air.

'Amy McDiarmid,' Richard said, 'I'm arresting you for the murder of Conrad Gardiner, Jimmy Frost, Father Luc Durant and Pierre Charpentier.'

Amy looked with wild eyes at the Police, and then she threw the can of petrol onto the floor where it glugged out the remainder of its contents, and pulled a handgun from her waistband that she pointed at Richard.

'I don't think you are,' she said, her voice tight with anger.

Amy then pulled a Zippo lighter from a pocket and held it up in her other hand.

'You take even one step towards me, and we all go up.'

CHAPTER NINETEEN

None of the Police officers dared move.

'Don't do it,' Camille said.

'Why not?' Amy said darkly.

'Because they're all dead. You did it. You won. Didn't you?'

As Richard marvelled at how quickly Camille had reoriented herself to the reality of who the killer was, he also saw Amy draw herself up a touch taller and raise her chin proudly. She was delighted by Camille's assessment.

'But *what* did I do?' Amy asked. It was clear she wanted to have her brilliance affirmed.

Camille put up her hands to keep the conversation as calm as possible.

'We don't need to do this here,' she said.

'No, I want to know what you know.'

'We'll tell you back at the Police station.'

'No, you don't give me orders. Start talking. Now.'

As Amy spoke, she flipped the lid on the Zippo lighter open with a metallic click.

Camille, who'd hitherto rated their chances of talking Amy 'off the ledge' as quite low, now realised that, since she had no idea how or why Amy was the killer, she was going to have to put her life in the hands of one of the most insensitive men she knew.

'Sir . . .?' she said to Richard, hoping that he'd understand how high the stakes were.

'I'm not explaining myself to anyone,' Richard said.

'I think you should,' Camille said.

'I'm not a performing monkey, Camille.'

'We're underground, sir,' Fidel suddenly blurted, 'in a room that's full of petrol and a woman's holding a lighter. Sir, please can you do as she says?'

Richard could see from the looks that both Camille and Fidel were giving him that they really, *really* wanted him to explain himself. And it was certainly true that Amy was indeed holding a lighter inside a room that was no doubt filling with petrol fumes.

Richard sighed.

'Okay,' he said reluctantly before turning back to Amy. 'But I should say, I only realised you were a possible suspect yesterday. As well you know, all along we've presumed that this case was about Pierre Charpentier wreaking revenge on his old gang members. Just like you wanted us to. And the fact that Conrad spent all of Pierre's cash while he was in prison was a piece of good fortune for you that made it all the more credible that he had to be behind the murders. After all, Pierre was released from prison on day one, he discovers his cash has vanished, and he threatens to kill the rest of his gang on the same day – and then the gang start getting killed three days later. It's hard not to draw conclusions. But Pierre's missing cash had nothing to do with the murders. Not directly. Because I ultimately realised there was another reason why Pierre's gang started to die after Pierre had been released.'

'Which was?'

'You had had to wait twenty years until Pierre was released before you could get your revenge. After all, it's not usually possible to murder someone while they're inside a maximum-security prison. But once Pierre was out, you enacted your plan, didn't you? And it's something of an irony, because while we kept presuming that the murders could only have been planned after Pierre was released from prison, all of the evidence kept pointing to them being premeditated – although we didn't know that they'd been *years* in the planning. Because that's how long you've been planning this, haven't you?'

'But what made you think I was a suspect?'

'Simple logic. After all, it just didn't make sense that someone as scared as Father Luc would tell anyone where he was going into hiding, least of all someone he already suspected might have wanted him dead. So how did the killer know where Father Luc was hiding? Well, there was one possibility. Because I knew that Father Luc had said the address of his retreat out loud at least once – in front of us in the Police station. So how could the killer have overheard that? It seemed like a long shot, but it occurred to me that there was one way – if the killer had managed to install a listening bug. Was that even possible? And that's when I remembered that there had been one person other than Father Luc who'd been in the Police station, and who could have installed a listening bug. Natasha Gardiner. And what was more, I remembered how she'd fumbled her handbag to the floor when she'd been with us. So had she installed a bug then?

'As it happened, a cursory sweep of my desk soon proved to me that she'd done no such thing, but I'd started looking for a listening bug so I decided I'd finish the job. I searched the rest of my desk, and even the walls, and that's when I found the USB plug. And that's what really flummoxed me. Because, as had been the case with Father Luc, there was no way Natasha had gone anywhere near the wall while she was in the Police station. I was her alibi. Just as I'd been with Father Luc. Neither of them had gone anywhere near that particular wall at any time. I was sure of it.

'But it was very definitely a listening bug, so who could have placed it there? Whoever it was, they must have had access to the station when no-one was looking. And that's when I remembered that there had been one person who'd been in the station unsupervised during the case. And that was you. Because, just after Camille and I had finished interviewing Natasha Gardiner following the explosion on Conrad's boat, we returned to the Police station and I saw you and Dwayne leaving it together. And while it seemed impossible to imagine that you were the killer, I had to acknowledge that it would have been a relatively simple matter for you to find a spare wall socket to put the USB charger into while Dwayne wasn't looking.'

'But why would I do that?' Amy asked, the challenge clear in her voice.

'Good question. Why would you come to the island, get hold of untraceable mobile phones and a handgun – which, as I said at the time, would have been easy enough for someone who'd spent time in prison. Like you have, Amy. As for the USB bug, I imagine that you'd already sourced that before you even left the UK. Because it was always your intention to come to Saint-Marie in time for Pierre's release, and then murder him and his three other gang members. Wasn't it?'

'Don't avoid my question. Why would I do all this?'

'Because all along there's been someone in the case who we'd not taken seriously enough. André Morgan's girlfriend. Because that was you, wasn't it?' As Richard said this, Amy's grip on the handgun tightened. 'You were the woman he fell passionately in love with, and I think you fell passionately in love with him. As you told me when we had our chat, you first came on holiday to Saint-Marie when you were nineteen. Which, doing the maths, would have been just over twenty years ago. When André was still alive.

'And it was while you were here that you fell for André Morgan. And started leading him astray, as his parents saw it. I suppose we'll never know exactly how André met Pierre, but I believe a good boy like André wouldn't have started hanging out with someone as dangerous as Pierre without someone influencing him. In fact, although I'm not a betting man, I'd wager you were deeply involved in convincing André to hook up with Pierre.

'Anyway, André's parents never knew the identity of their son's girlfriend, but they made one simple mistake. They presumed that she was an islander rather than someone from abroad who was here on holiday. That's why André's dad Stefan told me that André's girlfriend was still somewhere on Saint-Marie. But he was wrong. The girlfriend who'd led André astray had never been from Saint-Marie. She was a Brit. And that's the real reason why no-one's seen her since. When André went to the UK, she went with him. Of course she did. She was going home. With her new boyfriend. Although she didn't return to her home town of Edinburgh. She went to London and set up a life with André as he started his new job at the Bond Street jewellers.

'I think you realised that André was "the one" for you, didn't you? And with him at your side, you'd be able to put your suffocating family and low-scale drug dealing behind you. With the money André was about to make from his share of the robbery, you'd be able to settle down with him forever. But Pierre was far more dangerous than anyone knew. Even his own gang members. And, knowing that if the Police ever worked out that André had been involved, he'd be able to offer up Pierre's identity, Pierre shot him dead.'

'And it was all your fault,' Camille said.

Everyone turned and looked at Camille, surprised by her intervention.

'You're to blame for all of this,' she continued. 'If you hadn't introduced André to Pierre, he'd still be alive.'

'It's not true,' Amy said, but the Police could see that she didn't quite believe it.

'Either way,' Richard said, wanting to take back control of the conversation, 'after André was murdered, it was you who went to a phone box, called the Police, and tipped them off that the robbers were from Saint-Marie, wasn't it? You put on a Caribbean accent to hide your identity, but you'd been living with André for months, I can't imagine it would have been hard for you to adopt his accent for the phonecall.

'And, thanks to that tip-off, the Police started looking on Saint-Marie and Pierre went to prison. But none of the jewels were recovered, and none of the other gang members went to prison. I can't imagine how frustrating that must have been for you. You'd lost the love of your life, and also his share of the heist, and three of the four gang members had got away scot free – not forgetting the fact that they'd all got to share the cash from the two-million-pound heist. Whereas you had nothing. Less than nothing. So then what?

'We know you returned to Edinburgh, and I think this is when your drug dealing stepped up a level. When you started selling heroin and fencing stolen goods for your criminal friends. You were a full-blown criminal, and I think you were driven almost entirely by anger at André's murder.'

Amy's jaw tightened, and Richard realised his words were hitting home.

'And then, in the blink of an eye, you were serving a prison sentence yourself. A young woman from a respectable part of Edinburgh, I can't imagine how much that must have hurt. How being rejected by your own mother and sisters must have hurt. And I think you blamed Pierre and his gang for this as much as you blamed them for André's murder.

'And things didn't improve after you left prison. You'd been ostracised by your family, and you couldn't make headway in your life. You were on benefits. You struggled with debt. And, again, I think that when you considered the life of happiness and riches Pierre had deprived you of, you put the blame for your failings squarely on Pierre. I can imagine why. It can't have been easy, a bright woman in her thirties unable to get a proper job because of her criminal record. And it was during this time that whatever fantasies you had about exacting revenge on Pierre became more concrete.

'That's why the murders were so elaborate. You've been planning them for years. Because, in your fantasy version of all this, it wasn't enough just to kill them, was it? You also wanted the Police humiliated. After all, they'd failed you twenty years ago when they weren't able to arrest three quarters of the gang, or recover any of the money. That's why I think you left rubies at the scene. You wanted to create a famous case where the Police were utterly humiliated. That was also part of your revenge. And how you must have laughed when you met a real life Policeman in a bar. And not just any old Policeman, but one as easy-going as Dwayne. Because you realised, all you had to do was woo him, and then he could be your man on the inside while you went on your killing spree.

'Pierre was first, wasn't he? He had to be if your plan was to work. You hotwired an old Citroën CX from the car park by Honoré harbour, using techniques you'd picked up when you were jailed twenty years ago. And I imagine you followed the taxi that picked Pierre up. It wouldn't have been hard. Pierre was focused on meeting the rest of his gang and getting his share of the loot. But I don't imagine you expected the rest of his gang to arrive so soon after he got to his house, so I think you were forced to wait until you knew they'd definitely cleared off and Pierre was left alone. But this was a stroke of good fortune for you. Because there was now a witness who'd partly seen three men with Caribbean accents and dark-coloured skin visit Pierre that morning. When your car turned up later on, it's no surprise the partially sighted witness presumed that it was one of the same men. Just as we did. But it wasn't, because on this occasion it was a woman with a Scottish accent and fair-coloured skin.

'That's why our witness overheard Pierre saying "I thought I'd never see you again" to this person. It always was an odd thing to say to someone he'd seen only an hour or so before, but it makes far more sense when you realise he was speaking to someone he hadn't seen for twenty years. But now you'd arrived, I think you spun Pierre some lie. Maybe about where his share of the money was. Either way, you convinced Pierre to leave with you, not that he thought he'd be gone for long. That's why he left his cigarettes and money behind in his house. But you had other plans for him.

'You drove Pierre straight to the cemetery, where you parked on some bleached pea shingle gravel that the cemetery had recently bought – meaning it got in the tread of the car you'd stolen. Not that you realised it at the time. You then took Pierre into the cemetery, and I can't imagine how he must have felt as you approached the Morgan family crypt. After all, he knew he'd murdered André, and you'd been André's girlfriend at the time. He must have realised you were up to something once you reached it.

'And here's the next clue that shows that only you could be the killer. You see, the door to the crypt wasn't forced in any way. It was opened with a key. So, seeing as Stefan didn't use his copy, how was the crypt opened? Well, there is one other copy in existence. It was made by André twenty years ago. And seeing as he's no longer alive, the only person who'd likely have that key is the person who he used to come here with. His girlfriend.

'And killing Pierre in a crypt was so clever, really. After all, where better to hide a dead body than among other dead bodies? But it was also poetic justice for you, wasn't it? You wanted to kill André's killer in the same room as where André had been laid to rest. And then, the genius of your plan was, once Pierre was dead, you could use his dead body to create a false trail for us to follow. You took his hand and pressed a fingertip onto a SIM card that you then put in the phone that you used to blow up Conrad's boat. And if the phone sank to the bottom of the sea – meaning we never found his fingerprint – you made sure we'd get the message that Pierre was behind the murders by also putting one of Pierre's fingerprints on a chunk of concrete that you then used to smash in the window of Conrad's study.

'But you were even cleverer than that. Because, having secretly killed Pierre, it was time to announce your arrival on the island with a big, explosive bang. And for that, you were able to exploit the fact that you had a Policeman as a boyfriend. That's why Conrad was murdered on a Thursday morning. It was all planned for a time when you knew Dwayne would be at home "studying" with you. When I knocked on the door, you must have been delighted to realise you were now getting two Police alibis for the price of one. And, although you were only wearing a towel at the time, when you left me on the doorstep talking to Dwayne, it would have been a simple matter to go to your burner phone, ring the mobile you'd previously set on Conrad's boat, and set the explosion off.

'Then, once Dwayne and I went down to the harbour, you got dressed, went down to Conrad and Natasha's house and waited. Then, once Natasha learned that it was Conrad's boat that had blown up and left in a hurry, you smashed in the window with the incriminating bit of concrete, climbed in to Conrad's study, trashed the place and then placed a ruby on the desk.

'And here, you made your only mistake. Not that it would be revealed as a mistake until much later on. Those rubies you left at the scene to show the Police up were ultimately going to be your downfall. Because, as you guessed, we'd fail to find a single shop on the whole island of Saint-Marie that sold them. But, when we were trying to work out where they'd come from, our Commissioner of Police suggested that maybe Father Luc had got them from a clerical haberdashery shop, and that rang a bell with me. Although I couldn't work out what it was, and I only got there once I'd realised that only you had been in the Police station – essentially unsupervised – since Conrad's murder.

'Because, during our conversation the other night, you couldn't help but reveal to me that you've been working as a shop assistant in a posh department store on Princes Street in Edinburgh. And what's the one thing all posh department stores have? A haberdashery department. So, not really daring to believe that I was right, I called the haberdashery department of the only department store on Princes Street, and they told me that they did indeed sell fake rubies. By the way, how am I doing?' Richard asked Amy, and he was gratified to see that her gun hand had lowered, although she still held the Zippo lighter high in her other hand.

'Keep talking.'

'Well, having announced your arrival with such a bang, the remaining murders were far more straightforward. You spied on Jimmy Frost until he went to his office late at night, got him to let you in, and then you shot him dead – making sure to leave a ruby behind which had one of Pierre's fingerprints on. In case we really weren't getting the message. And then you killed poor old Father Luc Durant, having broken into his house when you first got to the island and seen that he took sleeping pills to get to sleep. I wonder if that's when you realised that you could use them on him to make it look like he'd committed suicide?'

'I bet he was the easiest to kill,' Camille said. 'After all, he already agreed with you that he was guilty for André's death. In some ways, I imagine he welcomed being blamed for it. But the thing is, he's not really to blame for André's death, is he? You are.'

This drew a sharp intake of breath from Fidel, and fury flashed in Amy's eyes.

'Not that you like to admit it. But it's why you've kept yourself so busy planning these murders. Because the truth is, if you hadn't persuaded André to go to London and take part in the heist, he'd still be alive today. Your perfect André. You'd have settled with him. Married him. Had children with him. But it wasn't to be. Because of what you did.'

As Camille spoke, Richard was amazed to see tears start to sparkle in Amy's eyes – the arm that was holding the lighter also seemed to waver – and Camille started to approach her slowly.

'All those years of happiness you were denied. All because of one bad decision you made. You let Pierre into your life. A man you've now killed. You've got your revenge. It's all you've dreamed of all these years. That's what matters. Pierre's gone. As are the other members of the gang. They've all gone. And now you've got no reason to hurt any more.

André can rest in peace. His killer has been killed. It's over, Amy. It's over.'

And with that, Camille had ghosted so close to Amy that she was able to reach out lightning fast and grab the lighter with one hand, and Amy's gun hand with her other. And, as she did so, Amy seemed to come out of her reverie and started to struggle to get free, but Fidel was up to her in a flash, knocking the gun from her hand and whipping out a pair of handcuffs that he fastened to her wrists.

And Richard stood rooted to the spot throughout it all.

Then, as Amy struggled to get free from Fidel and Camille, Camille called over to her boss, 'Okay, sir, we need to get out of here, right now.'

Richard was still trying to catch up with events, but all he could think was, through her speed of thought and swift actions, Camille had just disarmed a woman who was holding a gun to them all. The thought popped into Richard's mind that he could have kissed her in gratitude, although he was quick to squash it. But he could have hugged her, that felt more plausible. Not that he ever would, of course. He was sure that if he did, she'd arrest him for assault. And there was the small matter of the fact that they were already standing in a bunker that was full of petrol and a murderous woman who'd been intent on setting fire to it.

'Sir! We need to get out of here.'

'Yes. Of course, Camille,' Richard said.

They had to get out of there, his partner was right.

There's not a day I don't think of him. André.
Every day, he's with me. The life we should
have been having together. It was his idea I
do this. Or at least he didn't stop me when
I planned it. And I think he looked over me.
While I was getting everything ready. He was
my guardian angel, making sure it went alright.
And I know he was with me when I saw the rubies
in the store. It just felt right to leave
them with each body. Your boss was right. I
wanted these to be famous murders. But there
was something else to them as well. I wanted
to frighten the rest of the gang. I wanted
them to know they'd be next. And I thought
I'd done it, I really did. Until I listened to
that day's recordings and learned how there
was a specialist Forensics team coming in from
Guadeloupe to sweep the crypt. I knew I had no
choice. If no-one had been there for years, I
couldn't take any risks. I knew I'd have left
a hair or something in there you'd be able to
find. That's why I was going to torch the place.
But now it's over, I don't know how I feel.
I'm not sure I feel anything apart from happy
I did what I set out to do. The men who ruined
my life are gone. Who've haunted me for twenty
years. Who took André from me. Do you have any
idea how that feels?

DS Camille Bordey: What about Dwayne?

Amy McDiarmid: What about him?

DS Camille Bordey: You used him.

Amy McDiarmid: So? He's a copper. He can handle it. And he'll know. We had good times.

DS Camille Bordey: You don't care about what you've done at all, do you?

Amy McDiarmid: I'm sorry about Dwayne. I liked him.

(Tape switched off)

Interview of Amy McDiarmid terminated at 18.57pm

Everyone on the island of Saint-Marie was surprised at how quickly Dwayne seemed to recover from the discovery that his girlfriend had killed four men since he'd started dating her. There was obviously an element of denial and embarrassment that explained his desire to 'move on', but Dwayne returned to his usual levels of bonhomie with such aplomb that everyone genuinely believed he'd made a full recovery.

He was still somewhat standoffish with Richard, though, and Richard had been warned by Camille not to push back. This didn't seem fair to Richard. After all, as far as he was concerned, he'd essentially identified and then caught a serial killer single-handedly, but Camille still behaved as if he was somehow at fault. All Richard could conclude was, life was so very unfair.

Perhaps the only clue that Dwayne was hurting in any way

was his announcement, a few weeks later, that he was going to stop studying for his sergeant's exam. He said he wasn't cut out for it, and when Fidel and Camille tried to convince him otherwise, he refused to listen. He just kept on saying that he was better off staying an ordinary Police officer.

That same evening, entirely by chance, Dwayne found himself locking up the Police station at the same time as Richard was leaving. Dwayne could see that his boss had something on his mind, but he wasn't that interested in talking to him – a fact Richard was also able to see for himself.

'You don't need to sit the sergeant's exam for me to know what a good copper you are,' Richard said awkwardly.

Dwayne turned to look at his boss.

'What's that?'

'You don't need to be a Sergeant for me to know how good you are, Dwayne.'

'Even though you think I slope off from work?'

'Look, I don't want to get into a fight, although you're right, your methods sometimes leave something to be desired.'

'What?'

'But it was you who solved the biggest case this island has seen in years.'

Dwayne frowned.

'You mean Amy?'

'Of course.'

'But that was you. You solved it.'

'You misremember, Dwayne. I was completely stuck. I

didn't know what to think. And it was you telling me to approach the case logically that helped me solve it. And the fact that you kept asking me to work out what was "bugging me".'

A slow smile appeared on Dwayne's face. He couldn't help himself.

'You're right. It was me.'

'Seriously, I couldn't have done it without you.'

Dwayne took a moment to realise that he had indeed been the key to unlocking the whole case.

'Thanks, Chief. And you know, I should thank you.'

'Why?'

'Someone had to man the Police station when you went out and caught her, and you made sure that person was me.'

'It only seemed fair to spare you.'

'Anyway, thanks. And while we're talking, you should know, Chief, there's maybe another reason I can't take the exam.'

'Oh? Why's that?'

'I never did any revision. I didn't even pick up a book.'

'I know. I'm trying to gloss over that part.'

'I'm just not a books person.'

'Don't keep going on about it.'

'But I'm glad to have got that off my chest. It's been weighing on me. Knowing I was kind of in the wrong, even though it wasn't my fault.'

Dwayne waited for Richard to make some kind of superior comment, but he was surprised when he his boss sighed.

'Well, if we're talking about getting things off our chests, I think I owe you an apology as well.'

'You do?'

'I really should never have looked up your girlfriend on the Police Computer Network.'

Richard wasn't sure how he'd feel if he admitted this, and he was surprised that, even though he was still sure he'd been in the right to look up Amy's record, saying that he'd been in the wrong seemed to lift the fug of shame that had followed him ever since then. It was a stunning revelation for Richard. Saying 'sorry' really did seem to make you feel better.

'Don't worry,' Dwayne said sadly, 'I get it. You were suspicious of her. So you looked her up. And you were right to be.'

'But I wasn't, really. Not at that time. I just looked her up.'

'You weren't suspicious of her?'

'Not really. I was just worried for you.'

'You were?'

'I didn't want her hurting you.'

'What?'

'After all, we didn't know who this woman was.'

'Wait, wait, wait, wait,' Dwayne said, as though he'd just discovered that up was down and left was right. 'You were being my *wingman*?'

Now it was Richard's turn to be surprised.

'I have no idea what a wingman is.'

'You had my back.'

'Is that what a wingman does?'

'Well, that changes everything. Everyone needs a friend to look out for them. Thanks for that . . . wingman.'

Dwayne came over to his boss, slapped him on the back – inadvertently winding him in the process – and then turned and headed off down the stairs.

Once he'd gone, Richard found he couldn't move. This was mainly because he was still struggling to get his breath back, Dwayne having slapped him really quite hard. But it was for another reason as well.

Dwayne had just called him his 'friend'.

Was that true? Richard thought to himself. Did Dwayne really consider them both to be friends?

The thought warmed Richard inside.

From the empty car park beneath the station, Dwayne suddenly stopped and called back.

'Hey, I'm meeting Camille and Fidel at Catherine's bar for a drink. You want to come?'

'No, thank you,' Richard called back, on the grounds that he'd started an excellent jigsaw of a Bavarian Castle only the night before, and he'd already spent much of the day looking forward to spending the evening finishing the sky.

'Oh,' Dwayne said, and it slowly dawned on Richard that Dwayne was genuinely disappointed. And as he had this thought, Richard also realised that 'going for a drink' was something friends did with each other, wasn't it?

'But when I say "no, thank you",' Richard called out, suddenly realising how he could save the situation, 'what

I really mean is that I don't want you buying me a drink, because I want to buy *you* a drink.'

Dwayne didn't speak for a few moments.

'You're getting the drinks in?' he eventually asked.

Richard realised that his Bavarian Castle would just have to wait.

'You know what? For one night only, I think I am.'